THE STILLNESS IN THE AIR

Jason and Azazel: Apocalypse
Book Four

V. J. Chambers

Punk Rawk Books

THE STILLNESS IN THE AIR
© 2010 by V. J. Chambers
www.vjchambers.com

Punk Rawk Books

ISBN: 978-0-9841206-4-2

Printed in the United States of America

10 9 8 7 6 5 4 3 2 1

THE STILLNESS IN THE AIR

Jason and Azazel: Apocalypse
Book Four
V.J. CHAMBERS

ACKNOWLEDGMENTS

I am indebted to the help of many people in the writing and editing of this book. First, a huge thank you to Cindy Slayden, a resident of Columbus, Kentucky, for helping me with a little firsthand knowledge of the town. I'm sure I've screwed up a thousand things, however. They are my errors, not hers.

Additionally, an enormous thank you to my wonderful beta readers who read a draft of the book and helped me clean up errors. Thank you so much Stacey Wallace Benefiel, Melinda Desy, and Raina Tash. I am forever grateful.

Thanks go out to my followers on Facebook for reading daily updates on word count, offering help and encouragement, and just being awesome in general.

Finally, I'd be lost without Aaron Lennox, who lives with my craziness while I'm writing, and is always patient, sweet, and beautiful.

BEFORE...

October 2012

I picked at a piece of lint on my sleeve, evading the question. "There was a guy," I said. "I haven't seen him in a few years."

The counselor nodded, leaning forward. "It didn't work out?" she asked.

I pushed my hair away from my forehead. She couldn't possibly understand how painful it was to talk about this. "We were teenagers, you know? It was that kind of crazy, silly sort of thing you think is love when you're seventeen. But..."

"It wasn't love?"

"He was violent," I said. "Not to me. He was always nice to me, but he'd get really angry sometimes, and he'd kind of go crazy." I paused. "Actually, that's not true. He wasn't always nice to me. There was this one time. One time, he almost killed me."

"So it was an abusive relationship?"

No! Well. "It was...it was just intense. I did things when I was with him. Things I didn't think I'd ever do. I still sometimes remember those things. Dream about them. I had a sort of problem with alcohol for a while. It was just better to get away from him. To get away from all of it. You know?"

"And there hasn't been anyone since?"

I shrugged, not looking up. "I've dated a couple guys. But...as screwed up as it sounds, being with them, it's like...it's boring. There's no spark, you know?"

"It's common for women who are abused to feel an excitement, to miss the adrenaline of the relationship, even though they know they were being hurt."

The counselor didn't know what she was talking about. And she was getting me off track. "Look, I didn't come here to talk to you about my relationships. I just heard that I could get prescriptions through the college for free. And that's all. I've been taking this pill for years. Will you give me the pills or not?"

"I just think it's possible, from what you've told me, that these pills are cutting you off from your emotions. Clearly, at the time they were prescribed, you were in a state where you weren't functioning. But it's clear that you don't have the same kind of trauma in your life. Maybe it's time to face yourself again."

"No," I said. "No, that's not it. Not at all." I needed the pills to stop me from being able to influence people with my mind. But if I told her that, she'd think I was nuts. "Never mind. You're obviously not going to help me."

"You have to talk about this to someone. If it's not me, then please tell me you have a friend or a family member — "

"Everyone in my family is dead," I bit out. "And no, this isn't something I ever want to talk about. Mostly, I just want to pretend it never happened."

Which wasn't easy. Things that Jason and I had done had pretty much permanently screwed up the world. When I'd used my powers to convince all of the Sons to commit suicide, I'd effectively killed off three quarters of the U. S. government. Now the

8

government belonged to a bunch of Wiccan tree-worshippers – The Order of the Fly. I'd given up hope that things would ever go back to the way they used to be. I got up out of the chair, ready to leave.

"I'll write you the prescription," said the counselor.

"You will?" I said. That was great. That was awesome. I sat back down. "Thanks."

"But I have to say that I wish you'd make some appointments with me. Maybe twice a month. To talk about this. I think you need to process what happened to you."

That was the last thing I needed. "I'll think about it," I told her. She smiled. "You do that."

I watched as she scribbled on her prescription pad, wondering why I hadn't just lied to her. I could have easily have just said, "No, I'm not in a relationship. No, I haven't had any serious issues with relationships. I just want to focus on school right now." Why had I opened up to her? I knew it was stupid to open up to psychiatrists. They never understood. They never really believed me.

I'd only come here for pills. Hallam and Marlena might be working for the government these days and since the government was overrun by the Order of the Fly, they might think it was practically criminal to suppress one's magical talents, but I didn't care.

The counselor ripped the prescription off of her pad and handed it to me.

"Thanks," I said. As long as I had the pills, I didn't have any powers. That was the way I liked it.

The lights in the office abruptly switched off, along with the

9

hum of the fan overhead. The room went dark. I blinked, trying to force my eyes to adjust. I could barely make out the face of the counselor, who was frowning. "Was there a storm?" she muttered. "Maybe something just tripped a breaker."

I shrugged. We both stepped out of her office and into the hallway outside, which was just as dark. The college counselor's office was in the lower level of the freshman dormitory, and above me, I could hear whooping. Freshmen seemed to think anything at all was an excuse for impromptu parties. I'm sure they were all hoping the lights stayed out. It would probably mean cancelled classes.

I said my goodbyes to the counselor and made my way through the hallway to the lobby of the counselor's office. A student work study was on her cell phone behind the desk, babbling excitedly, "My laptop's got a battery, and I'm looking at it on the internet. The power's out all over the state. We're gonna be out of class for sure!"

I rolled my eyes. Predictable.

Outside, the sky was blue and clear. No storm. Not even a cloud. There were faint imprints of purple and pink dancing over the horizon. I squinted. What? Aurora borealis? In New Jersey? During the afternoon?

What was going on?

CHAPTER ONE

April 2013

Kieran slammed the door of the beat-up Subaru we'd been driving. "So this Jason guy was like your high school sweetheart or something?"

I stepped out of the car myself, stretching. It had been a long car ride. I took a look around. We were standing in front of a church, which looked a little worse for wear. It had a high bell tower, which looked proper and picturesque, but the addition on the back of the building stuck out like tennis shoes on a prom queen. "Sort of," I said. "There wasn't much about it that was sweet, though."

The Kentucky air was warm, but we knew that since we'd been driving with the windows down the whole way. I peeled my shirt away from my back. It was stuck there with sweat. The car we had was equipped for air conditioning, but using the a/c was a complete waste of gas, and it wasn't like we had easy access to gasoline these days.

"Right." Kieran stepped over the trailer on the back of the Subaru and opened the trunk. We'd been dragging a motorboat with us all the way from Georgia. "He's psychotic or something."

Psychotic? That was putting it a little strongly.

Kieran handed me my bag. I didn't know why he was suddenly so talkative anyway. We'd barely said anything to each other on the eight-hour drive to Columbus, Kentucky. Things between Kieran and me were a little awkward.

I took my duffle and slung it over my shoulder. "He's not psychotic. Not exactly."

Kieran shoved his shoulder-length sandy hair behind his ears and grinned. "He tried to kill you, didn't he?"

Only once. And he hadn't exactly been himself during that moment. Of course, I guess Jason's sense of self was a lot different than what I'd originally thought it was. Especially these days. I shrugged. Was there any point fighting about it? "He's kind of psychotic, I guess."

Kieran lifted his own duffle out of the trunk. He half-grinned.

Damn it. Why did he have to be so freaking gorgeous? It would be a lot easier if he weren't. Of course, if he weren't beautiful, things wouldn't be awkward, because I never would have —

"Azazel!"

I looked up, looking for the person who was yelling my name. Marlena was at the door to the church, just under the tower. She was grinning.

I hiked my bag up on my shoulder and strode toward her. "Marlena, it's so good to see you."

She met me three steps away from the door and enfolded me in a tight hug. "I know," she said into my shoulder. "It's been too long." Marlena was black and British. I loved the lilting sound of her accent. And she was the closest thing I had to an older sister or a mother figure. I'd missed her.

She released me, and I stepped back to present Kieran. "This is Kieran."

"Your bodyguard?"

"Her partner," said Kieran, offering her his hand.

She shook it, raising an eyebrow. "Partner?" She smiled at me, mischief dancing in her eyes.

Kieran winked at me.

I cringed. "Not like that," I said. It had only been once. And I'd been drunk. And... I wanted to change the subject. "Where's your husband, the man in charge?"

"Hallam's inside. He's fiddling with the radio. It's down again." Marlena motioned us inside.

Inside the church, it was darker, despite the fact that the windows, originally stained glass, were all busted out. The air was much warmer, even though a breeze fluttered through the broken glass. I tried to remember what air conditioning felt like, or what electric lights looked like. It had been over six months since I'd experienced either.

"We got the transmission that you were coming," Marlena continued, walking us into the sanctuary, "but it went down the next day, and we haven't been able to get it back up." The sanctuary still looked like a church. There were plush pews lining the rectangular room. Most of them were covered with sheets, blankets, and pillows. Apparently, people were sleeping in here. The front of the room no longer contained a pulpit, however. A few drums containing gasoline were stacked against the wall and several pallets of bottled water. I knew the look of the provisions well. They came straight from the Order of the Fly emergency shipments.

Marlena walked through the aisle between the pews, heading straight back through the church. We followed.

"Has the situation changed?" Kieran asked. "Anything we should know about that headquarters couldn't tell us?"

"No," said Marlena. "He's still here. He still wants to see you." She paused and looked over her shoulder at me.

I cringed again. I'd been dreading this ever since Georgia. I didn't want to see Jason. I didn't want to see him at all. "That's not the only reason I came," I said. "You told headquarters something about the Key of Asher."

We stepped up onto the platform that used to contain the pulpit.

"Sure," said Marlena, "and you can talk to Lily about that after you see him." She stopped at a door at the back of the platform, her hand on the knob. She looked at me, and then she cast her eyes down on the floor. "He's different."

"We haven't seen him in years," I said. What did she expect? Or did she think I'd kicked him out of the house for no reason? He wasn't different, anyway. He'd always been that way. He'd just gotten worse at hiding it.

Marlena turned the knob and opened the door. "Well, if anyone can get through to him, it's you." She smiled at me.

It was my turn to look away. Get through to him? Whatever.

We walked out of the sanctuary and into a dim hallway. A little bit of light streamed through two open doors on either side of the hall. Inside one, I could see rows and rows of stockpiled ammunition. Guns were hanging on the walls. Inside the other, a group of people were crowded around a radio.

"So that's still the plan, then?" Kieran asked. "We want to recruit him? We want Azazel to convince him to join us?"

"Of course that's the plan," said Marlena. "What else would we want to do with him?" She waved into the room with the radio. "Hallam!"

Hallam's shaggy head looked up. When he saw me, his face lit up. "Azazel, you're here!" He broke away from the others, dusting off his hands. He looked older. His face had more lines. He'd grown a full beard and mustache. There was a streak of gray in his beard.

Still, I was glad to see him. Hallam had been lots of things over the years: a guy I was terrified was going to kill me, the overbearing father figure I'd never wanted, and overall, a good friend. He was British too. I also dug his accent. He hugged me even tighter than Marlena had, nearly crushing my ribs. I oomphed as he released me, trying to catch my breath to introduce Kieran again, but Hallam was already pumping his hand. "Kieran, I presume?"

Kieran smiled. "Azazel didn't tell me this was going to be like a family reunion." He grinned, looking annoyingly attractive again. "Actually, she hasn't been talking to me much lately at all."

I glared at him. "Should I see Jason now? Is there any reason to wait? Anything I should know?" The sooner I got this ridiculous mission out of the way, the sooner Kieran and I could get back to Georgia. Hopefully, I could get us reassigned to separate units, and I'd never have to see him again.

Hallam shoved his hands in his pockets. "You don't want to rest after your drive?"

"Rest?" I repeated. I laughed. I guess I sounded a little bitter. "I haven't really had a chance to rest in six months. I doubt that's going to change any time soon."

Hallam nodded. "He's been tied up in the back room for days. He and a bunch of the locals have been giving us problems ever since we arrived. After we captured him, and he saw me, he's been asking to see you."

"I didn't want to tie him up," Marlena said, pleading with me to understand.

"He and his little group injured a member of our party," Hallam said. "We had no choice."

"It doesn't bother me that he's tied up," I said. But it did, a little. Not because I cared if he was uncomfortable, but because it didn't make any sense. Jason had broken out of a maximum security holding cell in England. There was no reason for him to stay tied up in a church in Kentucky. No reason at all. I swallowed. "Take me to him."

Hallam sighed. "If you're sure."

"I'm sure."

Hallam pulled some keys out of his pocket. They jangled

16

as he walked down to the end of the hall and opened up one of the rooms. All four of us went inside.

The room had a smashed piano in one corner, and stacks of bent folding chairs in another. There was one window, high up on the far wall. It was still intact. It was closed. The room was stifling.

Jason was against another wall, his arms tied above his head. The rope was secured against a coat rack that was bolted into the wall. He wore a ragged t-shirt that clung to his muscular chest and a pair of cut-off jeans. He was sweating and his dark hair was pasted against his forehead. His eyes were closed.

Marlena reached for my hand and squeezed it. I let her, but the scene didn't bother me. Well, okay, it did. But not because I felt bad for Jason. I didn't give a flying fuck what happened to Jason anymore. It only bothered me because I was seeing him, and I really didn't want to have to look at him again. I pulled my hand away.

"Hi babe," said Jason without opening his eyes.

Oooh. So I was supposed to be impressed that he knew I was here without actually seeing me? Big deal. I crossed my arms over my chest.

Jason opened his eyes. He caught my eyes with his own. I clenched my teeth. He looked the same. "Didn't you miss me? I missed you," he said.

"Somehow, I've soldiered on without you," I said. I wanted to leave. I wanted to run out of the room and never look at him again. But they wanted me to try to get him on "our side." So I'd try.

"I want to talk to Azazel alone," said Jason, stretching his arms as best he could.

"Jason," said Marlena, her voice cracking. Jason and Marlena had known each other since they were kids. I'd heard him once refer to Marlena as the big sister he'd never had. It was killing her to see him like this. "We just want to help you."

"Just Azazel," Jason repeated.

"No can do," said Kieran, from behind me. He stepped forward, touching me on the shoulder. "They sent me here to protect you."

I stepped away from Kieran, shying away from his touch.

"They sent *you* to protect her from *me*?" Jason laughed. "They really underestimate me, don't they?"

Kieran's eyes darkened. "I'm not leaving her alone with you."

"What is he? Your idea of a rebound?" Jason grinned. His skin crinkled a little around his eyes. It never used to do that. It looked good on him.

I shook myself. Don't find Jason attractive, I told myself. Think of Jason in that car garage that night, with the body just a few feet away from him. Think of Jason telling you it was an accident, as if that made it all better. "It's been years, Jason. I'm past the rebound stage. Kieran and I work together. That is all."

"Yeah? Well, he doesn't look at you like a co-worker," Jason smirked. He wriggled against the ropes that held him.

I could see that they were a little loose. Damn it. He'd be out of them in two seconds. Hallam knew Jason. Hallam had trained Jason. How could Hallam be so stupid? "I only want to talk to Azazel."

I turned to Kieran. "It's okay. I can handle him."

Hallam nodded. "She can. She's talked him down from worse."

Kieran didn't look happy about it, but he nodded once curtly and headed out the door.

Hallam put a hand on my shoulder. "We'll be right outside if you need us."

I nodded, pulling my pistol out of its holster inside my shorts. "I've got a gun."

They left. Marlena looked like she might start sobbing. I shut the door after them. I didn't turn around right away. I just stood, facing the door, staring down at the gun in my hand. I thought about turning quickly, before he had a chance to see what I was doing, and squeezing the trigger three times in succession. My aim wouldn't be good the first time, because I was turning, so I might miss. He'd have a chance to get free of the ropes. He'd go for the window, maybe, or the door. But he didn't have cover, and he wasn't armed. I could get him in the chest, I was sure. Maybe the head. And he deserved to die. He did. But…

I flashed on his arms around me while I was screaming, awakening from a nightmare. I thought of his deep voice, his gentle hands. I thought of how much he seemed to care about me then. I couldn't do it. Not all of him deserved to die. There was a part of Jason that was worth keeping alive. I just wasn't sure how deep he'd buried that part.

"You look beautiful." His voice was husky. "I had forgotten how beautiful you are."

I turned around, bringing up the gun. "Shut up," I growled.

He laughed. "Damn. You were always so sexy with a firearm. I'm getting all hot and bothered."

I reholstered the gun. "What gives, Jason? We both know you could be out of here in five minutes. Why the charade? Why stay tied up here?"

Jason laughed again. He slid his hands out of the ropes, easy as pie. Standing, he massaged his wrists. "I wanted to see you. You always hang up on me when I try to call."

He hadn't called in over a year. Part of that time, he couldn't, because no one really had phones anymore. Not on the east coast, anyway. For a few days after the blackout, the landlines had worked, until the generators in the stations went down or the people manning the phone companies had run screaming for home. Very few people even had landline phones anymore, though, anyway. At least half the cell phone service went out the instant the solar flare hit. It must have knocked out some satellites in space. Everyone else's cell phones stopped working as soon as they couldn't recharge them.

But before the lights went out, he did call me. Usually once every few months. It didn't matter if I changed my number. He always found me. "Well, I'm here now. What did you want to talk to me about?"

Jason crossed the distance between us in three steps. I started to take a step back from him, but before I could move, I was in his arms. He pulled me tight against him, one hand on the small of my back and the other tangling itself in my hair. I had forgotten what it felt like when he touched me. His caresses were white hot, searing into me. I didn't fight it. I was consumed by the sensation. His lips pressed against mine, and I opened my mouth to him, letting his tongue probe me. Fireworks exploded at the end of all my nerves. I melded my body against his, my arms going around him, exploring the sculpted perfection of his back, his shoulders. Ah, God. Jason.

And then I pushed him away.

He was startled, so I threw him off balance. He tried to step backwards to correct his loss of center, but he stumbled and thumped to the floor on his backside. I had my gun out again, trained on him.

He held up his hands in surrender.

"Don't ever do that again," I said.

"Right. Because I could tell how much you hated it."

I decided to ignore his sarcasm. I was angry. "You and a bunch of locals kept Hallam's group from getting west because you wanted to make out with me? Seriously?"

"No," said Jason. "I stayed tied up in this room, because I wanted to talk to you. I wasn't planning on trying to kiss you." He took a deep, labored breath and shifted his gaze to the ceiling. "Can I stand up?"

21

"I don't think so," I said.

"Are you going to shoot me?"

"I haven't decided yet."

He lowered his hands. His voice went low and intimate. "I don't think you'll shoot me."

"I might," I said. "I'm not seventeen years old anymore, Jason. You can't charm me that easily."

His eyes raked my body appraisingly, taking in every nuance. "Yeah. You're not seventeen."

I half-wanted to shoot him just for that. " *What* do you want?"

"I've only ever wanted you."

"That's not true. You used to want to be a normal guy. You used to want to have normal experiences, to live in a John Hughes movie."

"I'm not normal," he replied. "And in case you missed the memo, it's the freaking apocalypse. The lights went out. There is no normal."

"It's normal out west," I said, teeth clenched. My arms were starting to shake. I lowered my gun so Jason wouldn't see, but I didn't put it away. I hated it when he started talking about how he wasn't normal. It was his excuse for everything, and it wasn't enough. Not anymore. I was through forgiving him.

"If it's normal out west," Jason said, "then why haven't they sent any rescue teams to help us? Where's the freaking Red Cross?"

"The Red Cross' Administrative Headquarters was in

D.C.," I said. But he was right. It didn't make sense. Even if the east coast had no power, and most companies were based there, why hadn't the rest of the entire United States responded to the crisis? Why hadn't other countries responded to the crisis? We couldn't communicate with anyone. We didn't know.

"There's no reason to go west," Jason said. "All I want is for your precious Order of the Fly to pack up and get the hell out of here."

"How can you say there's no reason to go west?" I asked. "We need help. People are dying. If you'd seen the things I've seen, you'd realize that."

Jason shrugged. "How can you be sure the people out west even want to help us? It's the freaking Bible belt. Face it, Azazel, when your precious Order of the Fly took over the government, all of the people out there hated it."

"Maybe they're trying to help. Maybe they can't. But whatever is happening, we know they had power. Right after the outage. We have to get across the river. And you and your little goons are blocking us."

Jason stood up. He walked over to the broken piano and began to plunk some of the keys. They didn't make any noise. "Here in Kentucky most people weren't crazy about the Order of the Fly either."

"Columbus was liberal," I said. "They got that Democratic candidate here—"

"Because it's a poor state, and they needed federal funding. Not because they agreed with the OF's agenda on religious freedom." He looked at me. "Understand, I don't care if they want to use magic, and they want to promote the rights of Wiccans and pagans. I never cared about that, you know that. But I'm not letting anyone go west."

He wasn't? Why did he care? "Why not?"

Jason crossed the room to me and took my hand. I pulled it away. He let his own hand dangle in the air for a few seconds and then he dropped it. "Things are good here. Now."

"What? Things are not good. There's no electricity. It's chaos."

"Yeah. There's no...there's no government. There's no authority. There aren't people with tons of power trying to throw their weight around and force people to do stuff they don't want to do. Everyone is free."

Was he insane? "There are mobs. There are gangs of people stealing food and gasoline, shooting innocent people. There are turf wars and starving babies. People are not *free* ." I'd been travelling up and down the coast, trying to help the military keep order. I'd seen what the world had become.

"That will stop," said Jason. "Soon. I'm just not going to let the OF stick their noses into this and ruin everything. I will stop the OF. After I stop them, I can help everyone else. I can bring everyone back together, and we can all have freedom. We can live without anyone looking over our shoulders."

Kieran was right. He was psychotic. I took a step back, shaking my head.

"Can't you see it, Azazel? You and I were made for this. You wouldn't be working with the OF if they didn't recognize your talents were perfect for this situation. All our lives, people have prophesied that we would be important if something like this happened. We are the key players here. Why don't you help me? Leave the OF, and help me — "

"Help you what?" I said. "Rule the world?" I felt cold all over. Jason was mentioning things from our past, things that I thought I'd buried when I'd made every single one of the men chasing us kill himself.

"Help me help the world rule itself," said Jason. "With your powers, we could — "

"I'm not using any of my powers," I said. "Not anymore."

Jason looked shocked. "You're not?"

"You know what happens if I do!" He'd been there when we found out. He'd watched the tiny casket get lowered into the ground. He'd known that it was all my fault.

"Azazel, even Agnes told you that we were important to the future of the world. You and me. We're supposed to be part of this massive change that's overtaking everything. This power outage is the first step. And if you just run from who you are — "

"Who am I, Jason? Am I Kali? Am I the vessel? Your dark counterpart? The person who's supposed to save you? The person who's supposed to kill you? If this is the apocalypse, am I the messiah or am I the anti-christ?"

"We're both all of that," he said, his eyes burning. "But

apart, we're nothing. You and I are made to be together. We are soul mates. You can't keep running from me. Not now. If you used your power, you'd—"

"No."

Jason must have heard something in my voice that told him I was serious, because he didn't say anything. He was close to me now. He reached out and stroked my cheek. I recoiled.

"Don't touch me." My voice was hoarse.

He was quiet for a little longer. When he did speak again, he was quiet. "You know that what happened was an accident. I didn't mean for him to get hurt. I wish you could forgive me."

"I wish it wasn't so easy for you to forgive yourself." I turned and walked to the door of the room. "They sent me here to try to convince you to join the OF and help us return order to the world. I guess that's a lost cause."

"I'll never join them. I don't deal well with people telling me what to do."

That was true, as far as it went. He'd never been particularly good with any kind of authority. I put my hand on the doorknob. "You might want to tie yourself back up again."

He rushed to me, grabbing both my hands. I tried to pull away, but he held me firm. "Azazel, is there any way you'll come with me? Please?"

He was just as exquisite as he'd always been. Dark, dark hair. Huge dark eyes like pools I could swim in. His heart-shaped face. I didn't know if I would ever look at him and not feel a stirring inside me. I'd always want him. But that was all.

"I love you," he said. "I'll always love you."

"I can't ever love you again." My voice was shaking. Was it from rage? Fear? Pain? I wrenched my hands away from his.

He looked wounded, like a little boy. Then he squared his shoulders. He laughed. "Tell Hallam, tell Marlena, tell the Order of the Fly to leave. Leave, or I will make you leave." His mouth twisted into a cruel, satisfied smile.

I crossed my arms over my chest. So it was going to be like that, was it?

"You know me," he said. "You know I can do it. They don't know what they're up against. Make them see that it's impossible to win against me."

"It's not impossible," I said. "If anyone's your match, it's me."

Jason chuckled. "I taught you everything you know."

I shook my head. "Not everything."

Jason turned the knob on the door.

My hand went to my gun. "You're not just going to walk out of here."

"Watch me."

I drew the pistol, flipping off the safety.

Jason's hand paused on the knob. He looked at me. "Are you fucking that Kieran guy?"

I was caught off guard. "What? No."

He moved too fast. His hand was on my wrist in a second, twisting. I let go of the gun. He caught it with his other hand.

Damn it. He had me. Jason pointed the barrel of the gun at my face. Fine, then. I could play dirty too. "Maybe once," I said. "He didn't need me to show him where my clit was."

Jason made a little growling sound in the back of his throat and seized my arm, twisting it. Good. I'd gotten to him. He yanked me against him, my back against his front. He put the gun against my temple. He breathed in my ear, "It's like our first date, babe."

Right. Me, Jason, Bramford, crazy Satanists, and Jason with a gun to my head. Except back then, I'd been sure Jason wasn't going to shoot me. Now, I didn't know.

Jason opened the door. He walked me into the hallway.

"Sorry," I said to the shocked faces of Hallam and Marlena. "He didn't go for it."

CHAPTER TWO

Kieran went for his gun.

"You draw that, I blow her head off," said Jason.

Marlena had her hand over her open mouth. She was shaking her head back and forth, like she couldn't believe it.

Only Hallam kept his cool. "You expect me to believe you'd shoot Azazel?" he said. He drew his own gun out of his shoulder holster.

Jason didn't shoot me. Instead, he moved the gun away from my temple and pushed me into Kieran. "You expect me to believe you'd shoot me, Hallam?"

Kieran and I went sprawling onto the floor, a tangle of arms and legs. We extracted ourselves and scrambled to our feet.

Jason pushed past Marlena, shoving her into the wall. He sprinted down the hallway.

Hallam yelled, but he didn't shoot.

Kieran struggled to free his gun.

Jason burst through the door into the sanctuary.

Kieran went after him.

Hallam and I didn't move.

I heard shots, muffled through the door. It unglued my legs. I raced after Jason and Kieran, throwing open the door to the sanctuary. Hallam and Marlena were hot on my heels.

The sanctuary was empty. I darted up the aisle and out the door, crashing into Kieran on the outside steps. He steadied me with one arm, peering fiercely around the church, his gun at the ready.

"He got away," said Kieran.

Of course he did. That wasn't relief I was feeling, was it?

I heard Hallam sigh behind me. "What's happened to him?"

* * *

Hallam's office was off the side of the church, part of the ugly addition that had been built on. There was a sleeping pallet in one corner, and a desk in the other. It was covered with maps and other pieces of paper. The computer that used to sit on it was junked and stashed against the wall, its screen shattered. Computers were worthless without electricity.

The four of us sat on some folding chairs, and I explained what Jason had said to me.

Then Marlena started crying, for real, which was a big deal, because Marlena was tough and I'd never seen her cry. "I just don't know what happened to him."

Hallam put his arm around her. "I hate to say it, but I think Azazel was the only thing keeping him tethered to this world." He looked at me. "When you left him, he just snapped."

Right. Fine. Blame me. Hallam and Marlena had known Jason longer than they'd known me anyway. I guess they were on his side.

"This isn't Azazel's fault," said Kieran. "That guy is nuts. Wasn't he trained to be like the ultimate mass murderer or something anyway?"

Hallam studied his fingernails. He'd been the one who'd done a lot of that training. But he'd been ordered to by the Sons of the Rising Sun, a twisted secret society bent on world domination. And Jason and I had gotten rid of them. In the end, it was really me who was the mass murderer. I'd convinced them all to commit suicide, screwing up the entire world. Maybe it all was my fault.

"I'm not blaming her," said Hallam.

"Of course not," said Marlena. "I was there when you two broke up." She looked at Hallam. "If you'd done something like that—"

"I would never do that," Hallam said.

"The point is," said Kieran, "he's not going to join the OF. So we need to radio in and see what they want us to do about it. Do they want him destroyed?"

"No," said Marlena.

I shook my head. "That's not our problem, Kieran. We came here to talk to him. We did. Now, if I can just get the Key of Asher, then Kieran and I can leave."

"Maybe if you talked to him again," said Hallam.

"No," I said.

"But you were always able to get through to him," said Hallam. "Even at the Sons' Headquarters, when he'd gone completely insane, you were able to stop him."

"He was never able to stop, Hallam," I said. "You and I both know that. He's never been quite balanced. And I was just lucky that time in England. Because he shot at me. And if I'd hit the floor one second later, I'd be dead."

"This guy is dangerous," said Kieran. "I gather that he's charming. Sociopathic people often are. But he uses people like pawns to achieve his own ends. You can't let him manipulate you."

"Jason isn't sociopathic." Marlena leaned forward in her chair, fire in her eyes.

"He fits the profile," said Kieran.

"He's not sociopathic," I said.

"Excuse me," said Kieran, "but I don't know if you're being honest with yourself about this. You were essentially in an abusive relationship with him, and I don't think it's fair to ask you to confront your abuser—"

"He didn't *abuse* me."

"He tried to kill you. I just saw him holding a gun to your head."

I took a deep breath, trying to steady myself. "We had an unhealthy relationship. Yes. He's not a great guy. But he's not abusive or sociopathic. He has empathy. He feels guilt. He was just brought up in such a way—"

"Don't defend him," said Kieran. He looked around at us. "All three of you. You make excuses for him."

"You don't understand," said Hallam. "You don't know him."

"I do," I said. I looked at Kieran. Was he right? Was I

32

defending a man who'd abused me? What was Jason if not a clever, cunning killer? How many people had I seen him kill? Sure, sometimes he cried later, but did that make those people any less dead? "Hallam, he doesn't want to let you through because he doesn't want the OF to tell him what to do. He hates authority. He's always been violent."

"He protects the people he cares about," Hallam countered. "He saved your life too many times to count, Azazel. He saved mine too."

"Protects?" I repeated. "After Jason appeared in my life, I spent years being chased and shot at. Because of him, my entire family is dead. Because of him, I had to learn to kill people. If I'd never met him—"

"Those things were not all Jason's fault," said Hallam.

He was right. I rubbed my face with my hand. "He didn't always do it to protect people," I said. "Like Marlena said, when I broke up with him, he was out of control."

Hallam massaged the bridge of his nose. "Indeed."

We were quiet.

"You want my advice?" I said. "Break camp in Columbus and try to cross the river somewhere else. He wasn't wrong when he said that the force of people you have here is no match for him."

"But you're a match for him, Azazel," said Hallam. "You're powerful. The things you can do are astounding."

"No," I said. "Because I won't be here. I'm taking the Key of Asher and reporting back to Georgia. Because I've fulfilled everything that I was supposed to do here."

"You can't just leave," said Hallam.

"He's right," said Marlena. "Jason still loves you. I know he does. If only you could—"

"No," said Kieran, "you can't ask her to see him anymore. This man traumatized her. So lead us to Key of Asher or whatever, and we'll leave tomorrow morning."

Marlena got up and came to me. She knelt next to my chair. "Azazel—"

I turned away. "Kieran's right."

Hallam sighed. He stood up too and walked to the door. "Lily's out with a few others scouting for fuel and food. She should be back this evening. She's got the Key of Asher. You can talk to her." He opened the door and gestured to the hallway. "I'll show you where you can sleep."

* * *

One of the rooms in the back, the one where all the guns and ammo were stored, had been partitioned off with sheets into separate, small sleeping areas. Kieran and I both had small sleeping pallets. We spent the rest of the afternoon staying busy. Kieran offered to help with the radio, and I went out back where Marlena and few of the women were working on making food.

Some of the group had been hunting. They'd killed some rabbits. They were skinned and cleaned. We were cooking them on an old charcoal grill, along with wild onions that a few of the others had found. Rabbit wasn't something I would have eaten before the lights went out, but I had to admit that meat sounded nice. Kieran and the group I

34

worked with the in south subsided almost entirely on canned food and powdered pasta meals. At least there were still large supplies of prepared herbs there for the taking in abandoned grocery stores. If we couldn't get west, though, and get help, things would go even further downhill. It was amazing to me what losing electricity had done to civilization. All our pretty, fancy little toys and tricks were suddenly meaningless. We were primitive, struggling to survive like animals. It frightened me.

After dinner, we sat around the smoldering coals of the grill as twilight set in. I listened to the chatter and laughter of Marlena, Hallam, and their group. They were one of the scouting units. Their mission was to get west. They'd been on the move for months. While they were frustrated with the fact that Jason had halted their progress, I could tell they enjoyed the chance to wait it out here for a bit. The more permanent encampment seemed to suit them. It was a warm, spring day, but as the sun set, the air grew colder. I shivered in my t-shirt and shorts for a bit, but then I went back in to get some warmer clothing from my duffel.

As I was emerging from my little sleeping area, now in jeans and a sweatshirt, Kieran met me at the door. Scant light filtered in through the windows of the room, turning the guns into long, black shadows. I could barely see the features of Kieran's face.

"Hey," he said. "I just came to check on you."

I gestured to my new outfit. "I was cold."

"Right."

I started to push past him, but he stopped me.

"Are you okay?" he asked.

"I'm fine." I didn't need Kieran to comfort me. I was glad he'd had my back when we were talking to Hallam and Marlena, but that didn't mean we were best friends or something.

I started for the hallway.

"Look," said Kieran, "I didn't ask for them to assign me to come with you."

I stopped and turned to him. His hair was catching the last bit of light from outside. It glowed, surrounding his head like a halo. "I know."

"When we talked right before we left, you said we were cool."

"We are cool."

"Okay, so why the silent treatment? Why are you treating me like some asshole?"

I rolled my eyes in the darkness. I didn't have time for this. "I'm sorry I hurt your feelings."

"That's not what I mean. I just don't see why we can't be adults about this."

"I don't see how being adults means we have to be best friends."

"You know, I was drunk too."

"Oh thanks," I said. "This has been real comforting, Kieran, but seriously." I stepped into the hallway.

"Come on," he said. "I didn't mean it like that. I mean, you're gorgeous and smart and awesome. I would have done it if I wasn't drunk, but—"

I closed my eyes. "I just want to pretend it didn't happen." Which would be a lot easier, if I wasn't still waiting for my—

"I don't," he said. "We were lonely. Both of us. The world exploded. It's okay that we needed some comfort, some human contact. It can just be that. We can still be friends."

"We have never been friends. And I'm sorry, but just because I got wasted and let you play hide the salami with me does not mean we're a couple or buddies or that I have to tell you how I'm feeling."

"Azazel."

"Let's just find the Key of Asher and get the hell out of here. Please?"

I started down the hallway.

"Fine," he muttered. "Sure." He paused, and then called after me, "Was it really bad or something?"

I stopped. Turned. It had been awesome. Really awesome. The best since Jason. But if I told him that... I opened my mouth.

And then I heard the screaming, outside of the church. Kieran and I exchanged a look of alarm and then we both scrambled towards the door.

CHAPTER THREE

Everyone was outside, standing in a tight bunch. One of the women was still screaming. I ran forward, pulling people aside to see what was going on. They were standing around a bundle of cloth, stained red.

I swore.

"Don't look at it, Azazel," Hallam said. "We found it at the edge of the woods. There was a stirring like a deer or something, but we think someone left it there."

But I had to. I knew what it was, but I had to see it and make sure. I knelt on the ground next to the bundle and pulled aside the edges. Some of the blood — I was sure it was blood — got on my fingers, but I didn't bother wiping it off. I just opened the bundle, like it was a Christmas present. The cloth was white. Maybe it was from a sheet. The edges were fraying. It was tough to see what was in it at first, because there was so much blood. But I stared at it and forced my mind to recognize what it was seeing. One toe. Several fingers — most were pinkies, but one was a thumb. They'd come from more than one person, because the thumb was definitely male, and so was one of the pinkie fingers. The other belonged to a female. I couldn't tell about the toe.

I rocked back so that I was sitting in the grass, my knees

at my chest. "He did this for my benefit."

"Who?" said Marlena.

"Who do you think?"

Hallam was rubbing his forehead with his hand. "It's the scouting party. The ones who I sent out for fuel and food. The ring on that finger belongs to Lily."

"Jason didn't do this." Marlena's voice had gotten shrill.

"He's done it before," I said. I stood up. "He did it to his mother."

"Listen to me," Marlena said. "Listen. When that boy was five years old, he fell down outside on the sidewalk, and he scraped his knee, and I bandaged it for him. He is not capable of—"

Hallam drew Marlena into his chest. She quieted. Then she pushed him away and walked off, putting distance between herself and the body parts.

"He cut off body parts of his mother?" Kieran asked me in a low voice.

"She wasn't a very nice lady," I said. "Not that it makes it okay."

Hallam's face was pale. He stroked his beard nervously.

"This is a message," I told Hallam. "He said he would make you leave. You need to do what I said. Break camp. Find a way around him."

"I'm not leaving my scouting crew with him," Hallam said. "They're still alive, don't you think?"

I nodded.

"The woman in the scouting crew had the Key of Asher,

39

didn't she?" Kieran said.

Hallam glared at him. "For God's sake! What's so important about the grimoire anyway? She's lost a finger."

Kieran was right. Damn it. I needed that book of magic. I'd come miles and miles for it. I took a deep breath. "We'll get the scouting party back."

"Oh, how do you propose to do that?" Hallam laughed wildly.

"You said it yourself," I said. "If anyone can take Jason on, it's me. We'll get them back." And the grimoire.

"We need to radio this in," said Kieran. "I think I've almost got it fixed. Hallam, do you want to give me a hand?"

Hallam looked from Kieran to the bundle of body parts on the lawn. He threw his hands into the air.

In the distance, the crickets were chirping.

* * *

I was used to sleeping on hard floors and on the ground. Ever since I'd been recruited to work for the government, I'd been doing just that. There was no electricity, people were going crazy, and I was travelling all over the coast, trying to gather up as much gasoline, natural gas, and other fuels as I could. They needed me because I could influence people's brains. Make them do things. I helped a lot. If we went into a community and started pumping out all the gasoline from the neighborhood gas station, people tended to get annoyed with us, whether we were the government or not. We could subdue them with the threat of force, usually. If that didn't

40

work, using some actual force usually did. But the government liked having me around so they didn't have to shoot civilians. I could just convince everyone to walk away.

But I hated doing it. I hated using my power or magic or whatever you wanted to call it. I'd put my foot down about a month ago. "No more," I'd said. The government might not understand the true nature of my magic, but I did. I didn't know exactly why, but the power had a perverse sensibility. It liked to wreak havoc and cause destruction. If I tried to use it a different way, it would goad me and seduce me. There was a voice I always heard. It was raspy and ghostly. It liked blood. It always tricked me. No matter how I tried to keep people from getting hurt, it always made me do it.

I did not want to hurt people anymore. I hated it. Killing people had destroyed me. Maybe I'd done it in self-defense before, but I didn't like the way it made me feel. Hard. Emotionless. And sometimes...oh God, sometimes, I even felt like I enjoyed it. That was what scared me the most about the power. The thought that maybe the voice didn't come with the magic. Maybe it was just me. Maybe some part of me liked killing things. It made me nauseous even to consider it.

No matter how hard I tried to do good, I always managed to only do evil, awful things. Maybe the mobs of people didn't get mowed down by army machine guns, because I convinced them to go home, but they all threw themselves off a bridge the following day because they were so depressed about the state of the world. (It happened in Tennessee.) Maybe they began shooting each other down like dogs in the street. (That was in Virginia.) The people in charge told me I was being paranoid. They said the events weren't related. I tried to explain to them that my power had caused it, and that I'd felt it. They didn't care.

They told me to come and get an ancient grimoire called the Key of Asher from a woman on a scouting party here in Kentucky. They thought the grimoire could help me learn to focus my magic, make it stronger. But I'd heard that the Key of Asher contained a ritual that would allow me to cleanse myself of all power. Get rid of magic entirely. That was what I planned to do.

Then the government couldn't use me anymore. I'd have peace. It was all I wanted.

Also, cleansing myself of power would get rid of the dreams.

I might have gotten used to sleeping on hard floors, but I'd never gotten used to the dreams. Before the lights went out, I took meds that got rid of them and made me sleep like a baby. But now I couldn't find the pills anymore. They were prescription, and they weren't common. By now, what little supply of them there had been seemed to be gone.

The dreams were prophetic. Sort of. They were always tangled up in symbols and imagery I couldn't understand and interwoven with my own fears and personal demons. For a few months, I'd worked on trying to decipher them. Usually, I couldn't. Now, I just suffered with them. I wished they were gone.

I'd inherited this lovely cocktail of powers from my late grandmother, who was a gypsy. She hadn't used her power for anything other than destruction either, but at least her powers had limits. She'd only been able to influence impressionable minds. I'd never run into a mind I couldn't manipulate. Maybe someday, I'd run into a block, but thus far, no.

Sometimes getting drunk made the dreams go way, sometimes not. And when I was drunk, I made great decisions, like sleeping with Kieran, which had made my life much more complicated than it needed to be. Getting drunk was never a good idea. I didn't know why I still did it occasionally. Honestly, it was less and less of a problem these days, anyway. Alcohol was harder to find than food.

I didn't have any problem going to sleep inside the church that night, despite the fact the floor was hard and flat and I didn't have a pillow. None of the things I'd seen that day kept me awake—not Jason, not the bundle of body parts. I crawled into my little sleeping pallet, burrowed under the blankets they'd given me, and fell to sleep immediately.

Where the dreams were waiting.

In my dream, I was back in the mansion my grandmother had left me in her will. I was living there with my brother Chance, his girlfriend Mina, their little daughter Jenna, Jason, Hallam, and Marlena. The dream started out nice. Jason and I were cuddled in our bed, spooning. He was

43

asleep, gently snoring at my neck, his arm curled possessively around my hip. I felt cocooned in his warmth.

Then the crying started. It was little Jenna, screaming her head off across the mansion. I snuggled closer to Jason, waiting for Mina or Chance to feed Jenna and stop her squalling. *You do it* , rasped a voice inside me. *Shut that brat up.*

I felt queasy. The voice bothered me. It always urged me to do things that scared me. But what was wrong with quieting Jenna so we could all get some rest? The screaming kept up, building into a frenzy, louder and louder. Finally, someone tapped on my door.

I slid out of bed, throwing on a robe. Mina was at my door. Her hair was frazzled and there were hollow dark circles under her eyes. "She won't eat," she said. "She won't be quiet."

I followed Mina to Jenna's nursery, where Jenna was lying on her back, flailing her arms and legs and yelling her head off. Her little eyes were scrunched up in agony. Her face was turning red from the effort of it. I did what I always did. I picked her up and put her over my shoulder, walking and rocking with her. And as I did so, I reached out with a little bit of my magic and touched her tiny mind. I willed her to be quiet, to be calm.

And like she always did, she stopped screaming.

I handed her to Mina, who looked so grateful as she popped the bottle into Jenna's mouth. Jenna sucked contentedly. "Thank you, Azazel," said Mina. "You're a miracle worker. She always gets quiet for you."

I just shrugged, ready to go back to bed and sleep next to Jason. "Guess she just likes me."

And all of this could have happened. It did happen, many times, on many nights. But this was a dream, not a memory, and that's why, in the dream, the flies started crawling out of little Jenna's ear.

At first it was just one. The tiny black bug made its way across Jenna's soft forehead. I brushed it away, but there was soon another one, and another one. They began pouring out of her ears in a swarm, enveloping us.

Mina and I cowered, arms up against the whirlwind of flies, buzzing madly around us.

Little Jenna spit the bottle out of her mouth. "Mommy," she said.

Never mind that she was too young to talk. In the dream, it seemed perfectly normal.

"Mommy, you shouldn't let Aunt Azazel do magic on me anymore."

"Magic?" whispered Mina.

"I thought it was harmless, Mina," I told her, pleading. "I never thought..."

Flies started crawling out of little Jenna's mouth, out of her eyes and nostrils. Her body was turning gray.

Mina held up her rotting child to me. "Azazel?" she whispered. "Azazel, what did you do to my baby?"

I woke up then. I sat straight up. It was dark and silent in the church in Columbus, Kentucky. The crickets were still chirping somewhere in the distance. Now, I couldn't sleep.

I used to wake up screaming from the dreams, but I'd trained myself not to. I did the best I could to wake myself up before they got really bad. That dream had more to it. I'd dreamed it before. Sometimes, if I let it go on, little Jenna's dead body would chase me through the house, begging me to save her.

I threw aside my blankets and quietly dressed in the dark. I would go for a walk. Columbus was a small town, but maybe it had a drug store or a pharmacy. I hadn't been able to stop at one on the way to Columbus, because Kieran was with me, and I didn't want him to know.

I managed to make it out of the church without colliding with anything in the dark or making a lot of noise. Once outside, I stood in cool night air, breathing deeply to calm my racing pulse and letting my eyes adjust to the dark. Gradually, the street ahead of me became something other than unidentifiable black blobs. I was able to see that there were a few buildings down the street, one with a sign that I couldn't read.

I set out down the silent road.

Upon further inspection, I could see that the building was actually a car garage or something. It wouldn't have what I needed. But across the road was a store that had an ice container in front, the white letters were peeling, but still recognizable and gleaming in the moonlight. Ice meant a convenience store. A convenience store meant over-the-counter medicine and condoms. They might have what I was looking for there. It was a small town. Would women really drive all the way to another town to buy these if they needed them?

The door to the convenience store was locked, so I busted one of the windows with a rock and reached inside to unlock it. I couldn't believe no one had rooted through this place before.

Inside, however, I realized I must have been wrong. Many of the shelves were cleared out. People had been through here all right. But someone had still locked the door. Had the owner of the store simply let people in? Hadn't there been looting here? There had been looting everywhere else.

I found the aisle with the ibuprofen, maxi pads, and Nyquil. If they had it, it would be here. Most of the medicine was still on the shelves. I searched through it three times, hoping maybe they were hidden behind something else, or that I'd just missed them the first time through. But no.

There were no home pregnancy tests. None, and my period was a week late, and I'd slept with Kieran three weeks ago.

I sat down on the concrete floor of the store. I didn't care that it was filthy or cold. I just sat there for a while. I couldn't be pregnant, could I? I didn't want to be pregnant.

Maybe someday, yeah, it would be nice, or at least it would have been if the lights hadn't gone out. I could have seen myself, in five years or so, married to a nice guy, working a steady job, begging him to go out and get me pickles and ice cream or something. But not now. Not in this messed up, destroyed world. And not with a man I'd only had sex with because I was drunk and scared and lonely. It couldn't be true.

* * *

The radio crackled. Hallam, Kieran, Marlena, and I were sitting in the radio room the next morning. Kieran and Hallam had gotten it to work, and had contacted OF headquarters. Even though the OF was the U.S. government, things were so different these days than they used to be. I'd gotten used to thinking of them as the Order of the Fly a long time ago. Old habits died hard.

When I accidentally convinced all the members of the Sons of the Rising Sun to commit suicide, I had no idea what kind of effect this would have on the world. The Sons were an influential bunch. Their membership extended not only to the slavishly devoted Brothers, who were a cross between monks and James Bond (and, incidentally was what Hallam had been), but to rich and influential men all over the world. The upshot of this was that when they all killed themselves, over three quarters of the world's governing members were suddenly gone. Heads of corporations were dead. Certain influential journalists were dead. It was truly an event that brought the world to its knees. And it was my fault. Oops.

Afterwards, theories abounded. Terrorism. A widespread suicide pact. But the one that was the most popular by far was the theory that this was a sign. The end of the world was coming.

The Order of the Fly didn't think the world was coming to an end. They thought this was a sign that their time had come. The OF had long been aware of the Sons, since the Sons had swindled them out of a great deal of money back in the 1800s, when they were just another new-agey type order floating around, trying to do magic. The difference was, that unlike the Hermetic Order of the Golden Dawn (that people like Aleister Crowley and W. B. Yeats were members of) the people in the OF really could do magic. The Sons sensed their power as a threat, and squelched them.

I came in contact with the OF right after the mass suicide. A woman named Agnes, who had been a bit of a mentor to me in Italy, put me in touch with them. They were supposed to be able to help me learn to use my powers.

The Order of the Fly was busy trying to get its people elected into as many government positions as they could, and they succeeded in having enough to essentially overtake the U.S. government. This didn't bug me too much. Overall, the OF was made up of good people. Not all could do magic, but all believed in tolerance, fair-thinking, and being open-minded.

There were some people in the country who it did bug, though. To them, the Order of the Fly sounded Satanic. Having been raised by Satanists, I knew they were way off base, but one girl can't change the mind of half the country. Things were getting pretty bad before the lights went out. There weren't just protests and walk-outs. Things like bombs and shoot-outs were happening. It was like America was turning into Ireland.

Maybe it was like Jason said. Now that the lights were out, the people on the other side of the country had decided to let the OF fend for itself. But I hoped not. I really hoped not.

On the radio, Hallam's immediate superior, Phillips, was talking. His voice sounded flat and staticky. "I thought you had the ringleader captured. Over."

"He escaped," Hallam said. "Over."

"Can't you capture him again, over?" Phillips asked.

"If I might add something?" I asked.

"Go ahead," said Phillips. "Over."

"Jason allowed himself to be captured and allowed himself to stay captured. He could have escaped at any time, but he didn't. He was toying with us. He's quite skilled, and the force we have here isn't capable of taking him down," I said. "I suggest we do nothing more than go in covertly and get the scouting mission out, then break camp and try to go around him." I paused. "Uh, over."

Phillips didn't answer for a while. Finally, he said, through the static, "That's a negative Wakefield team. We'd like you to hold your position and take no offensive action. Over."

"But our team is being tortured," Hallam said.

"Junkin's group to the north of you is making good progress. They may be able to get across the river within a week or so. If we can get them across, then we'll be in a better position. Until then, I don't want to risk the safety of

50

the remainder of your group on trying to rescue a few. If this ringleader is as dangerous as you say, it doesn't seem wise at this juncture. Over."

Hallam argued with Phillips a little more, but Phillips wasn't budging. Our orders were to wait it out. To do nothing. There was no word on Kieran and I. We weren't told to report back south, and I didn't bring it up. I needed to get my hands on that grimoire. As long as there was some chance I could get to it, I was staying.

Finally, Hallam ended contact with Phillips. "I can't believe this. My people are being tortured, and I've been ordered to do nothing about it." He stood up and kicked the metal folding chair he'd been sitting on. It fell over with a clatter.

Marlena rushed to him. "Hallam, calm down," she said, putting a hand on his shoulder.

It was nice watching the two of them. They comforted each other. They were there for each other. Of the three couples that had lived in my grandmother's mansion, they were the only one that was still together. I could see why. They were a team.

Hallam took Marlena by the shoulders. "They count on me," he said. "They won't expect to just be left there."

She put a hand on his cheek. "I'm sorry."

"We could just go anyway," I said. "That grimoire is with the Lily person you mentioned and —"

Hallam pushed Marlena aside and stared down at me. "You and that wretched book. There are people there.

People who are losing pieces of their bodies. Besides, if she were captured, I'm sure the last thing she was worried about was that book. The Key of Asher is probably lying on the ground somewhere in the woods."

I stood up. "You don't think the book is there?"

"I highly doubt it."

Well, then. Maybe I didn't need to be so gung-ho about breaking into Jason's camp.

"Do you even care about those people, Azazel?" Hallam asked.

"Of course I do," I said. But I needed to think. Was there any way I could find the Key of Asher, if I searched for it? Maybe we could retrace the scouting party's steps and figure out where exactly they were taken.

"I don't think you do," said Hallam, and the way he looked at me hurt. He looked disgusted. "Yesterday, Kieran was saying that Jason was sociopathic, but are you any different? You're both the same." "Hey," said Kieran, standing up. "She's concerned, okay? But we have our orders."

"They didn't give you orders," said Hallam. "Just me."

"I just need to find the grimoire, Hallam," I said softly. "It's important. Of course, if you'd like to assemble some people to break into Jason's camp and look—"

"Why risk lives, when you could end this in seconds?" Hallam's nostrils flared.

Marlena put her hand on Hallam's shoulder again. "Hallam, it's okay."

"It's not," said Hallam. "Azazel, you could stand right here and make all of them crazy or make all of them want to throw themselves in the river. All of those locals Jason has working for him. It would be over."

I looked down at the ground. "I can't."

Marlena peered around Hallam. "Why can't you?"

Kieran raised his eyebrows questioningly.

"There are consequences to using this kind of power," I said. "It always turns out worse."

Marlena stepped forward, taking my hand. "You can't still blame yourself about Jenna, can you, Azazel?"

I shook her off. "It was my fault. When I use the magic, something bad always happens. I won't use it again. I won't." And then, I turned on my heel and left the room.

* * *

Before...

September 2009

Jason pulled the car up to the curb of the Order of the Fly's campaign headquarters. The building was nothing exciting – three stories of boring brick and square windows. On the lawn, there were six or eight people picketing. They held signs that said things like, "Get the Witches out of the Whitehouse" and "Hocus Pocus and Foreign Policy Don't Mix." They looked pissed off.

I opened the passenger side door and put one foot on the asphalt.

"Sure you don't want me to come in with you?" Jason asked.

"I'm fine," I said. The picketers were always outside the building. I leaned across the car and kissed his mouth. "Pick me up

53

in an hour?"

"You got it," he said.

I made my way inside amidst shouts of, "Witch" and "Nutso" and "Communist." The picketers didn't exactly always make a lot of sense, but they were part of life these days. Not a day went by that the news wasn't covering a demonstration or hosting a debate between OF supporters and the Christian right.

Once indoors, I knew my way around. This was my fourth session with Lucy, a psychic who was able to gauge when I was able to access my power. I hadn't been able to manage it thus far. I waved to the girl behind the desk. Her name was Gina or Georgia or something. She always remembered my name, but then, my name was a little distinctive.

Lucy was waiting for me in her office, a room filled with several plush chairs, shag carpeting, and numerous hanging houseplants. Lucy said that atmosphere was important to using magic. I wasn't sure I wanted to embrace that I was actually doing magic. It made me sound like a five-year-old or something.

After we exchanged greetings and made some small talk about Lucy's kids and Jason's health, she asked me if I'd been working on the exercises she'd given me last week.

I flung myself into one of the plush chairs. "I've been trying, but nothing's happening," I said. "No matter how relaxed I am, I can't influence anyone to do anything, let alone thousands of men all over the earth to kill themselves all at once. Are we sure I did that?"

Lucy chuckled. "Of course we're sure. I sense enormous power whenever I'm around you."

I sure didn't feel like I had enormous power. I felt overwhelmed by the world. Mina, Chance's girlfriend, was hugely pregnant. Whenever I could, I did my best to make sure she kept off her feet, which meant running errands for her and ordering ridiculous amounts of food for her to eat. (No one in our house really knew how to cook.) I was just starting my first semester of college, and I didn't have a major yet. Everyone kept asking me what my major was, and I kept feeling stupid. I felt so behind in all my classes, due to the fact I hadn't really had a proper senior year of high school. Technically, I hadn't graduated from anywhere, even though the Sol Solis School had issued Jason and me diplomas. There hadn't been much left of the school, of course, after I'd made most of the teachers kill themselves. I was ecstatic to be so close to Jason, and to be able to have a normal relationship, but sometimes it felt like there was pressure from all directions. A little bit of power would be nice right now. It really would.

Lucy and I got started with our session. She had me close my eyes and lean back in the chair. She began to speak in a soothing voice, telling me to relax and think of a warm, dark, empty place. This was how all the sessions started. Apparently, in order to master my power, visualization was very important. Grounding myself in an imagined space provided my mind a space to work from. Or something.

I did as she asked, immersing myself in warmth and darkness. There was nothing there, not even my body. Everything was dark and warm and comfortable. I felt, like usual, that I might go to sleep.

"I've been telling you to imagine your power filling this space,"

55

said Lucy's voice, velvety and comforting, floating into my dark warmth, "and it hasn't been working. Today, instead, I'd like you to imagine that there is a container in the room. You can make it look however you'd like."

I imagined a huge glass bottle in the middle of my dark space.

"The container has a cap or a lid," continued Lucy.

I imagined the glass bottle capped tightly.

"Inside this container," said Lucy, "is your power. You've put it all inside the container. Now, you need to let it out, by opening the cap or lid."

Oh, what the heck? Nothing ever happened anyway. I imagined popping the cap off the glass bottle.

"When you open the container, your power rushes out."

My power looked like soda in my imagination. It foamed over the lid and spilled out into the darkness.

I felt an odd tingling feeling in my stomach. It was as if the warmth from the dark space I was imagining was spilling out into my body. The tingling began to spread over my torso, into my limbs. It flowed up my spine, bubbling like Coca-Cola, and I felt it nudge the back of my brain.

"I feel something," I gasped to Lucy.

"So do I," said Lucy. "You've done it. You've released your power!"

She sounded excited. I was too. "What should I do?" I asked.

"Slowly open your eyes," she said, "and see if you can still feel it when you do."

I eased my eyelids open. Lucy was sitting across from me in one of her chairs. The room looked exactly the same. But suddenly, I

56

could feel Lucy's brain. I couldn't read her thoughts or anything like that, but I could get a sense of what she wanted. Right now, more than anything, she wanted me to be able to use my powers. Cool! "I can feel it," I told her. "I can feel you too. What you're focused on right now."

"Good," said Lucy. "See if you can stretch out further, beyond this room."

I imagined my power as a bubbling liquid, spreading out through the building. I couldn't make out individuals, but I could feel the divergent desires of many, many minds. Suddenly, it seemed easy. I could...make everyone want to dance the mambo!

Lucy stood up and began to undulate her hips. Ha! I was doing it! I was controlling her. I got up out of my chair and ran to the door. Flinging it open, I looked down the hall. Everywhere, everyone was dancing the mambo. No way! This was fabulous.

My head felt bubbly, like the power was dancing around inside my brain. It was surging, growing more powerful by the second. The things I could do with power like this! Geez. I could —

Make them all stab each other, whispered a ghostly voice from inside my head. I pictured it for a second. All of the people in the office wielding whatever weapon they could find. Scissors. Pens. Pencils. Letter openers. Blood would be everywhere, soaking into Lucy's shag carpet...

The people weren't mambo dancing anymore. Now, they were stalking out of their cubicles, heading towards each other, their faces ugly.

No. I didn't want this. I stuffed the power down, pulling it together and shoving it back inside the glass bottle. I slammed the

57

cap back on.

Everyone shook themselves and went back to their desks. I breathed a sigh of relief.

Lucy called to me from inside her office.

I turned to her. "Are we sure that my using this power is a good idea?" I asked.

CHAPTER FOUR

Kieran found me in the out building of the church, which apparently wasn't being used for anything. It was piled with junk that Hallam and Marlena's group must have moved from the church. Desks, computers, phones. Once I think it might have been the church's office. I had crawled underneath one of the desks in the room and was clutching my knees to my chest, concentrating on not crying.

Kieran found me in five minutes. He sat down next to me on the floor.

I glared at him. "Go away."

He studied his fingernails. "I get that you might not want me to come and talk to you, after what you said to me last night. But Hallam and Marlena are upset too."

"No one needs to talk to me," I said. If I talked, I might burst into tears. I'd never cried in front of Kieran. Before the thing had happened between us, Kieran had just been one of the guys. I did my best not to show weakness in front of them. Now, I was acting like a little girl. I hated it.

"Hey, it's really understandable. This is a stressful situation for you. Having to see Jason again must have been pretty disturbing."

"It's not about that." What was it about, anyway?

"Everyone's stressed out. Sometimes I have a hard time too."

God. I didn't want Kieran to sympathize with me. Kieran was half the problem anyway. If I'd never gotten drunk with him, half of my problems wouldn't exist. Yes. That was good. If I just got angry, I could keep back the tears. "You have no idea what's going on with me," I said.

"I don't. I wish you'd tell me."

I crawled out from under the desk and got to my feet. I looked down at him. "Do you? Do you really?"

He stood up too. "Really," he said. "I want us to be friends."

"That's not going to happen."

"Okay." Kieran took a step back. "Look, I don't know why you hate me so much. You seemed to like me fine before. If I'd known that having sex with you would make everything so weird, I never would have done it."

"It's not just the sex." I mean, it was because of the sex, but I could love 'em and leave 'em. I wasn't weak.

"Sure, whatever. I'm sick of this junior high crap, though. We had sex; it was fun; it didn't mean anything. Let's get over it." He started out of the building.

I jammed my hands in my pockets. Good. He was leaving. That's what I wanted.

I don't know why I called after him. "I want to get over it, but I can't."

He stopped and looked at me. "What's that mean?"

I walked over to him. I didn't want to yell this across a

room. "I'm late," I said.

"For what?" He looked puzzled.

"My period," I said, "is late."

Kieran didn't say anything. His eyes widened. His adam's apple bobbed. He took a huge, shuddering breath.

I stepped around him and walked out of the out building, back towards the church.

Kieran caught up with me in a few minutes. He stopped me and turned me around to face him. "We used a condom," he said.

I shrugged. "I think it was old. And they don't always work anyway."

He shook his head. "This can't be happening."

"Tell me about it," I said. I kept walking back to the church. Kieran didn't stop me again.

* * *

The rest of the day was tense. Hallam didn't want to talk to me. Marlena was with Hallam. Kieran avoided me. I spent the day with two members of the group who were hunting. I tried to get some information from them about where the scouting party (including Lily and the grimoire) might have gone. They gave me a basic idea of the layout of Columbus, Kentucky, which was a very small town. Most of the houses in and around it were abandoned. They figured that most of the locals had joined Jason. Jason was apparently camped out in Columbus-Belmont park, some historic memorial to a battle in the Civil War. The abandoned houses were most likely the places the scouting party would have hit.

Eventually, they made me stop talking, because they said I was scaring the animals away. It was probably a good thing that I did, because shortly after that, someone shot a deer. That was a lot of meat. It was too bad we no longer had refrigerators, because there was no way we'd be able to eat all of it before it went bad.

I didn't stick around long enough to watch the guys gut and clean the meat. Too gross. Ugh.

I helped with cooking dinner again and with cleaning up afterwards. There was no laughing and chattering during our evening meal that day, only silence. Everyone seemed grim or angry.

I headed back to my sleeping area shortly after eating. I hadn't been able to get back to sleep after my dream last night, and I felt pretty tired. The odds were good I'd have another nightmare tonight, but maybe if I went to bed early, I'd get in a few more hours. One of the guys who I'd been hunting with was already in the room when I walked in. His name was Gus, I thought.

I said hi and made my way through the partitions to my own little area.

He called after me, "Is what Hallam says true?"

I ducked back out from behind the hanging sheets. "About what?"

He looked a little embarrassed. "About being able to influence all the people in the park. Making them jump in the river or something."

Great. I wished Hallam hadn't been so forthcoming about

my abilities to everyone else. "I don't like doing that kind of thing," I said. "It's all death and destruction and blood and—" How could I make him understand that so much of my life had been swallowed by violence? How could I make him understand that I just didn't want to hurt people anymore?

"But you'd be able to get the others back," he said.

I sighed. "Look, I'm sorry. I can't do it. I told Hallam that."

He bit his lip. "It's just that one of the people in the scouting party is my wife. They sent back her finger and…" His face twisted. He looked like he might start crying.

I lowered my head. "I'm sorry."

"If there was anything you could do, I beg you, please, do it," he said. There were tears in his voice.

I wouldn't look at him. It would be too much. I already felt guilty enough. "You don't understand," I managed. "It's destructive. It's wrong. I can't hurt all those people."

"Please," he repeated, sounding so empty and hollow.

I darted back into my sleeping area. I didn't say anything else to him, but I heard him sobbing. I hated hearing men cry. I'd heard too much of it ever since the lights had gone out. I just yanked the covers over my head and tried not to listen.

Exhaustion claimed me, and I fell asleep.

The dreams were waiting.

I sat on a plush couch, piled with silks and velvets. I was surrounded by opulence: elaborate paintings framed with gold, dangling crystal chandeliers, thick soft carpeting, and expensive furniture. Servants came in and out of the room, bearing trays laden with fruits and meats. I felt like an Egyptian queen as I lounged there. All that was missing were men in loincloths fanning me with huge leaves.

Instead, Jason appeared behind my couch. I smiled up at him. He looked just as beautiful as he always did. "Hello, love," I said.

He leaned over the back of the couch and kissed me, long and deep. I wanted to pull him down on top of me and run my hands over his body, but he pulled away after the kiss, stroking my forehead. He crossed the room to another couch and settled on it.

"Darling," he said, "we have prisoners to deal with."

I sighed. "More of them?" I pouted.

"Yes," said Jason, "well, it's hard work ruling the world."

He was so right. It was. Oh, how we suffered. I caught his eyes with my own and we shared an empathetic look. Only we understood what this was like.

"Well," I said, "bring them in."

Jason waved his hand carelessly at the servants.

A door on the other side of the room opened and several guards escorted two men inside. The men were dirty and grizzled. They were chained hand and foot. They had scabs and scars crisscrossing their hands and faces. Still, there was a look of determination in their eyes, a fire. I smiled at Jason. Between the two of us, we'd put that fire out. It was what we did best.

The men were forced to their knees in front of us.

One of the guards stepped forward. "These men are members of the Resistance, your Worship. They have committed crimes of treason against your empire."

Jason raised his eyebrows. He addressed the prisoners. "The punishment for such crimes is death. Are you aware of this?"

The men stared straight ahead, refusing to answer.

"Your emperor has asked you a question," I said. "Answer him."

They were stonily silent.

I narrowed my eyes, sending a tendril of magic across the room towards the men. At once, they grimaced in pain. "Answer your emperor," I repeated.

"Yes," one of the men replied, but he still didn't look defeated. He still looked angry. We'd break him, though. Of course we would.

Jason smiled at me in thanks. "We can kill you one of two ways," he said. "The first way is quick. It will be over in seconds. The pain will not last. The second is long and excruciating. You will feel more pain than you thought possible and it will go on for quite some time, until your body cannot handle it." Jason paused. "I'm sure you would prefer to die the first way. And we can arrange that. All we need to know is the location of the Resistance base. Where are the Resistance leaders?"

"We'll never tell you that," said one of the men.

I smiled. "Oh good. I was hoping they'd pick the second

option. It's so much more fun."

Jason reached his hand across the arm of the couch. I did the same. "So was I, my love," he said. "So was I."

Our fingers brushed. Our hands met and clasped. The power danced through us, like electric current on wire. We turned to the two men. The power burst from us. They writhed and screamed and bled and hurt.

Jason looked at me tenderly. "I knew you'd come over to my side eventually, darling."

* * *

I woke up screaming. I hated it when I did that. I tried not to scream usually. But this dream was new. I'd never dreamed about Jason and I torturing someone before. The euphoria I'd felt causing pain in the men disturbed me more than anything. Was this a prophetic dream? Was there a possibility that something like this could happen?

I only screamed once, but I woke up Kieran. He was on the other side of the sheets hanging to my right. Immediately, he shoved them out of the way and crawled into my sleeping area, his eyes wide, his gun drawn.

I sat up, pushing his gun down gently. "It was just a dream," I whispered. "I'm sorry. Go back to sleep."

He squeezed his eyes shut and opened them again. "You're okay?"

I nodded.

He flipped the safety on the gun back on and stowed it back in his sleeping area. "You want to talk about the dream?"

"You don't have to be nice to me," I said. I'd been kind of bitchy to him earlier.

"Sure I do. I'm a decent human being, right?"

It would be nice not be alone with this dream. "Yeah, I want to talk about it." I motioned towards the door. "Not in here. We'll wake people up."

There wasn't anyone sleeping in the sanctuary. Apparently, with the scouting party kidnapped, there was enough room in the rooms in the back. Kieran and I sat down on one of the pews. It was dark. All I could see of Kieran were shadows. Somehow, it made it easier to be vulnerable. To talk to him. I told him about the dream. "It was just so creepy. To think that I could take that much joy in someone else's pain. I felt like some kind of super villain or something."

"Hey, it was just a dream. You're not like that at all."

But my dreams weren't "just" anything. They were omens, portents, and warnings. "Sometimes I wonder if I am. Hallam said that I only cared about the grimoire. He was kind of right. And that guy was begging me to use my magic to save his wife, and I said no. But if I use the magic, I'm afraid I might turn into that. Into something evil."

Kieran shook his head. He took my hand. "Nothing about you is evil."

I tried to make out his features in the darkness. "You don't know me very well, Kieran."

He brushed my cheek with his knuckles, a quick caress. "Sorry," he said.

I almost wished he'd do it again, but I knew it was only because I felt lonely and scared. That was the reason I'd gone to bed with him in the first place. I couldn't make that mistake again. I didn't care about Kieran like that. I didn't think I was really capable of caring that way for someone. Not after Jason. Not ever again.

"Do you think you dreamed about Jason because you saw him the other day?" he asked.

"Maybe," I said.

"What happened between the two of you, anyway? When did the relationship go bad?"

I sighed, staring out into the darkness. "In some ways, it was always bad, I guess. We were only really happy together when we were on the run. When we had a common enemy. Whenever we were safe, things started unraveling."

"Because he was violent?"

"Yes. No. Maybe. We were both violent, that was the thing. I killed my own brothers. I shot my best friend. I made all the members of the Sons kill themselves. I destroyed the world."

"Hey, come on. That's not your fault."

That was nice of him to say, but we both knew it wasn't true. "Jason and I would both just get...jealous. And we'd get crazy because of it. But he got so crazy that he..." I sighed. Sometimes the weight of how much Jason had betrayed me overwhelmed me. I'd forgiven him so many times, but what he'd done the last time was simply unforgivable.

Kieran didn't say anything. He just squeezed my hand. We sat there in the night, holding hands on the church pew. Neither of us spoke again for a long time. It was nice, just being next to him. It was comforting.

Finally, Kieran said, "About what you said earlier?"

Oh God. I didn't want to think about that. "I'm sorry I told you."

"I'm not. I'm glad you told me. I have a right to know about something like that. Don't you think?"

"Yeah. I guess so."

"What are we going to do?"

What could we do? "Wait. See if my period comes."

Kieran shifted next to me. "And if it doesn't? If you're..."

Don't say the word. Don't say it.

"...pregnant?"

"I'm not. I can't be. I can't have a..." I licked my lips. "I would be a horrible mother."

He squeezed my hand again. I pulled it away.

"Don't be like that," Kieran said. "We got into this mess together. We can deal with it together. Let me be there for you."

I shook my head, but I wasn't sure if he could see in the darkness. "I feel tired. I should go back to sleep."

Kieran sighed, sounding frustrated. "You can't keep me locked out forever."

I stood up.

"If you're pregnant, it's my baby too," he said. "I deserve to be part of this."

What?! "Deserve?" I repeated. "Because you managed to get some sperm past a latex barrier? Deserve?" I stalked off.

Behind me, I could hear Kieran swearing.

* * *

"I just think it might be a good idea," I said. "Part of reason I came here was to find that grimoire, and if you're right, and it's lying on the ground somewhere, I need to find it. It's important."

Kieran and I were talking to Hallam in the radio room the next morning. He was standing with his arms crossed over his chest, looking annoyed. I knew that look on Hallam quite well from when I was a teenager, and he was pissed that Jason and I were sleeping in the same bed. Sometimes it seemed like Hallam never approved of me.

"What about provisions?" Hallam asked. "You expect us to provide you with water and food for this little searching expedition you've planned?"

"The way I figure it," said Kieran, "your scouting party failed to bring in any more food or fuel. Azazel and I can look for the grimoire and try to bring back some supplies. It's a win-win for you, Hallam. Otherwise, we're just here in your hair, eating your food anyway."

Hallam sighed. "I just wish you were as concerned over the lives of the people who were captured as you are over that stupid magic book."

"I am concerned," I said. "But the orders said to sit tight and wait."

"What if he kills them?"

70

"He won't," I said. But I wasn't sure. Jason might. I didn't know him nearly as well as I used to.

"Azazel, are you sure you can't just use your power to—"

"No!" I said.

Hallam sighed again, more heavily. He shot a glance at Kieran, who shrugged.

"Maybe you should do it," Kieran said. "It would make everything a lot easier."

I wasn't using magic. I wished everyone would stop asking me to do it. "I need the grimoire," I said. "It will help." Maybe lying could buy me some time. Once I had the book, and I'd purged all power from my body, then they could complain all they want, but it would be done. No one would ask this from me anymore.

"All right, then," said Hallam. "Go try to find it."

"Great," I said. "Kieran and I will leave this afternoon."

We packed sparingly, bringing some supplies for camping and a little water. Hopefully, we'd find some food in some of the abandoned houses. We thought about taking the car, but it seemed like a needless waste of gasoline. We needed the fuel to get back to Georgia, or wherever we'd be headed after this. Instead, we decided we'd be walking.

I wasn't thrilled with the prospect of spending a few days alone with Kieran, because things were so weird between us. However, I trusted Kieran, and I knew him better than the others in the camp. I couldn't ask Hallam to spare one of his own people to help me find the grimoire. Kieran had been assigned to help me with this mission. Kieran was the person I was taking.

We set off in the afternoon. The sun was still bright in the sky. It was warm, but not nearly as warm as it had been the day we arrived. The spring heat fluctuated. Tomorrow, it could be cold. I didn't know how similar the climate of Kentucky was to West Virginia, where I'd grown up, but I knew back home it wasn't unlikely for an occasional frost to happen at this point of the year. I hoped it wouldn't get that cold. If it did, Kieran and I would have to snuggle for warmth. And somehow, I thought he would enjoy that more than I would.

We checked the houses that lined Polk Circle, but they were quite close to the church, and had probably already been raided. Sure enough, there was next to nothing there, and no sign of the grimoire. We thought, however, that the scouting party had probably been captured closer to town. After all, Jason's people were camped out in the state park, which was right next to the river. Would they have spread out so far trying to find this scouting party?

We were trying to find supplies, but my first priority was the grimoire, so I insisted we search close first. Kieran and I decided it made sense to work in ever widening semicircles, branching out from the entrance to the state park. We searched until it got dark, but didn't find the grimoire. We did, however, find some canned food, which we stacked and left to gather up on our return trip. There was no reason to carry all that heavy stuff with us when we were coming back this way.

As the sun started to drag heavy in the horizon and the sky turned bright colors, we came to one last house, which we decided to check out before we made camp. If the house was suitable, we might even sleep there that night. The house was two stories, with a wide veranda-style porch on the front. It had white siding. It sat alone in a field. The grass was high. One lone straggly tree adorned its front yard. A swing hung from the branches. For the most part, the house looked inviting, if a little forlorn.

Kieran and I had to break in. The doors were locked, as if the people inside were just on an extended vacation. Kieran smashed out a window in the front door. We were able to unlock the door that way and get inside.

The house was stuffy inside. It didn't smell good.

"We're not sleeping in this stench," Kieran said, and I agreed with him. I'd rather sleep outdoors than smell this.

"Let's just check out the kitchen and get out of here," I said.

"Go for it," said Kieran. "I'm going to duck into the garage and see if there's any gasoline or cars I can siphon."

We parted ways. The kitchen was at the back of the house. I made my way through a messy living room. Used plates were still sitting on the coffee table. Articles of clothing were scattered over the floor. These people were slobs, I decided. The stench got worse as I got further into the house.

The kitchen had one of those swinging bar doors, like a saloon in the old west. I swung though it and was greeted with a disgusting sight.

A man sat at the kitchen table, clutching a shotgun. What was left of his head was slumped to the side of his lifeless body. His face was just gore — brain matter and blood. There were flies crawling all over his body. They made a sickening buzzing sound.

I wanted to throw up. I backed out of the kitchen, bumping against the swinging door on my way out. "Kieran!" I yelled.

I knew this kind of thing had happened. For some people, it had been too hard after the power outage. At first, we'd thought it was nothing. After all, sometimes, the power goes out. Hospitals had generators, so did many grocery and department stores. We were aware that it was massive and that transformers up and down the entire east coast of the U.S. had been knocked out. We knew that millions of people were without power. But... it was just a power outage. We expected to be up and running again by the end of the day. We didn't understand that the transformers couldn't be repaired. They had to be replaced. And we had neither replacement transformers nor the means to build new ones. Not without power.

Weeks passed. No power. Hospitals couldn't function. Battery operated appliances couldn't be recharged. Cell phones stopped working. It was October — neither too hot nor too cold, so people weren't dying yet from exposure, but people were dying in hospitals. People were starting to panic. That's when the riots started and the looting. And then things just kept getting worse and worse.

Some people couldn't handle it. Some people killed themselves. Apparently, that's what this guy had done.

"Kieran!" I yelled again.

And that's when I heard it. Wailing. From upstairs.

It was a baby.

I ran up the steps as quick as I could. At the top, there was a bathroom and three bedrooms. I looked in each, looking for the source of the crying. In the first, two children, maybe six or seven were lying on their beds. They'd both been shot. I closed my eyes and backed out of the room. Oh my God. What had this man done? Had he shot his entire family and then shot himself?

It certainly looked like it. The second room contained a woman, also lying on her bed, shot through the head.

Jesus.

I could still hear the crying. I opened the door to the third bedroom. It was a baby's room. The walls were yellow, with a strip of wallpaper around the middle. Little zoo animals marched around the walls—chubby elephants and wide-eyed zebras. There was a crib on the far wall. The mobile over the crib was zoo animals as well. I walked to the crib and looked down into it. The baby was squalling as loud as he could. I thought he was a little boy. He was wearing a blue onesie with trains on it. What had happened? Had the man saved the baby for last? Hadn't he been able to shoot the baby? But how could he bear to leave the baby alive to starve to death? Certainly, that was crueler than a shot to the head. I shuddered, wondering how long the baby had been here by himself.

He was still screaming as I lifted him out of the crib. I pulled him close, cradling his head against my shoulder and sliding my hand under his bottom. I began to walk around the room and bounce him gently, cooing to him.

Kieran appeared in the door to the bedroom. "Holy crap!" he said.

I looked at him helplessly. "Will you look through the kitchen for some formula?" I yelled over the baby's cries.

CHAPTER FIVE

The baby was sleeping. I'd found some diapers and changed him. He had a heck of a diaper rash. (And that had been the grossest diaper I'd ever changed.) I was cradling him in my arms. His little mouth had gone slack against the bottle I was holding.

Kieran was watching me with interest. "You sure do know how to take care of babies," he said.

"I helped with my niece a lot," I said.

"Huh," he said. Mercifully, he didn't ask any more questions. There was nothing I wanted to tell him about little Jenna. I never wanted to talk about that. Ever.

We were sitting in the living room. The sun was going down. It was dark. God. It was always dark. I missed electricity. "I don't want to stay in here with all these dead bodies," I said.

"Okay," said Kieran. "But what are we going to do about this baby?"

"Take him with us," I said. "We'll have to go back to camp. We can come back and look for the grimoire later."

"But do we need to pack up baby supplies?"

He was right. We didn't get our tent pitched until it was very dark outside. I let Kieran work on building a fire while

I tried to get the baby supplies into the packs we'd brought with us. I was sure that there wasn't anything we could use back at the church. I didn't know if there were supplies to be raided in the nearby convenience store or not, but I knew that we needed to get all the formula, bottles, diapers, and baby clothes we could. Of everything, the diapers were the bulkiest. Kieran wanted to leave them behind, but I wouldn't. He said that people used cloth diapers before the advent of disposable ones and considering there was a finite supply of them, we might as well get used to that. I told him that he could wash the cloth diapers if he felt that way. He caved and let me bring the disposables.

With a fire built, Kieran and I heated up some cans of chili and ate next to our tent. The baby was snoozing inside. I'd made him a little bed of blankets away from our own sleeping bags. The last thing I wanted to do was roll over on the baby and kill it. This happened more often than people thought.

I watched Kieran eat, the fire dancing on his face, lighting up his long hair. He was a good looking guy. He was nice, too. Decent. If I were really going to have a baby, he wasn't the worst pick for a father ever. I didn't think he'd run off or leave me in the lurch or anything. I thought he was a pretty stand-up guy. Still, the whole idea felt too foreign to really wrap my head around. I couldn't believe that there could actually be a tiny being growing inside my body.

Actually, it sounded kind of gross. If I were pregnant, wasn't I supposed to be releasing hormones that would help me bond with the little creature? Maybe that came later. I stared down at my flat stomach and willed it to stay flat. I was only a week late. My period would come. Maybe it was stress. Maybe I'd lost too much weight. There were lots of things that could be going on.

Inside the tent, the baby woke up and started fussing. I left my chili and went in to get him. I didn't know if he needed another bottle already. It hadn't been that long since I fed him. Sure enough, he quieted as soon as he was in my arms.

He was lonely, poor guy. How many days had he lain by himself in that house, his family rotting around him? It made me feel sick. I tickled his tummy, and he gave me a huge toothless grin. Kieran came around the fire and sat next to me, peering at the baby.

"Did you see his name anywhere?" he asked me.

I shook my head. "Nope."

"He's very cute."

"Yes," I cooed to the baby, "this little guy is adorable."

"Well, that's what we'll call him, then," said Kieran.

"What?"

"Guy. You said he was a little guy. Guy's a good name. It's very masculine."

I laughed. I brushed his nose with my forefinger. He grabbed at my finger with his tiny hand. "You like that, Guy? Is that a good name?"

He gurgled and smiled.

Kieran reached in and tickled his chin. "I think he likes

it." Guy grasped Kieran's finger. It was crazy, how big Kieran's fingers looked next to Guy's tiny ones. Kieran smiled at me over the baby. "He's got quite a grip."

"Yeah," I said. "Babies go through a stage where they love to grab stuff."

"Cool," said Kieran, looking at Guy again. He gazed at the baby. "Very cool." Guy and Kieran made gurgling noises at each other for a bit. The two of them were fun to watch, I had to admit. "We could do this," Kieran said.

He caught my eyes.

"Kieran, we don't even know if—"

"We could, though, I mean, don't you think?"

I sighed heavily. "There's way more to babies than diapers and formula and finger grabbing."

"Sure, I know that," said Kieran. "Can I hold him?"

I handed the baby to Kieran, who look a little terrified at first. He wasn't sure where to put his hands. After I assured him that he wasn't going to break the baby, he relaxed a little bit. The warm light from the fire lit up the angles of his face and the swell of the muscles on his arms. He was a big guy, but he held Guy so tenderly. I had to admit that I kind of liked the way it looked, Kieran holding the baby by the fire like that. It was comforting. I hugged my knees to my chest and took the sight in. Kieran would be a good dad. Definitely.

"So," said Kieran. "What else is there to babies?"

"Come on," I said, "are you serious?"

"Totally. You have to feed them and change them, right?

And once I get to be okay with washing dirty diapers, that's not going to be much of a problem."

"Feeding them," I reminded.

"Well, not to be crass, but doesn't nature sort of cover that part? I mean, you're going to be equipped to feed the baby once it's born with your—"

"Stop," I said. I was not entirely comfortable with Kieran discussing my breasts as a food source. Okay, sure, that's what they were actually for and everything, but... "I guess you're right, but that whole idea makes me feel sort of ooky."

"How come? It's totally natural."

"Well, of course, *you* think it's neat. You're a guy."

He shrugged. "Okay, then, we'll find formula. We work for the government. Shouldn't be a problem. What else?"

"That's a problem," I said. "The fact that we work for the government. How am I supposed to take care of a baby when I'm gallivanting all over the U.S. trying to gather up fuel?"

"I guess you'd have to take maternity leave."

"Do you think they'd let the chick with the nifty magical powers take maternity leave? And besides, it's not like the baby will be able to take care of itself right away. There aren't schools anymore, exactly, or day care centers. This is a full time job for at least fifteen years."

He laughed. "It's not ideal. But we could do it."

Another horrifying thought occurred to me. "There aren't hospitals, anymore, Kieran. How would I have a baby without a hospital?"

"It seems to me that babies predate hospitals." Kieran shifted Guy in his arms.

"Yeah, and there used to be a huge infant mortality rate," I said.

"Whatever," said Kieran. "I think the delivering mother is doing most of the work there. Somebody just needs to be around to catch."

"And to make sure the baby's not breach and that there's no umbilical cord wrapped around its neck and to administer the epidural—oh, God. There are no more epidurals. Or heart rate monitors. Or—" I broke off. God. I couldn't be pregnant. I just couldn't be.

Kieran was quiet for a few minutes, and then he said gently, "Azazel, if you're pregnant, there's nothing we can do about it."

Right, I thought bitterly. No more abortions either.

"If we have to make it work, we will," he said. "We can."

I shook my head.

"I'm just saying, whatever you need from me, whatever I can do, I want to do."

"Look, let's just wait, because maybe it's all a false alarm. Maybe I'm not pregnant." Please, don't let me be pregnant. Please.

Kieran looked into the fire. The dancing flames illuminated all the hollows in his face. He looked older and more serious than he usually did. "I lost my family right after the lights went out. After that happened, I was kind of destroyed, you know? I, um, I just didn't want to ever care that much about other people again. It hurt too much."

Should I touch him? To comfort him? Or would he think that meant something else? I knew how he felt. I'd lost my family too.

Kieran kept talking. "Back in Georgia, before we left, Thomas said something to me. He was teasing me because he said I was watching you a lot."

"Kieran, you don't have to—"

"No, I want to tell you this. If there's a baby, that's scary. It's really scary. But, it might be nice to have someone to take care of. I kind of miss feeling that about another person." He looked up at me. "I think I might feel that about you."

"Kieran, I'm not—"

"Yeah, it's okay," he said. "I'm not pledging my everlasting love or something. And you don't have to feel anything for me at all. I just wanted you to know that I'm here, and I'm going to try to take care of you. That's it."

I chewed on my lip and didn't say anything. That was sweet, so why did it make me feel awful? "We should sleep," I said. "We've got to lug all this baby crap back to camp tomorrow."

He handed me Guy. "I'll be in a little bit," he said.

I was asleep before he got into the tent.

* * *

I had a dream about talking flies. There were a bunch of them. They were all standing on a half-eaten piece of cantaloupe in a trash can. Abruptly from above, a human hand reached down and tied the trash can closed, leaving them in darkness. A few escaped but the others were trapped inside the bag.

There was panic. The flies flew against the stretched plastic, screaming.

But one of the flies nudged another fly. "This is it," he said. The flies all had tinny little voices, like Alvin and the Chipmunks. "This is our chance."

The other fly didn't seem much interested in what the first fly was saying. "Go away," she said.

"It's the end of the world," said the first fly. "We're important. We are special flies with magical powers."

The girl fly just laughed at him. "We're flies," she said. "Nothing we do matters."

"Sure it does," said the boy fly. "If it didn't matter, then why would you be so interested in trying to stop me?"

The girl fly rubbed her two front legs together and didn't answer.

"If it doesn't matter," said the boy fly, "then why won't you join me? We can rule this trash bag together!"

The girl fly flew away from the boy fly.

Then the dream sped up, like time-lapse photography. The flies laid eggs. The eggs hatched. The trash bag was thrown in a landfill and covered with other trash bags and dirt. The flies all died.

I woke up and stared up at the top of our tent. Kieran was lying on his side, his eyes closed. Guy was twitching in his sleep. They both looked peaceful. I burrowed into my sleeping bag. Was it true? Did we matter at all? Were we nothing more than flies in a trash bag to the universe? The sun had wiped out our transformers and left us without power. We were a civilization forced to its knees. It was odd, I thought, because all the stories and predictions about the apocalypse involved humans doing something wrong. Nuclear bombs or pollution. It was weird that when it really came down to it, as destructive as we might have been or as powerful as we might have thought we were, it only took one overactive flare from the sun to cripple us. We were nothing.

* * *

I woke up the next morning to Kieran hovering over me with a hand over my mouth. My eyes opened wide and I tried to struggle away from him, but he held a finger to his lips, signifying me to be quiet. Cautiously, he moved his hand away from my mouth and gestured outside of the tent. Now, I could hear footsteps and muffled voices. Who was it?

But it was pretty obvious who it must be. Our people wouldn't be out here. It had to be Jason's people. Perhaps this was how they'd captured the scouting team. They weren't going to capture us. I got my gun out, which I always kept close while I was sleeping, and sat up. Kieran also had his gun drawn. Together, we softly crept to the door of the tent. Kieran mimed unzipping the tent quickly and jumping out with our guns drawn. I nodded. It was a good plan. With any luck, we'd get them by surprise.

But there was one thing we had forgotten to take into account with our little plan. Guy.

He woke up at that moment and started screaming.

Kieran and I both sat back from the door, exchanging a look. Whoever was outside knew we were inside at this point. And they knew we had a baby. I holstered my gun and picked up Guy. He didn't stop screaming.

Kieran glared at me.

Since I wasn't sure why we were being quiet anymore, I just said, "Look, he's hungry. He's just going to keep crying."

Kieran rolled his eyes.

"See?" I said. "This is why it would be hard to have a baby."

Kieran unzipped the tent and got out. He had his gun in his hand, but he wasn't pointing it at anybody. I climbed out after him, still holding Guy. There were two men outside the tent. I say men, but they were really teenage boys. Neither of them looked older than eighteen. They both had big guns, which they put away immediately when they saw the baby.

"What are you folks doing out here?" one of the boys asked, his eyes trained on Guy as if he hadn't seen a baby in years. Strangely, the sound of the boy's voice seemed to calm Guy down. He swallowed one of his cries, hiccupped once, and was quiet.

Kieran started to say something, but I elbowed him.

"We're just passing through," I said. "I'm Ella, this here's my man Jim, and our baby Guy." I did my best to imitate the easy drawl the boy had. It wasn't hard. I'd grown up in West Virginia. Talking like I was from hickville only meant I needed to stop concentrating on pronouncing everything properly and talk the way that came most naturally.

"Passing through?" asked the other boy. "Why aren't you just staying put where you live? There ain't any real reason to go no place."

"Well," I said, "we heard they got power on the other side of the river. That's where we're headed." How would Jason's people field that? What kind of lies was Jason telling them?

The boys crossed their arms over their chests. "You don't want to go on the other side of the river, ma'am."

I cocked my head to the side. "Why not? Ain't they got power?"

"They have power all right," said one of the boys, "but they've all gone crazy over there."

"There's a dictator," added the other boy. "He won't let anybody do anything. It's like communist Russia or something."

Inwardly, I groaned. Trust Jason to cook up a story like that.

"You all might just want to head back with us," said the first boy. "We got a nice little camp out in the park. It's real nice. We're all real friendly folk. People have been showing up at our camp from all over too. You'd be welcome."

"Yeah?" said Kieran, who couldn't fake an accent at all and wasn't even trying, "then how come you guys have guns?"

People had been showing up, huh? And Jason was taking them in? What did Jason want with all these people? It didn't make sense.

"Well, for the same reason you got a gun, mister, I reckon," said one of the boys. "Because you never can tell about outsiders."

"But you all seem nice," said the other boy. "In Columbus, we all take care of each other. This power outage thing wasn't nearly as big a deal to us as it was to some. See, back in 2010, we had such a bad ice storm that we were out of power for over a month. And nobody got out of line then."

"Exactly," agreed the other boy, "here in Columbus, we've got each other's backs. We gave to other people what they needed, and they helped us out too. No rioting or shooting each other here, no sir."

I guessed I believed that. Small towns tended to work in more subtle ways. For instance, here in Columbus, no one was shooting each other, but they were all following Jason around and doing his bidding. I bet that there wasn't an easy way to get out of that either. Small towns were good at creating all kinds of peer pressure. Heck, my hometown had been jam-packed full of Satanists. Nicest people on the outside, though, really. It also explained why the store I'd been in hadn't shown any signs of looting. Probably, the store owner had just shared with the community.

I looked at Kieran. "I don't know, honey. I'm not sure if I

don't want to see the other side of the river for myself." How would they react to that? Were they going to force us to come with them? If they did, I was going to have to hurt them. I didn't want to, but I couldn't be Jason's prisoner either.

"Ma'am," said one of the boys. "We're not letting anybody across that river. It's for your own safety."

"You heard the man, Ella," said Kieran. "We might as well just head back on home."

I steeled myself, waiting for them to insist that we come back with them.

But instead, one boy just said, "If that's what you folks want to do, we ain't gonna stop you."

"You might want to come by our camp just to see it, if you'd like."

"No thanks," said Kieran. "We're just going to feed the baby and be on our way."

"Okay, then," said a boy. "Just you folks watch out. There's those crazy witch ladies that live out here, pretty close by, and once you get into town there are some meddling government folk. They shouldn't come out this far, but if they do, you just watch yourselves."

We thanked them. The boys shook Kieran's hand and ambled off into the distance. Weird. So, Jason was patrolling the area, and he was actively trying to recruit people to his encampment. He wasn't forcing people, though.

"They never would have believed us if it wasn't for the baby," said Kieran. "I don't know. I think babies are lucky."

Guy started screaming again. I raised my eyebrows. "Lucky, huh?"

* * *

After breakfast, Kieran and I started back for the church. It had been a lot easier on the way in, because we hadn't had to carry Guy or all his stuff. Even switching the baby back and forth, we found ourselves taking more breaks. We were sitting down on one of these little breaks and had perched on a fallen down tree. I was feeding Guy. Kieran was rubbing his arm and complaining that babies sure were heavier than they looked, when a woman's yell interrupted us.

"It's them!" cried the female voice from behind us.

We got up in a hurry, Kieran pulling his gun. (I was pretty annoyed that the baby kept me from having a gun out at any time.)

Two women were approaching us from behind. They were both wearing jeans and t-shirts. One had a short, pixie hair cut. The other wore her long hair in a ponytail. The ponytail chick waved at us like we were long lost relatives. "You're here," she said, as she approached. "I can't believe it."

I pulled Guy close, protectively. Kieran showed the women his gun.

"You guys want to stop right there," he said.

Ponytail waved her hand dismissively. "Oh, you don't need the gun. We're not going to hurt you." She kept right on walking, even though the other woman trailed behind

90

her, looking a little concerned. Once she was right up on us, she offered her hand. "I'm Nancy," she said.

Kieran and I both stared down at her hand. Kieran switched his gun to his other hand and shook her hand. "I'm—"

"Kieran, right?" she said, grinning.

Kieran dropped her hand. "How do you know that?"

"Carol, I told you they were real, and that they were coming," Nancy said excitedly to her companion. "I told you!"

Carol stopped a few paces behind Nancy, putting her hands in the air. "Don't shoot us, please. Nancy's a little nuts, but she's harmless, I swear."

Nancy turned to me. "You're Azazel, right?" She put a hand on the back of Guy's head. "And this is little Guy?"

The lady was creeping me out. "Do you work for Jason?" I asked, even though that wouldn't explain why she knew who Guy was.

"The Wodden guy?" asked Carol. "Oh, no. The rest of the community would never have stood for us camping out at the park with them. They've been calling us witches for years."

The boys had said we needed to watch out for "the witch ladies." Was this them? Why did people think they were witches? How did they know our names?

"You don't have to worry," said Nancy. "We're going to help you. And we've been waiting for Guy for ages. It seems like ages, anyway." To Carol, "Come over and look at him.

He is so precious."

"I'll keep my distance until he puts his gun away, thanks," said Carol.

"Kieran, put the gun away," I said. "They seem harmless."

"Except she knows our names," said Kieran.

"She's right about that?" Carol said. She looked surprised. "Nancy thinks she can see the future. She's been babbling about people bringing us a baby for the past two months."

Kieran put his gun away. "Azazel can see the future too. She has dreams."

Oh, God, seriously? That's what made him feel at ease? Some chick claiming to have powers? What was the world coming to? Anything was believable these days, it seemed. The world was screwed up without electricity.

Nancy and Carol invited us to lunch. Their house was an old farmhouse. All the windows were open. They had pink curtains fluttering in the breeze. They had a few chickens and two goats. I could also see that they'd planted a garden recently. I guess they'd be okay here, even without power. For lunch, we drank goat's milk and ate fried eggs. It was amazing to have fresh food besides meat.

Nancy and Carol said that Columbus had never been the most welcoming of communities to them. They were lesbians. Before the power outage, people had mostly left them alone. After the power outage, they said that people got downright hostile.

"They were convinced that we were witches because we grew herbs and did a lot of natural homeopathic medicine," said Carol. "Sounds like something out of the middle ages, right?"

Before the power had gone out, Nancy had used a sperm donor to get pregnant. Unfortunately, she'd lost the baby sometime in November. She credited it to stress. It had been hard for both of them, especially Nancy. But then, she'd started having dreams.

"I saw him in my dreams all the time," said Nancy. She was holding Guy now, feeding him his bottle. He seemed very content. "I knew his name was Guy. I knew he was our baby. And I knew he was coming to us."

"I thought she was nuts," said Carol. "I thought it was some kind of coping mechanism to deal with the miscarriage."

"But he is ours, isn't he?" Nancy asked. "You are going to leave him with us, aren't you?"

It made sense. How would we take care of a baby back at the camp? We weren't equipped to do that. And we were all a little busy trying to get west. Nancy and Carol were the best fit. I thought they'd be good mothers.

"So, the dreams started after the power outage?" I asked them.

They had. And something else strange had started at that point too. Carol recounted to me a story about cutting herself while chopping some vegetables (some of the few fresh ones left from the stores at that point). Nancy had been able to heal her, somehow. She'd done it twice now.

"I don't know why this is happening to me," said Nancy. "It's almost like the fact they started calling us witches came true or something."

"You said Azazel has dreams," said Carol.

"They don't make any sense," I said. "Last night I dreamed about talking flies."

"You did?" said Kieran.

I shrugged.

Kieran took another long swig of goat's milk. "Azazel has more powers than that, though. She can influence people's minds. Huge groups of them."

"I don't like to do it," I muttered.

"I've dreamed about flies too," said Nancy. "There were a bunch of them. They were carrying a big book on their backs. They were grunting. They were trying to hide it from the vessel."

"Not the vessel again," Carol groaned.

The vessel? I felt a little twinge of nervousness. It couldn't mean me, could it?

"Yes," Nancy said. "The vessel. The book was called the Key of Ashes or something."

"The Key of Asher?" I said. "You dreamed about the Key of Asher?"

Suddenly Nancy looked at me in an odd way. "Yes," she said. "They took it to the park, where the Wodden guy is. To keep it from you." She paused. "You're the vessel."

The twinge deepened. Nobody had called me the vessel

in a long time. "What do you mean?" I asked.

Nancy's eyes seemed to glaze over. "I have dreams sometimes, about things... They don't make sense to me. There's a sun, and the sun is inside a vessel, something that contains its fury. Then the vessel tips over. The sun spills out. And the sun is so bright, it dries up everything. All the grass gets burnt and curly." Guy started crying. Nancy shook herself, as if trying to bring herself back to reality. She handed Guy to Carol and got up. She went to the sink. The window over it was open. The breeze made her ponytail flutter. "You're the vessel aren't you?"

I went over to her. "No one's called me the vessel in a long time," I said. "And it isn't true, anyway. My grandmother made it all up. She forced people to think bad things about Jason and me."

"Jason." Nancy turned to me sharply. "That's the Wodden guy, isn't it? The one in the park? He's the sun."

"The Rising Sun," I said softly. "But it isn't true, what you're saying. It can't be. You're saying that I caused the solar flare? That breaking up with Jason made him bad?" If I was the vessel, and I was covering Jason up while we were together, then it seemed her dream stated that when I left him Jason was free to burn up the world. Like a solar flare. But that was silly, because Jason couldn't cause solar flares. I mean, could he?

"I don't know what the dream means," she said. "I have other dreams though. Like the flies."

"It's stress," said Carol. "They're nightmares. She can't

sleep. I don't like them."

I took her hand. "They don't always come true," I told her. "Sometimes, I think they're just possibilities. We dream them so we can stop them."

But Nancy didn't look comforted. Instead, her eyes bulged and she dug her fingernails into the palm of my hand. Her mouth opened, and she started to speak, but her voice didn't sound like her own anymore. It sounded a little older, and a little deeper. I knew the voice, just like I knew the words. "Your power feeds his. Together, the things you will do. The terrible, terrible things you will do. Do you know what he is capable of?"

Michaela Weem. Michaela goddamned fucking Weem! I tried to yank my hand away from Nancy's. I didn't want to hear the rest of it. I'd heard it before. I didn't need to hear it again.

But she didn't stop. "Ah, I see that you do. I see that you have seen his face. His true face. Do you think it will stop, Azazel? No! It will only get worse. Soon it will be thousands upon thousands of bodies heaped on a pyre. And you will lie dead as he feasts on your guts!"

I pulled harder on my hand, trying to make her let go, trying to get away from her. "No," I said. "None of that is true. My grandmother put those visions in Michaela's head. She made all that happen."

Nancy's fingers dug in tighter. Her eyes burned into mine. And her voice wasn't Michaela's anymore, but it wasn't quite her own either. "It doesn't matter where the visions come from. If enough people believe them, they are true. You will find him sitting alone. He will be crying, like a little boy. You will put your hand on his forehead, and you will reach inside with your mind. You'll squeeze something in there. Something vital. He'll look up at you for that last moment, wondering why. He'll whisper that he loves you. And then...he'll die."

I swallowed hard. I put my hand against Nancy's forehead in much the same way she'd just described. I reached inside. And I made her *let go of me!*

We broke apart, both stumbling and gasping. Nancy clutched her head. "Augh!" she screamed.

I started swearing. I wanted to run for the door, but I didn't. I couldn't because, suddenly all around me, the world was buzzing with flies. They blocked me. They stopped me. I blinked once. Hard. And they were gone.

Nancy was shaking herself again. She rubbed her face. "Like a brain freeze," she muttered. "Like too much slushy, too quick."

Kieran and Carol were both on their feet.

"What did you do to her?" Carol demanded. Guy whimpered in her arms. Carol went to her girlfriend and touched her face. "Are you okay?"

Nancy took the baby from Carol, grinning. "I'm fine. I'm fine. That was crazy! What was that?"

"I don't know," I said. What was I supposed to say? I think you channeled Jason's crazy mother and then had a vision where you predicted the way I would kill Jason?

We left not too long after that. I don't think any of us were much in the mood for visiting after Nancy's outburst. Kieran tried to talk to me about whether it was a good idea to leave the baby there or not, but I was preoccupied. I said the baby would be fine. We were right to leave him there. I also insisted we just go straight back to the OF encampment. I believed Nancy's dream. Jason had the Key of Asher. It wasn't lying around outside, lost in a scuffle. Jason had it.

Kieran tried to engage me in conversation. He wanted to know why Nancy's outburst had freaked me out so much. He wanted to know about my grandmother. I didn't want to talk about any of it.

All I could think about was what Nancy had said. She'd envisioned me killing Jason. When I'd met Jason, people had wanted me to kill him, but I'd refused. Now Jason was hiding out, cutting off people's fingers and making threats. She'd echoed the words Michaela had said to me all those years ago. Was it possible that Jason really was going to become the monster she'd envisioned?

A long time ago, I would have argued against it until I was hoarse. Back then, I didn't believe there was darkness inside Jason. Now, with everything I'd seen, I wasn't sure anymore. Maybe I should have killed him when I had the chance.

CHAPTER SIX

The OF encampment was in a tizzy when we arrived. Kieran and I had trouble finding Hallam and Marlena. No one seemed to be able to talk to us. People were outside the church, standing in groups of two or three, frantically talking to each other. Several of the women were crying.

Kieran grasped the shoulder of one of the guys outside, wrenching him from his conversation. "What's going on?" he asked him.

It was Gus. He looked past Kieran at me. "Everything's falling apart," he said. "Headquarters won't let us do anything." He glared at me. "Why won't you stop this?"

"Where are Hallam and Marlena?" I asked, but Gus had already gone back to his conversation.

Kieran and I went into the church, dropping off what supplies we'd gathered in the sanctuary. We searched each room, calling for Hallam and Marlena. Finally, we found them in Hallam's office. There was another bloody bundle on Hallam's desk. I went to it. There were more fingers. More toes.

I gulped and stepped away.

Kieran stayed behind me, peering down at the gory pieces. I watched Marlena, sitting dejectedly on a folding chair, while Hallam glared out one of the windows. Both of them looked beaten and tired.

"This is insane," said Kieran. "Did you really report this to Headquarters?"

No one said anything.

"Well, should I get on the radio myself?" Kieran asked.

Hallam turned away from the window. His voice was like ice. "Did you find your magic book?"

"No," I said. But I was pretty sure I knew where it was. And I was going to get it. The body parts were just a good excuse.

"We found some food," Kieran said. "We dropped it off in the sanctuary. Did you radio headquarters or not?"

"They told us to stand down," said Marlena. She was staring at the floor.

"They're well-armed," Kieran admitted. "Still, I don't get the impression Jason's just going to stop at cutting off fingers."

"The bundle came with a note," Hallam said. He handed it to me. The paper was stained with blood. It was Jason's handwriting. It said, "Still think I shouldn't drag it out, Hallam?"

Kieran reached for the paper. I handed it to him.

"I don't get it," I said to Hallam.

"The night with the girls. In the sorority house," said Hallam. "I said something to him like that. He was explaining to them why we were doing what we were doing, and I said, 'Don't drag it out.' I meant for him to just go ahead and kill them quickly."

Kieran still looked confused. As briefly as possible, I explained to him that Hallam had helped train Jason for the Sons. His father, Edgar Weem, had been a twisted man who thought Jason needed the ability to kill. He'd lied to Hallam and Jason and told them they were taking down a brothel, when in fact it had only been innocent sorority girls. Hallam and Jason had killed them all.

"This is all my fault," Hallam said. "I turned him into this monster."

"The Sons did it," I said. "And you're not a monster, Hallam. You choose not to behave like he does. Jason has a choice too."

"He's going to kill them," said Hallam. "Don't you think the note implies he's going to kill them?"

I considered. Jason might be bluffing. He knew that Hallam would react emotionally to the note. He might be trying to trick us. But I wasn't sure if I cared. Jason might be twisted and a criminal genius, but he wasn't infallible. He was out of control. Maybe I did need to just find him sitting down and reach inside his head...

But that didn't make any sense. I couldn't kill people with my mind. I could influence their decisions or plant triggers, but I couldn't just kill them.

"We're going after them," I said.

Hallam and Marlena both looked at me, a bit of hope in each of their eyes.

"We have orders from Headquarters," said Kieran.

I shrugged. "The OF doesn't know what's going on here."

"Wait," said Kieran. "You said that the group here was no match for Jason. He's got an entire town in there."

"She's going to use her powers, aren't you?" asked Hallam, sounding triumphant.

"No," I said, "I'm not." I walked out of Hallam's office and into the room with the stockpiled weapons. We had a good bit of ammunition and enough guns to arm everyone in camp.

"Why not?" Hallam called after me. The three of them appeared in the doorway.

Because I hated using magic. But that argument wasn't winning me any points these days, was it? "Kieran and I ran into two of the townspeople out there. Jason's spun some ridiculous lie to them that across the river the government's turned into a fascist state or something. They're just people. They're misguided. I'm not going to hurt them."

I turned to look at the guns again, thinking fast. If we stormed in there, all of us at once, we'd create quite a spectacle. No. "How long would you estimate Jason's been here?" I asked.

Hallam and Marlena gave each other quizzical looks.

"Not long before we showed up," said Marlena. "Maybe a month or two?"

"So, he won't have had time to really train all the people he's found," I said. "Right?"

"Absolutely not," said Hallam.

"Okay, then, so Jason is good at what he does, but

Hallam was trained by the Sons too. I was trained by Jason. Marlena, you've always been a badass. And I've worked with Kieran. He can hold his own." Although I had to admit that Kieran and I had never really been in a real fight before, I thought he'd be okay.

"Just the four of us?" said Marlena.

I nodded. "We can sneak in."

She agreed. "Right, exactly. The objective is only to get the prisoners and get out, not to take on the entire camp."

Furthermore, I thought the grimoire was in the camp. I could find a way to sneak off and find it.

"No," said Kieran. "No, we'd be violating orders directly. We were told to sit tight and wait it out."

"Wait until he kills them?" asked Hallam. "I don't think so."

Right. I wanted that damned grimoire.

"When?" said Hallam.

I thought about it. "Tonight," I said. The sooner the better.

* * *

There were problems with my plan. First of all, Columbus-Belmont State Park was 165 acres—way too much ground for the four of us to cover. We had no idea where Jason was keeping the prisoners. Hallam suggested we put off the actual raid until the following night, and that he and Kieran go in and scout it out.

Neither Marlena or I were having that. We weren't getting left behind. Furthermore, I pointed out that we had a

103

better chance of trying to get in once undetected than in trying to get in twice.

Instead, Kieran and I watched from a distance and saw that there was a guard placed at the gates to the park. They seemed to change up the guard every four hours or so. At twilight, the guard changed. We were all in place.

The trees were tall and dark in the vague light. The sky was turning purple in the west, over the river. Columbus-Belmont State Park looked practically untouched by the power outage. Its signs still stood proud by the entry roads, proclaiming its name. Kieran and I had been able to see a little bit of the campgrounds from where we'd watched earlier. There were RVs and tents set up. It looked, for all anyone would be able to tell, like a typical spring for the park. Lots of campers around the camping loop, all there to enjoy the serene beauty of unspoiled nature.

Hallam and Kieran looked at me anxiously. Marlena was calmly watching the guard.

"What if this doesn't work?" Hallam asked me, whispering furiously.

"It will work," I said. If it didn't work, I'd make it work.

As soon as we were certain the changing of the guard was done and that the departing guard was out of earshot, we took off for the gate, moving quickly but quietly.

The guard was lounging against the Columbus-Belmont State Park sign, his hands in his pockets. He was whistling.

We crouched in the shadows behind him. I nodded to Hallam and Kieran. "Now," I said.

The two darted forward, tackling the guard. He went down with a thud. Hallam covered his mouth so he couldn't cry out. Kieran secured his hands behind his back. They propped him up so that I could approach.

I put a gun under the guy's chin. "Hi," I said. "I'm gonna get my guy to move his hand. You're not gonna make any noise. That clear? Nod if you understand."

The guard's eyes were wide. He shifted his gaze between all of us, but he nodded. He was young, like the kids Kieran and I had seen earlier. Too young. I kind of hated being so harsh with him. It reminded me too much of the way I'd been forced to act when Jason and I were on the run. I didn't want to be this cold, callous woman, but it was worth it if I could find the grimoire and make this stop once and for all.

I inclined my head at Hallam. He moved his hand.

The kid yelled. "Help, there are invaders—"

I shot him in the arm. I didn't think twice about it. I just did it. I would have shot his face off, but then he wouldn't have been much good to us. The violent reflexes I had just kicked in like that sometimes. It was disturbing, but I didn't have time to worry about it right now. I had a mission to accomplish.

The kid screamed, a piercing shriek.

"Shut up," I told him, my gun back under his chin. "That was a warning. Now call out and tell anyone who might have heard you that that was a false alarm."

The kid's voice shook. "Sorry!" he yelled. "False alarm."

"Tell them you're fine," I said.

"I'm fine!" he yelled. He looked down at his arm. Blood was seeping through his jacket. He whimpered.

"Worried about your arm, aren't you?" I asked him.

He nodded.

"Well, the sooner you help us out, the sooner you can ask someone to bandage it up for you," I said. "Take us to the prisoners."

"Prisoners?"

"Your boss has been carving them up and sending us souvenirs. Now where are they?"

The guard whimpered again. "The lookout house. All the way back by the river. But you'll never be able to get to them. There are at least six guys guarding them. None of the people from town are supposed to know about them."

I stepped back. "Get him up," I told Kieran.

Kieran wrenched the guy to his feet. The guard didn't want to stand on his own, so I put the gun back on his head.

"You will show us where they are, or I will kill you. Do you understand?"

"Yes," squeaked the guard, who suddenly seemed able to put weight on his feet.

Kieran patted the guard down. He found a gun and a knife. We took both of them. I stood behind the guard, my gun on the back of his neck. Kieran and Hallam flanked me, their guns at the ready. Marlena brought up the rear.

"You lead," I told the guard. "And don't think about leading us right to someone who's going to shoot us. I guarantee you I'm fast enough to blow you away before they take me down." I leaned close, whispering in his ear. "Besides, you're my human shield."

"Please," said the guard, "they're guarding them. I can't take you without them seeing—"

"You get us close," I snapped.

He started walking. His limbs were stiff. We walked along the road, away from the camping entrance, further and further into the woods. I could hear the crickets again, and if I looked up, I could see thousands of bright stars. The stars were so much brighter these days. I'd never realized how much electric lights blotted out the sky. It was a gorgeous night.

We came in sight of a flag pole, obviously another entrance to the park. The guard veered off the road then and led us into the woods. He tramped over the leaves and branches, making a lot of noise.

I told him to tread more carefully.

He started sobbing. Maybe I was pushing the kid a little too far. I didn't really want to hurt him. I just wanted him to take us where we wanted to go. Still, I wasn't sure what we should do with him once we were done with him. He could run off and get Jason. Then what would we do?

Also, I really wanted a chance to look for that grimoire. How was I going to manage that?

The guard took us through the woods in a round about way, but eventually we reached a clearing. He stopped and pointed through the trees at a gazebo-shaped structure that stood on the edge of the river bank. It was round, with a pointed roof. The foundation was made of stone. There was a large stone chimney jutting out of the top of the building. Was this one of those things left over from the civil war? Had the soldiers stood in it, looking out over the river watching for the enemy's approach? Was there a chimney so they could have a fire in the winter? Wouldn't the smoke have tipped off the enemy to their location?

We could see that the lookout house was surrounded by armed men. It was too dark to see who was inside it. I glanced from the lookout house to the kid who'd led us here. I considered. The easiest thing would be to shoot him in the head. Of course, that would probably alert the guards at the lookout house to our presence. Still, I didn't want this kid running loose in the camp.

"How's his arm?" I asked Kieran.

"He's losing a lot of blood," Kieran replied.

Great. I didn't want to leave the kid out here to bleed to death. I had the kid take off his jacket. Marlena and I made a tourniquet to tie around his arm, hopefully stopping the bleeding. Then we tied him to a tree with the rest of the jacket. I didn't think it would hold him for very long, but that was fine. We didn't need too much time. At least, I didn't think so.

Hallam ripped some cloth off the jacket to gag the kid. We couldn't have him yelling out to the other guards and warning them.

The four of us crouched just inside the trees and spoke in low voices.

108

"There are six of them," said Hallam. "Four of them are in our sight." The other two were behind the gazebo. "If we all shoot at once, can we take those four out?"

"Are we shooting to kill, Hallam?" I asked.

He hesitated. I knew he was weighing the options. On the one hand, dead guards were dead and therefore out of the way. On the other hand, Jason hadn't killed any of our people. If we killed first, it would give him the reason to launch a full-scale attack on us. And there were a lot more people in their camp than there were in ours.

"I can't guarantee a kill shot," said Kieran. "Not with only one chance."

"Legs," said Hallam.

I nodded. Marlena nodded. Kieran sighed. "I'll try."

"Okay," I said. "So we shoot and then?"

"We shoot," said Hallam, "and wait. Hopefully the guys on the other side come around to see to their friends, and then we shoot them too."

"We shoot them in the legs, and they can still shoot at us," said Marlena.

Duh. Why hadn't I thought of that? Why hadn't Hallam?

He took a deep breath and set his shoulders grimly. "Shoot to kill," he said.

We each sized up our targets and took aim. I was shooting the guy closest to the river. Right then he was looking out over the water. I wondered what he was thinking. Then I told myself not to. But it wasn't fair. These guys were all young, and they were all just following Jason's orders. They didn't deserve to die.

"On three," whispered Hallam. "One...two...three."

I squeezed my trigger, bracing against the force of the shot. Immediately, I heard the sounds of the others' gunshots. The guys at the lookout house all tensed one second, looking up. Then the bullets hit them. My guy went down, clutching his chest. Good.

Hallam's guy's head exploded. Of course. Trust the guy trained by the Sons to make a shot like that.

Marlena's shot took her guy in the stomach, and he went to his knees.

Kieran's shot went wide. He didn't connect at all.

Kieran's guy began returning fire in our general direction.

I hit the ground. Kieran ducked behind a tree. Hallam and Marlena took cover as well. Kieran peered around and got off another shot. This time, his bullet drilled the guy in the neck. Nice. I was impressed.

Unfortunately, the other two guys did not come around the lookout house. Instead, they took cover behind it and were shooting at us from there. Marlena's guy was hanging on too. He returned fire, even though he was lying on the ground.

We exchanged bullets for a few minutes, neither side hitting anyone. I did my best to hit Marlena's guy, but he was difficult to see now that he'd flattened himself against the ground, just a dark shape in the shadows.

What were we going to do? If we broke cover and raced

for the lookout house, they'd see us. On the other hand, if we stayed hidden in the trees for too long, more of Jason's people were likely to show up. I knew Hallam would suggest that I use magic, but I wasn't going to. I could figure this out.

Darkness was hindering us, but it was hindering them too. We had that on our side. How could we use it? "Split up," I hissed. "I'll stay here and keep shooting. You guys creep around in the shadows."

The other three agreed. They broke off, each slinking out of the woods. Kieran crawled further down the bank, and headed for them that way. Marlena stuck to the edge of the woods and came at them from the opposite side. Hallam, daredevil, that he was, got on his belly and crawled straight for them.

I shot over and over again, trying to make it seem that there were still four guns on them. I don't know if they thought so or not.

One of my shots finally got the guy that Marlena had originally hit. He cried out, forced out a couple more shots, and then was still.

For an agonizingly long time, I couldn't see Hallam, Marlena, or Kieran. I tried to look for telltale movements in the darkness, but couldn't see any. This was a good thing. It meant that the others couldn't see them either. But it was terrifying.

One of the guys behind the lookout house shot a bullet that was almost too close for comfort. It wedged itself into the bark of the tree in front of me, inches from my face.

I gasped, stepping back. I couldn't return fire for several seconds.

They were going to realize I was the only one there!

I stepped forward to shoot again, but looking out, I realized Hallam was leading the prisoners out of the lookout house. Kieran had marched the other two guards out from behind the stone structure. They had their hands in the air.

I heard Hallam yell to Kieran, "Shoot them!"

Kieran hesitated. Then he leveled his gun and put bullets neatly in each of their skulls.

Marlena appeared out of the shadows, ushering the prisoners towards the trees. There were four of them. All seven people sprinted towards me.

Within seconds they were under the cover of the woods.

"We don't have much time," said Hallam. "People heard those shots. Jason will have reinforcements on the way."

"We'll cut through the woods," said Marlena. "It'll be safer than following the road into the camp." She started to lead the prisoners forward. Hallam followed.

Kieran stopped, staring at me with wide, hollow eyes. What was wrong with him?

"Go," I told him.

He started after Hallam.

I didn't move. I looked back at the bodies and the lookout house. I wanted that grimoire.

I thrashed forward through the underbrush of the woods to the prisoners. "Which one of you is Lily?" I asked.

One of the women spoke up. "Me."

"Do you have the grimoire?"

"Azazel," Hallam growled.

"They took it from me," said Lily.

I dashed back towards the clearing. "Go on without me!" I told Hallam.

"Get back here," Hallam said.

I didn't pay any attention.

Clearing the woods, I was in the open. The grimoire wouldn't be in the lookout house. It would be safe, inside shelter. Would it be inside a building on the grounds? Was there a building? Maybe Jason had it in camp. One thing was for sure. Jason had it. I had to figure out where Jason would be.

I darted across the clearing to the lookout house and crept behind it, kneeling in the shadows. Hallam was right. Reinforcements would be showing up soon. I could follow them back to Jason.

As luck would have it, Jason appeared in just a few minutes, followed by about ten armed men. Not all were young boys this time. A few were older—maybe thirty or forty. They wore black shirts and jeans, almost like a uniform. These men must be Jason's personal guard. His highest in command.

Jason and the men surveyed the bodies.

One of the men spoke to him. He didn't have a Kentucky accent. In fact, he sounded like he was from up north, maybe New York or Jersey. Had he moved here? A northern transplant? "I told you we shouldn't let the locals guard the prisoners."

The locals? These men weren't from Columbus at all then? Did they travel with Jason? What the hell?

Jason held up a hand to stop the man. "No, this is what I expected. If you had been killed, the people wouldn't be willing to drive the OF out."

Another guy smirked. "We wouldn't have been killed."

Jason smiled. "Exactly. This way, everyone will be outraged. They'll demand we do something. We'll have to show the OF who's boss."

Wait, was I following him? This was part of his strategy? He was trying to rally the people of Columbus to fight us? Jesus, he was playing Hallam like a violin. I had to warn Hallam that an attack would be coming, but then Hallam was smart. He knew what the consequences would be when he'd ordered us to shoot to kill.

"Should we go after them?" asked one of Jason's men.

Jason shook his head. "Not yet," he said. "Let them go."

Jason had his men load up the bodies on makeshift stretchers. They wrapped the bodies, two to a sheet. Then the men tied off the ends. Together, they dragged the bodies away from the lookout house, back to camp. Jason didn't leave, though. He walked into the lookout house and rested his arms on the railing. He stood there, gazing at the river, quiet. I could see the shadow of his profile. I was struck again by how attractive he was.

Inwardly, I scolded myself. I wasn't supposed to feel

drawn to Jason. Not anymore. It had been so much easier to forget about him when he wasn't around.

"I know you're here," Jason said, his voice soft, like black velvet.

CHAPTER SEVEN

I didn't move. He wasn't talking to me.

"Azazel," he said.

Damn it. He was bluffing anyway. There was no way he could have seen me. I'd keep quiet. Eventually, he'd assume he was wrong and shut up.

"I'm not an idiot," he said. "I know you're looking for that grimoire. That Lily chick told me before I threatened to cut off her fingers." He giggled then. He sounded completely insane. "I cut them off anyway, of course."

Jason strode to the edge of the lookout house. He was maybe three feet away from me. I didn't move. I was huddled in shadows. He couldn't see me.

"Now," he said. "Why would you want the Key of Asher? Maybe it's because there's a section that's supposed to purge someone of power completely." He knelt down so that he was eyelevel with me.

Shit! He knew where I was. He had to. What was I going to do?

"You constantly surprise me," he whispered. "That's why I can't stop loving you, I think. When you kicked me out, you were so caught up in your own issues with magic. I didn't think you realized I had any magic."

Jason had magic? That was silly. My grandmother had told me that I'd done it all. I'd placed the suggestions. I'd driven people crazy and made men kill themselves. It was me. Not him.

"Are you going to come out?" he asked.

I guess there was the fact that Jason had sort of come back from the dead once. That had been kind of creepy. And before, all the weird things had happened after Jason and I had kissed. I'd always figured that the kissing was just a coincidence. We'd thought that Jason had power, because everyone had been convinced that he had, from Michaela Weem to the Sons. It had been kind of ironic, I thought, when we realized that it had all been me, the whole time.

But maybe it hadn't been all me. Maybe...

"Or am I going to have to drag you out?"

I stood up. I drew my gun.

"Jesus, Azazel," he muttered. "Always with the guns."

"I want the grimoire," I said.

"Absolutely not," he said. "I won't let you try to get rid of my powers. Unlike you, I happen to like them."

What? Wait a second. Jason was completely confused about what I wanted with the grimoire. He thought I wanted to purge his powers, not my own. I didn't care about his damned powers.

I leapt on him.

He wasn't expecting it. We both went sprawling onto the stone floor of the lookout house. We struggled for a second, but I was on top, and I had the advantage. I pinned him, my knees between his legs, putting pressure on his groin, my gun pressed against his chest. "Tell me where it is," I said.

"You just can't handle not being close to me," said Jason. "I miss you too, babe."

"Tell me where the book is or I will shoot you," I snarled.

"I'm not going to tell you," he said. "And you're not going to shoot me."

Oh, that was what he thought, was it? "I'll find it another way," I said. I didn't need Jason anyway. He was psychotic. He was a killer. He'd ruined my life. I pulled the trigger.

Click.

I was out of bullets.

Jason looked stricken. "You pulled the trigger."

I fumbled for more bullets, but Jason wouldn't let me do that.

His arm came up hard and fast, knocking my gun out of my hand so that it skittered across the floor of the lookout house and dropped off the side onto the river bank.

He grasped my arm and twisted it behind my back, sitting up at the same time.

I cried out in pain. He wrenched the arm he held out from behind me and pushed me down on my back.

My other hand was free. I clawed at his face, digging at one of his eyes. His hold loosened. I was able to start to sit up.

He snatched that arm away and slammed me down against the floor.

My head cracked into the stone. I moaned.

Jason had both of my arms held down now. He was on top of me, and I lay beneath him, spread eagle.

He lowered his face to mine. "The last time we did this," he murmured. "I remember it being a lot more pleasant."

"Fuck you," I muttered.

He gave me a wistful look. "No. Not if you don't want to." His lips hovered close in the air, next to mine. "But I miss that. Don't lie to me and tell me you don't."

I turned my face away from his. There had to be some way I could get out of this.

His mouth was against my ear. His tongue darted out against it, something that always made me shudder in pleasure. My traitorous body did it this time too.

I struggled in his arms. "Stop it."

"We could have everything. We could usher this world into the next age. Don't you realize it's what we're made for? Be with me, Azazel. Forgive me."

"Never," I said.

Then I heard a gun being cocked behind Jason's head. "Let her go."

I looked up. Kieran? Jesus Christ, what was Kieran doing here?

Jason slumped against me. "Not him again."

"I swear to God," said Kieran. "I will blow your brains out all over her face if I have to."

Jason pushed himself up to his knees, his arms up. "I don't suppose I want you to see what happens when you shoot me just yet."

What the hell was that supposed to mean? I didn't have the time to puzzle it out, though. Jason was no longer holding me down, so I wriggled out from underneath him, rubbing the back of my head.

"Sorry about your head," said Jason. He sounded sincere, too. God, I hated him.

"Put your hands behind your head," Kieran rasped. "Get to your feet slowly."

Jason complied, making a face. "Really, Azazel, I'm kind of insulted. I thought I set the bar a little higher than this guy."

"Kieran and I are not together," I said, furious. If he'd just stop taunting me, maybe I could keep my cool long enough to figure out what to do.

Kieran glared around Jason's body. "Why are you telling him anything? Is it his business what's going on with us?"

Oh, wonderful. Now Kieran was convinced there was an "us." There was no me and Kieran. There was just a slight, miniscule chance I was carrying his bastard child.

Jason barked out a hard laugh. "You're breaking his heart, babe."

"Stop calling me that," I seethed. Had he called me that when we were dating? I didn't think he had. Where was my gun? I was going to load it, and then I was going to shoot Jason myself.

"Stop talking," Kieran told Jason, pressing the gun tighter against the back of his skull.

Jason's voice was low and rumbly. "Kieran, don't fall for

120

her. Don't try to protect her. She doesn't need protection. And you shouldn't read much into anything she lets you do. Azazel's a certain kind of girl. She's...what would you call it? I know. Easy. I only had to shoot a couple of guys, and she hopped between the sheets with — "

I was lunging for him, but Kieran beat me to it. He took Jason's shoulder, spun Jason around to face him, and clubbed him in the face with the butt of his gun.

Jason's head snapped to the side. Kieran drove a fist into his midsection.

"Kieran don't fight him," I said, but it was too late.

Jason doubled over, but raised his head slowly. He smiled at Kieran. Blood was trickling down the side of his face. "You should listen to her."

Jason dove for Kieran, fists flailing. He tore the gun from Kieran's hand and flung it over the railing. He punched Kieran's ribs, while his other fist upper cut Kieran's chin.

Kieran absorbed the impact, but took two steps back. He roared in rage and then jumped on Jason.

The two tumbled to the floor of the lookout house, Kieran on top. He hurled blow after blow at Jason, his fists crunching against Jason's face and chest.

Jason was laughing. He was bleeding. His right eye was swelling up, but he was laughing. He reached up and took hold of Kieran's neck, squeezing him and lifting Kieran away from his body with one hand.

Kieran's eyes bulged. His grabbed at Jason, but he was too far away to make contact.

In one movement, Jason pushed Kieran down on the floor and got on his knees so that he was on top of Kieran. Jason twisted Kieran's face sharply. There was a cracking sound.

I put my hand to my mouth. Had he killed him?

But Jason released Kieran's throat and Kieran gasped. He was alive.

Jason put his knee on Kieran's chest and drove his weight onto Kieran. More cracking. Kieran moaned. Jason stood up. He kicked Kieran's stomach. Kieran groaned, but didn't retaliate.

Jason faced me, wiping his nose with the back of his hand. There was blood all over his face.

"Easy," I said. I hadn't realized that would hurt me so much. Jason and I might have gotten physical kind of quickly, but I thought it had meant something to him.

"I didn't mean it," he said. "I was just trying to piss him off. After all, he's the one who's with you know, and I'm..." He looked down at the ground, his shoulders slumping, as if all of his anger was draining out of him. "You're not easy. You're..." He swallowed. "Every time you touched me, it meant the world to me. I couldn't have handled being alive that day in the hotel if it wasn't for you. I'm sorry." He reached for me.

I took a step away from him, shaking my head. It was always the same. He was always doing this. Hurting people, and then expecting that some crazy romantic speech was going to make it all better. It didn't make anything better. It didn't.

But we looked into each other's eyes for a few minutes, and I saw the hurt guy in the hotel room, who needed me to hold him to keep the darkness at bay. I had to stop myself from going to him right then and there and putting my hand on his bloody, swollen cheek.

Jason wrenched his eyes away from mine. "Get your boyfriend out of here. I think I broke his ribs."

CHAPTER EIGHT

It was a long walk back to the church, since Kieran was in a lot of pain. It had been hell just getting him to his feet. I was pretty sure Jason wasn't going to send anyone after us, but just to be sure, we went through the woods. I stopped to untie the guard we'd tied to the tree. He wasn't unconscious from loss of blood yet, so I figured he'd be fine.

Kieran winced with every step and his breathing was labored, but he wanted to talk, once we were relatively clear of the park and were certain no one was behind us. "So," he said, "explain to me again what you saw in this guy?"

That was the last thing I wanted to talk about. Jason. "You're lucky he didn't kill you," I muttered.

"Oh, really?" Kieran coughed and clutched his chest.

I sighed. "Thanks for showing up, though. I didn't know how I was going to get out of that."

"Dude just bugs me," Kieran said. "I don't like the way he looks at you. Or talks to you."

"Sometimes, he's an ass," I agreed.

"Sometimes?"

I glared at him. "Why did you follow me, anyway?"

"It's my job to protect you," said Kieran. "And the other night, what I said about caring about you. I meant that."

"Don't," I said.

"I'm sorry it makes you uncomfortable if I say that, but you're very possibly pregnant with my child, here, okay?"

"Shh!" I said, glancing around us in the woods to make sure no one was around.

"Seriously?" he demanded, and then winced again.

"Look, Kieran, he was right about one thing. Don't fall for me. I don't feel that way about you."

"Why not? Because your ex beat me up and you no longer respect me?"

"Kieran!" The man frustrated me beyond words.

Kieran put a hand on my shoulder and stopped me. He turned me to face him. I looked up at his face, which was oddly not nearly as bloody or swollen as Jason's, even though Kieran had taken the worst of the beating. His ponytail was messy. Strands of hair were falling out of it, framing his face. "I'm sorry, Azazel, I can't help it. I am falling for you."

I wanted to look away, but I just stared at him, feeling helpless. "Well, you shouldn't," I said. "I just leave destruction in my wake. I never do anyone any good at all."

His shoulder muscles tensed. "Are you talking about what you did to the guard tonight?"

I'd been talking about my powers, but I realized I'd probably been a little hard on the guard. "Did that freak you out?"

He half-shrugged. "You're a badass. You're tough. You just shot him in the arm. You didn't hesitate."

"Yeah," I said.

Kieran cast his eyes away, nudging the leaves on the ground with one foot. "I could hardly shoot those guards when Hallam asked me to. I can't believe I did it. One minute they were alive and the next..."

I took Kieran's arm.

"Ow," he said.

I dropped his arm. "Come on. Let's keep walking."

We walked.

"You haven't killed many people have you, Kieran?" I asked.

He didn't say anything.

"It gets easier," I said.

"Yeah," he said, and his voice sounded hollow. "I bet it does."

* * *

Hallam was really pissed off at me, especially when he found out that I hadn't actually gotten the grimoire. When Kieran and I got back, he called me into his office. I sat on a folding chair. He paced the room and yelled at me for a long time, talking about loyalty and following orders and the importance of people over magic books. I just let him go the way I had when I was a teenager and he was lecturing me about sleeping in the same bed with Jason.

Eventually, Marlena popped her head in and told him to shut up. She turned to me apologetically. "He's just worked up because the prisoners are back and some of them may have infections from where Jason cut off their fingers."

Hallam glared at Marlena. "I don't need your help with this."

Marlena put her hands on her hips. "Azazel is not your daughter, Hallam. You don't have to lecture her like a child."

Geez. Finally somebody else besides me was saying it.

"I know that," said Hallam, slamming his hands down on his desk. "Some kind of guardian I made anyway. They're both absolutely out of control. Jason's cutting off people's fingers and Azazel's more concerned with magic books than people's lives."

I stood up. "Wait a second."

Marlena held up a finger at me.

I shut up.

Marlena walked to Hallam. She put one of her hands on his. "This is not your fault," she told him.

He pulled his hand away from her. "Everything's falling apart."

She sucked in a breath through her nose. "Maybe. But that doesn't mean you have to fall apart too."

Hallam snorted. "So now I'm falling apart, huh? You sure know how to make a fellow feel better, Marlena."

Marlena rolled her eyes.

I needed to figure out a way to get out of the room if they were going to argue.

But just then, someone stuck his head in the door. "Uh, sorry to interrupt, but there are two women here with a baby. They're saying something about dreams?"

Carol and Nancy! Excellent.

"I know who that is," I told Marlena and Hallam. To the guy at the door, "Take me to them."

The wounded prisoners were in the sanctuary, along with Kieran. They lounged on pews. A few were lying on pillows. Carol and Nancy were in the entrance. Carol was holding baby Guy. Nancy was especially excited to see me, but Carol looked a little annoyed.

"Thank God you're here," I said to Nancy.

"You need me, don't you?" she asked, grinning at Carol. "I told you the dreams meant something."

"We have five wounded people," I said. "They might have bad infections. And I think Kieran has broken ribs."

"Oh God," said Carol. "What happened to your boyfriend?"

I sighed. "He's not my boyfriend." Why did everyone keep calling him that?

* * *

Nancy got to work right away. She sat with each of the wounded people, putting her hands over their wounds. She squeezed her eyes shut. Her body shook. Then the healing would begin to happen. The wounds would begin to shrink. New skin would inch its way over the blood and exposed muscle. The skin would knit itself back together, and the person she was with would be whole again. I watched the injured as they stared in wonder at their healed bodies, twisting themselves to test if they were really unhurt. It was astonishing.

While this was going on, I filled Marlena and Hallam in on how we'd met Carol and Nancy and about Nancy's particular abilities. Hallam was intrigued. He wanted to be sure of the details. It had started after the power outage? She hadn't been able to do it before? I told him to the best of my knowledge that was true.

Now that Hallam wasn't screaming at me, I also told him about my run-in with Jason, and that he had the grimoire. I explained that Jason said he had powers and that he thought I wanted the grimoire in order to purge him of them. Hallam appeared even more thoughtful.

Afterwards, he gathered me, Kieran, Marlena, Nancy, and Lily in his office to talk. Nancy was exhausted, but exhilarated. She'd never healed so many people. She told us that she'd never felt quite so important or helpful in her life. It was wonderful to be able to make people feel better. We could all tell though, that it had taken a lot out of her. She was a little pale and her eyes looked a little too wide.

Hallam thanked her. "We're blessed to have you among us," he told her. "We can't express our gratitude enough. Is there anything we can do for you and your partner?"

Nancy just laughed. "Oh, I love his accent. Sure, hon, you and your wife can just keep talking English to me like that."

Lily laughed too. "It always did strike me as odd that the two of you were here and working for the American government. There's a story there, isn't it?"

"Oh, I've always been an expatriot," said Marlena. "I was born in America, but my parents were both British. That's why I talk this way. Hallam was just on the run from the Sons of the Rising Sun."

Lily and Nancy both raised their eyebrows.

"Evil secret society," I said. "Enough said."

"You're probably wondering why I called everyone in here," Hallam said. "It's just a little odd. There seems to be a sudden explosion in extra-normal abilities."

"Explosion?" said Lily.

"Well, we've got Nancy, Azazel, and then Azazel told me that Jason claims he can do things too," Hallam said. "Did you witness anything like that while you were in the camp, Lily?"

Lily considered, then shook her head. "He was just very interested in the grimoire. And Azazel, of course." She studied her hands, the two stumps where her pinkies used to be. "He's very compelling, I suppose. He got me to give him information. I mean, he was torturing me, but I got the impression I would have given it to him anyway, even if I hadn't been threatened."

"Hmm," said Hallam. "Maybe he's bluffing."

"We never did figure out how he came back from the dead," I said.

"He came back from the dead?" Kieran asked. "Like Jesus?"

"The bullet didn't cause as much damage as we thought, obviously," said Hallam.

"He stopped breathing," I said. "You couldn't find a pulse." I still remembered the way I'd felt in the attic of

Jason's mother's house. Jason's brother had shot him in the head, and I'd been sure Jason was dead. But when I'd put my lips against his, Jason's eyes had fluttered. He'd been okay. Had he come back to life? Healed himself? I used to think it wasn't possible, and that, like Hallam was saying, we'd overestimated the damage Jason had sustained. But in light of what Nancy could do, maybe Jason was capable of healing himself.

"The more I know about this guy, the more I don't like him," Kieran said.

"Well, at any rate," said Hallam, "it got me thinking about the nature of power and the nature of magic. Some of you know that I was trained by the Sons of the Rising Sun. They had very interesting ideas about power—sort of an amalgamation of all religious traditions. They believed it all described essentially the same thing and that the culmination of all of this would be in the Rising Sun—who they thought was Jason, of course. According to the Sons, all power was ancient and prophesied. Power was passed down along blood lines. It wasn't very democratic, I suppose." Hallam smiled.

"That's why my power doesn't make any sense," said Nancy. "I didn't inherit it. It just showed up."

"Yes, exactly," said Hallam. "Well, I first started working with the Order of the Fly immediately after the destruction of the Sons, when the American government was in shambles. Azazel was working through her own issues with her powers with their help. I thought I would find out a little about their philosophies."

The OF hadn't been of much help with my powers. They were ridiculously upbeat about everything, thinking that magic was for the good of humanity and everything else. They didn't understand that my magic did nothing but cause people pain. It was destruction, pure and simple.

"The Order of the Fly believes, quite similarly to some of the ideas spouted by poets and magicians in the early part of the twentieth century," said Hallam, "that magic can be invoked by certain images and ideas that gain great power — symbols, if you will."

Kieran leaned forward in his chair. "Yeah, I remember this from my training. The idea is that symbols gain power because they're recognized by the collective mind, right? Like everyone focuses on a cross for thousands of years, so it becomes a powerful symbol."

"Right," said Hallam. "But what if we took this a step farther? Nancy, you said that the people around here shunned you because they thought you were a witch, right? There was a powerful collective belief that you were a powerful being, and... now you are."

Nancy furrowed her brow. "That's true, I suppose."

Hallam looked at me. "Of all people, Azazel, you and Jason have been the focus of so many people. And they've all believed you were powerful."

Wait a second. I turned to Nancy. "You said something like that at your house yesterday. You said that it didn't matter where the visions come from. If enough people believed them, they were true."

"Did I?" Nancy said. "What I felt when I took your hand was so intense. There was so much turmoil."

I turned to Hallam. "Is this true, Hallam? If this is true, then what Jason is saying could be right. He could really be the Rising Sun. Not because the Rising Sun actually exists, but because enough people believed it did. He could have these powers because of that. And I could be..." God. What was I, if Jason was the Rising Sun? Was I the Vessel of Azazel, born to kill him or was I his consort, meant to love him?

Hallam shrugged. "If it's true, why is it happening now?"

"Maybe because the lights have gone out," said Lily. "People are much more superstitious now. There's less belief that the world is rational and safe. People are much more likely to believe in possibilities."

"Okay, but the people that thought Jason and I were powerful are all dead," I said. "Do they still count?"

"Symbols are powerful not just because people believe in them now, but because people have believed in them historically," said Kieran. "According to the OF, anyway."

Damn it. "But everyone thought something different about us," I said. "So what are we then?"

"Conflicted," said Hallam. "And possibly very dangerous."

"Okay," I said, "but we can get that grimoire back from Jason. We have to get that. If we can get that, it has a ritual that will teach me to purge all of our power. Both of us. I can wipe us clean. We won't be a danger anymore."

"Azazel," said Hallam, "I don't think that's the answer."

"The Key of Asher is more important as a tool to use magic for the good of others," said Lily. "The purging ritual is dangerous. It's not something to be attempted by a novice. I wasn't aware you even knew about it."

"Why do you think I wanted that damned book?" I asked.

"I didn't think you knew about Jason's power," said Hallam, confused. "You wanted the grimoire so you could purge his power?"

"No." I stood up. "No, I didn't want to purge his power. I wanted to purge mine. Why do you think I came all the way here from Georgia? It wasn't so I could see Jason again, that's for sure. I never wanted to see him again. I came so that I could get that freaking book, so that I could get rid of my power. I don't want it anymore."

Everyone looked shocked. No one said anything.

Fine. Screw them all. I stalked out of the room, slamming the door after me. I strode out of the church, onto the lawn. I'd walk up the street. I'd walk and walk and walk until I felt the anger seep away.

"Azazel!"

Great. Kieran. Why was he everywhere, all the time? I kept walking.

He ran up behind me. "Where are you going?"

"For a walk," I said, not stopping.

"I'll walk with you."

"No. Go away," I said.

He took my arm, and I shook him off. He took it again, harder this time, and yanked me to a stop, forcing me to face him.

"Are you serious?" he said. "That's why you came here? Because you wanted to get rid of your magic?"

"I'm serious," I said.

"How could you do that?" he asked. "How could you leave all of us in the lurch like that? We need your magic, Azazel. If we don't have it, our job is disastrous."

"Because of my magic, people get hurt," I said. "They always get hurt."

"You're crazy," he said, arms flailing. "Those are coincidences. Bad stuff happens all the time. And it's not your fault. You're not causing it."

"You have no idea," I said. I spun on my heel and started walking again. At first I didn't hear him behind me, but then the sound of his footsteps reached my ears. He was running to catch up.

"This isn't fair," he yelled after me. "You can't do this!"

I walked faster.

He was behind me, right at my ear. He was out of breath, but he just kept talking. "I was assigned to protect you, because you are important to us. We all depend on you. Every single one of us on the team. If it weren't for you, we wouldn't have been able to do all the good we've been able to do. And you want to throw it all away. I can't believe you could be so undeniably selfish."

I stopped. "Selfish?" I gaped at him. What did he mean?

"Yeah, selfish. You want a life where you don't have to work for the government and put yourself in danger. You just want to sit back and be out of the action. But that's not the way it works, okay? You have a gift. You have to use it for the good of humanity. Whether you like it or not. Okay?"

"What don't you understand about the fact that my 'gift' doesn't do any good for humanity? Even when I try to do good, terrible things happen."

"You want to see that, Azazel, but it's not true."

"It is true! You don't know what happened with my niece."

This didn't faze him. "No. You're believing a lie. And that's not all. That's not the only reason I can't believe you're trying to get rid of your power."

I clenched my teeth. "Okay. What else?"

"Tonight, I had to watch you go into a dangerous situation, where we were shot at. And then I watched that Jason fuck-face wrestle on the ground with you and try to hurt you, maybe try to rape you, I don't know —"

"Kieran, I've been doing dangerous things since we met."

"Yeah, and you have magic. So I said to myself that you could take care of yourself. And I shouldn't make an issue about it. But Azazel, you're pregnant—"

"We don't know that!"

" —and do you have any idea how scary it would be for me if I didn't know that you had that kind of power? That you couldn't protect yourself and our child —"

"God, Kieran, stop talking about it like that!" I screamed. I ran into him at full force and began beating my fists into his chest. At first I hit him hard, but then my punches grew weak. He grasped both my wrists. I sagged against him.

I convulsed into sobs.

Kieran pulled me close. He stroked my hair as I cried into his shirt. One of his arms was wrapped about my waist, and he held me tight against his body as if it were the most natural thing in the world. Right then, he seemed so strong and so powerful, and I felt so helpless and small. I didn't care if that was actually true or not. For the moment, it was too comforting to be in Kieran's arms and to let him whisper into my hair that everything was going to be okay. I clung to him, and I cried until I felt spent.

Even then, I didn't pull away. I snuggled closer against him. My hands wandered over his chest. He had a nice chest. I tilted my face up to look at him. He smiled down at me. The curve of his lips was so tender. He was such a nice, nice guy. What was wrong with me? Here he was, being awesome, and I was running from it. Did I have some block that kept me from being attracted to guys who weren't actually bad for me?

I slid a hand up around Kieran's neck, settling it behind his head. I moved his head down towards mine. He didn't need more encouragement. His lips met mine eagerly.

Kieran was a warm, enthusiastic kisser. His lips and tongue moved against my own. I didn't feel like the world was breaking apart. I didn't feel like my limbs were exploding. Instead, I just felt warmth spreading throughout my body, engulfing both of us. He made me feel drowsy, safe, like being wrapped in a blanket on a cold day with a cup of cocoa in my hands. Comfortable. Safe. Happy.

Then he pulled back. "Sorry," he said. He let go of me.

Suddenly, everything felt very cold. I hugged myself. "What's wrong?"

"You were upset," he said. "I shouldn't have taken advantage of that."

I rubbed at my eyes, trying to wipe off all my tears. God, I'd been emotional lately. Was that a sign of pregnancy? Jesus. "I wanted you to," I told the ground. I felt a little embarrassed.

"Sure, you did. When you were crying. But I shouldn't have kissed you like that. You needed me to comfort you, not jump you."

I giggled. "It was nice."

He laughed. "Nice, huh?" He shook his head. "Okay."

I was confused. "Is it bad that I thought it was nice?"

"No," he said. "It's fine. I thought it was much more than nice, though." He shoved his hands into his pockets. "We can just forget that happened, if you want. We don't ever have to talk about it." He turned and started back for the church.

I opened my mouth to call him back, but then I closed it. Maybe he was right. Maybe I'd kissed him because I was upset. Maybe we should just forget about it. Did I want a relationship with Kieran? He was gorgeous. He was sweet.

He was good in bed. I liked kissing him. He was completely supportive of my possible pregnancy. He'd already told me he was falling for me. Wasn't that enough?

What did I want anyway? I turned and looked towards the road that led to Columbus-Belmont Park. I thought of Jason's swollen face. I thought of his large, dark eyes. Did I want to rule the world?

I shook myself and headed after Kieran. I jogged to catch up with him, and when I did, I slid my hand into his. He gave me a startled look.

I smiled. "I thought it was more than nice too," I said. What was a little white lie in the grand scheme of things? Kieran was clearly the better choice.

CHAPTER NINE

I awoke in Kieran's arms. We were both zipped inside a sleeping bag that we'd gotten from the back of the Subaru. The morning breeze lifted my hair off of my bare shoulders. I opened my eyes, looking up at the morning sky, the grass and trees. I had done it again.

I shifted, maneuvering myself on to my back. How had this happened? Right, we were going to talk and we wanted to sit down, so Kieran suggested getting the sleeping bag. But I hadn't been interested in talking, I'd just wanted to kiss Kieran more. I guess I was afraid if we talked, he might realize that I wasn't sure how I felt about him at all.

Of course, a perfect reaction to a feeling like that was to have sex with him again. Damn it.

Kieran was only the fourth guy I'd ever had sex with. Besides Jason, I'd had a couple drunken hookups in college. Just like Kieran should have been. Nothing but a drunken hookup. That would have made things so much easier.

It wasn't that I was a fan of one night stands in general or didn't think that sex was better in a committed relationship with a person you loved. I thought that stuff. It was just that I had felt very, very deeply for Jason when we'd been together. It hadn't been that long of a relationship, but it had been very intense. We went through scary stuff together. Our lives were in danger half of the time. Everything about our relationship had been frantic and extreme. I killed for him. I would have died for him. And even though I couldn't be in a relationship with him anymore, it didn't mean that it was easy to start another one.

Even now. I gazed at Kieran's sleeping face. I liked him. I liked the way he made me feel. I liked how steady he was, and how much he cared about me. But I thought maybe something inside me was broken or something. I didn't know if I could really love someone ever again. After the all-encompassing, forceful love I'd had for Jason, love that I'd felt with every fiber of my being, I didn't know if anything else could ever measure up.

God. What was I doing? I was just going to screw Kieran up. Hell, I probably already had. What was I going to do?

Careful to be as quiet as possible, I unzipped the sleeping bag and slipped out of it. I found my clothes. Put them on. Darted away from Kieran to the church. I didn't know what he'd think or how he'd feel when he woke up alone. But I couldn't be there with him when he did. I felt too conflicted.

It was early, but Hallam was out back, piling charcoal into the grill for breakfast. He saw me approaching, but he didn't wave or call out. I decided I'd do my walk of shame through the front of the church instead of the back. But when Hallam saw me veering towards the front door, he called me over.

I debated for a second, but I walked over to him.

"Where were you all night?" he asked, setting the charcoal bag down on the ground.

I yawned and shrugged. "I think I'm going to try to catch another hour of sleep."

"Where's Kieran?"

Marlena opened the back of the church and came out. She had a sweater on, buttoned tight against the morning chill. "Hallam," she said, "she's a grown woman. Maybe it's none of your business."

Sure. Fine. Except when Kieran was hating me later, it was going to screw up the entire dynamic of the whole team. I was really good at messing stuff up, wasn't I?

Hallam's shoulders slumped. "You're right," he said to Marlena. To me, "I'm sorry."

"It's fine," I said, starting for the door inside.

"Hold on," said Hallam. "I wanted to talk to you about something." His voice sounded weary, like an old man.

I bit my lip. "Okay."

"You really came here because you wanted to get rid of your powers?" he asked.

"Yes," I said.

"Is this because of Jenna?" Marlena asked.

I folded my arms over my chest, trying to protect myself. I could hardly think about that, let alone talk about it. "It's because of a lot of things," I said. "If you think about the consequences of my magic, it's never really positive."

Hallam sighed. "I'm not going to argue with you about that. You seem convinced that it's true. But I have to admit the fact you want to get rid of your magic is disturbing, both to me and to the OF. I felt the need to radio headquarters about it."

My heart sank. This wasn't good. Headquarters was going to be pissed.

"They want you and Kieran to report to D.C. immediately. You're to leave as soon as you can pack your stuff," said Hallam.

Oh. Okay. Right. Why was it that everything in my life got worse and worse no matter what I did? I was only trying to make things better for everyone. Why couldn't anyone see that?

Marlena came close and put her arm around me. "I'm sorry," she said.

I leaned against her for a second. Comfort was nice, even if I didn't deserve it. "It's okay," I told her.

"For what it's worth," Hallam said, "I can't imagine what a burden this all must be for you. We expect a lot from you, Azazel. I'm sorry that your young life has been so harrowing. I'm sorry that Jason has become what he's become. I'm sorry that you have to carry the responsibility for the deaths of all the men in the Sons. It's not fair, and if I were you, I don't know that I could bear it either."

I moved away from Marlena. "I can handle it," I said. "It's not that."

"Listen," said Marlena, "what happened with Jenna...you can't know if what you did worsened the situation or not. Babies cry, Azazel. How would Mina and Chance have known she wasn't just colicky?"

I'd heard this argument before, from my own brother, his eyes red-rimmed with tears. I didn't want to hear it now. "Chance is okay, isn't he?" I asked. "I mean, you haven't heard anything otherwise?"

"No," said Hallam. "I suppose you can see him while you're in D.C."

"Yeah," I said. My brother had been taken into what might be called protective custody after the lights had gone out, but I didn't think it was so bad. He was allowed to come and go as he pleased. Mostly, anyway. There wasn't a lot of coming and going in a world where there was very little transportation. He was safe. That was the important thing. It had been one of my conditions before I even considered working with the OF. Chance had to be safe. As for Mina, his ex-girlfriend, with whom he'd had a child, well, we hadn't heard from her since the funeral. We'd heard rumors she'd gone out west. I hoped so. I hoped she was clear of this disaster, safe somewhere where televisions still worked.

I rubbed my face. "I'll start packing." But as I started towards the church door again, I saw Kieran making his way towards us, the sleeping bag balled up under one arm. I wanted to run inside and avoid him, but I was going to be spending another long, uncomfortable car ride with him. What was the point?

He didn't look happy. He stopped next to the three of us, shifting the sleeping bag to another arm.

"Headquarters ordered us to come to D.C.," I said by way

of greeting.

Kieran's eyes widened in surprise.

"I told them that Azazel wants to purge herself of power," Hallam explained.

Kieran shrugged. "Well, I guess that would do it." He shot a look at me. I looked away. "We need to leave right away?"

"As soon as you're packed," said Hallam.

"Better get packing," said Kieran. He went into the church. I followed him.

We didn't have a lot of packing to do. Mostly, we shoved our clothes into our packs. We stuck those in the Subaru, along with the sleeping bag we'd used the night before. Kieran unhooked the motorboat we'd pulled with us from Georgia. They'd need it if they ever got a chance to cross the river. And during all of this, Kieran and I said next to nothing to each other.

We stood outside the church, surveying the Subaru and the motorboat.

"I'll go say goodbye to Hallam and Marlena," I said.

"We should talk," said Kieran.

"We'll be stuck in a car together for a few days," I said.

Kieran took me by the elbow and dragged me away from the church, back down the road where we'd kissed last night. Once we were out of earshot of anyone inside, he stopped. He took two steps back from me, so that we were facing each other. He glanced at me, then glanced down at the road. He jammed his hands into his pockets.

I wondered if he was going to say anything.

Kieran took a deep breath, started to speak, then stopped. He tilted his head back. His hair was down. It hung free around his shoulders. Little strands of it glinted golden in the sun.

"I'm sorry," I said.

"No, this is my fault," he said. "I miss my family, and I have tried to turn you into something that you aren't."

"Kieran, I should never have slept with you again. I was—"

He held his hand up. "Stop."

I gulped down the rest of my words. I nodded.

"Okay," he said, tapping his foot and looking everywhere but at me, "when you told me you might be pregnant, at first I was really scared. And then, for a little bit, I was angry, because I didn't think this should be happening to me. I didn't want any of that. I felt like I barely knew you. Hell, I still barely know you."

"I'm sorry."

He waved his arms in my face. "No, seriously, don't say anything, okay?"

I nodded again, wondering where he was going with this.

He steadied himself and took another long breath. "Okay, so I was pissed. But then, I started thinking about everything, and I started to feel like maybe it was going to be okay, because this was, like, I don't know, a replacement. For what I lost. And that I should embrace it."

A replacement?

146

Kieran rubbed the back of his neck with one hand. "Right after the lights went out, everything started to get pretty hairy where I lived in Chicago. There were gangs and lootings and stuff pretty much right away. And my family got caught up in the cross-fire. These guys were drunk or on some kind of messed-up drugs. I don't know. But they broke into our apartment."

He stopped, seemingly unable to finish what he was going to say. He shifted on his feet and changed tactics. "I'd been at school, you know, when it broke out. My senior year. I was studying to be a phys ed teacher. But then the lights went out and they closed the dorms, and even though I was living on campus, it just seemed like I should go to be with my family. So I did.

"I hadn't been there for very long. Maybe a few days. My little sister—well, she wasn't so little anymore. She was sixteen. She was pretty, and we were just kind of getting to the point where we didn't get on each other's nerves so much. Like, we could tell that at some point soon, we could be friends, because we'd both be adults. Her name was Angie. I never realized how much I loved her. I don't know if I ever told her I loved her. Her whole life, I don't know if I ever once said that. But I did love her. So, so much.

"And my parents. They got on my nerves sometimes, but they were good, solid people. I depended on them. When those guys broke into our apartment, wanting whatever it was they wanted from us—I guess our food. Our TV. Any money we had. When they did that, I'd never seen my dad look so afraid. And I was afraid too. We didn't put up a struggle. None of us. We didn't fight them. They had guns. It probably would have been stupid, I guess. I thought, you know, that they'd just take what they wanted and then leave."

Kieran was talking to his hands now. His head was bowed. "And at first, it seemed like that's what they were doing. They were filling up these pillow cases with all our stuff, and they were cleaning us out. We were all sitting in the corner, like they'd told us to. One of them was making these comments about Angie, like how much of a hottie she was and other stuff. It was vulgar. I wanted to kill him. I wanted to rip him to shreds, but..."

"I didn't do anything," he bit out fiercely. "I just sat there. And I watched. And he..."

"Kieran," I whispered. I could guess the rest.

But Kieran kept going. His voice was getting tighter as he talked. He sounded so angry. "I watched them rape her. And when my father tried to do something about it, they shot him in the head. And when I tried to do something, they shot my mother too."

I put my hand to my mouth, too horrified to say anything.

"They left Angie and me. But Angie was so upset and hurt and I didn't have anywhere to take her. I didn't know what to do. Later that night, she started, like, bleeding, and I tried to get her to a hospital or to those rescue shelters they had then. The ones that existed for a while. But she didn't make it. She just bled and bled and bled and then..." He took a shuddering breath. "And then she was dead."

I reached for him, but he stepped back, out of my grasp. "I'm sorry," I murmured. It wasn't enough, but it was all I could say.

Kieran swallowed hard, and his jaw tensed. He wouldn't look at me. "I'm telling you this, because I hated myself for not protecting them. And I joined the OF, so that I could learn, you know, to be stronger. But I wasn't letting anyone that close anymore. Then, you told me that maybe I was having a baby. And I thought that this was my chance to redeem myself. Like, if I could protect you and if I could protect that baby, then maybe it would make up for the way I failed my family. Then maybe I could forgive myself."

I didn't say anything. I wanted to hug him maybe, or touch his arm, but I didn't know if I should, not after the way I'd just abandoned him in the sleeping bag that morning.

Kieran fidgeted with his hands, unsure of what to do with them. "That's why I pushed so hard for us to be together. It wasn't fair to you."

"It's okay."

"It's not okay. I was basically using you."

I blinked hard, trying to process all of this. First Kieran told me a long, horrific story that should qualify him for hours and hours of counseling, during which the counselor would eventually just give him some pills and tell him everything would be fine. (I know this. I shot my best friend in the head and the counselor wrote me a prescription. Seriously.) Then Kieran somehow made this an excuse for his actions. Then, he somehow decided his actions were bad and that he had hurt me in some way. The guy was even more screwed up in the head than I was. All I could say was, "I don't think so."

He looked up at me, holding my eyes with his own. "Yes, I was using you. I put you in this position to be something that you never promised me you could be. And no wonder you felt like you had to run away from that."

I thought my head was going to explode. "No," I said. "Sleeping with you again was cruel. I shouldn't have done that when I didn't know how I felt about you."

"No, that's my point. I don't know how I feel about you either. And we can't let this baby thing make us think that we should feel certain ways about each other when we don't really know anything about each other."

I nodded slowly, waiting for this to sink in. "So you're not mad at me?"

"Well, it totally sucked waking up in that sleeping bag alone. But while we were packing, I started thinking, and I decided that I couldn't be mad at you."

He wasn't mad at me. That was good. That was very good. But I was still confused. And I felt like we hadn't really addressed the whole story he'd told me, but I didn't want to bring it back up. It was too terrible. Who wants to talk about stuff like that anyway? "So you're not interested in me romantically?"

"I didn't say that," said Kieran. "I..." He blushed. "Obviously, I find you attractive."

I felt embarrassed too. "I think you're pretty easy on the eyes yourself."

"And we're, you know, physically—that's good."

I laughed nervously. "Yeah. It's good."

"So," he said, "we have this whole several days in a car thing planned. And I think it would be a good time to get to know each other."

Well, that sounded too healthy for words. I grinned. "Yeah. Okay. That sounds good."

He smiled and looked relieved. "Good."

I should have left it at that, but I couldn't. "Kieran, about your family, I—"

"It's cool," he said. "You don't have to say anything."

"I just..." I picked at the edge of my shirt. "I watched my parents get shot and killed too. It was years ago, and they were kind of messed up people, but I loved them." I paused. "You think you failed your family, but you don't know what it's like to really do actual horrible things to people. I have done things, Kieran, that I still can't really think about. Really, really bad things." I looked up at him. "So, you don't have to feel bad about anything around me, okay?"

"You're talking about the magic, Azazel, and I'm telling you that you haven't done anything—"

"I'm not talking about the magic. I'm talking about other stuff. The magic stuff was all an accident. I never meant for any of it to happen. But you think you failed your sister, because you didn't save her. But my brothers, they kidnapped me, because they wanted me to kill Jason, because they thought he was like the anti-christ or something. And to get away from them, I..." I glanced at the ground, then the sky, then my shoes, and then finally back up at Kieran. "I shot them both. I killed them." I didn't look away after I said it. I just watched him, waiting for his reaction.

"They kidnapped you? They tried to make you kill someone?"

I nodded.

"Those jerks," he said.

That was his reaction? Really? "Don't you care that I killed them?"

"It sounds to me like you were protecting yourself," he said. "I don't think you did anything that horrible at all."

I considered for a minute. "Even though now I don't even hesitate before I shoot kids in the arm?"

He shrugged. "Look, I told you I thought you were a badass. It's not a bad thing. Come on. They're waiting for us in Washington."

Right. Washington. Great.

* * *

With several gallons of gasoline closed up tight in the trunk of the Subaru, Kieran and I started off for Washington, D.C. Kieran was driving for the first leg of the trip, and I'd take over later. We'd barely pulled onto the E. Hoover Parkway when I saw them.

Just beyond the sign to Columbus-Belmont park, they were marching. It was an enormous group of people, mostly men and boys, but with a few women scattered in as well. They carried shotguns and rifles, the kind you'd use for hunting. They had grim, determined faces. They were heading into town.

"Kieran," I said.

He was watching the road. He hadn't seen them. "What?"

"Look." I pointed.

He glanced in the direction of the park. "Crap," he said. "It's Jason's people, huh?"

"It's got to be. They're going after Hallam and everyone else."

"What should we do?"

I considered. We had orders to be in D.C., but leaving Hallam in the lurch like this seemed like a bad idea. Jason's people outnumbered Hallam's by a huge amount. It was almost as if Jason had emptied his camp of people. Hmm. Jason's camp was empty. That would mean that no one was there guarding the grimoire. "Stop the car," I said to Kieran.

He pulled over. "We've got our orders, Azazel," he said.

"Screw the orders," I said, opening the car door.

"What are you doing?" he asked.

"Go back and warn Hallam," I told him. "There's something I have to take care of." I got out of the car and slammed the door.

I could hear Kieran yelling after me, but his words were muffled.

I didn't pay any attention to him. I scampered across the road and into the woods surrounding Columbus-Belmont Park. I didn't even look back to see if Kieran was following my instructions. He'd have to be a total dick not to warn Hallam, though.

It took me about ten minutes to get to the camping loop. It was right next to the main entrance, where we'd found that guard last night. I peered through the foliage in the woods at the camp. Like before, I could see numerous pitched tents, some campers, and a few RVs. There was a central fire pit. Several women, trailed by small children, were walking through the encampment. A few carried dishes. Maybe they'd been washing them in the river.

The question was where did Jason sleep? I tried to think it through. It was possible that Jason had won these people's loyalty by a show of solidarity. In that case, he'd sleep among them, in any one of these tents, wanting to appear as if he was just another of the people in town, nothing special.

On the other hand, Jason could have swept in like a king and demanded the best sleeping arrangements in the place, in which case he'd either be in a house or a deluxe camper somewhere away from the rest of the town.

Which was most likely? I didn't know. The Jason I knew wouldn't be leading a group of people at all. He hated it when people looked to him for leadership. Or at least, he'd hated it when the Sons had done it. Now? Who knew what he loved or hated?

There was another problem. How was I supposed to

154

explore the camp when there were people all over the place? It was daylight. I couldn't sneak around in the shadows. Somehow, I was going to have to find a way to hide in plain sight. Damn it. I really hadn't had much time to think this plan through, had I?

"For God's sake, Polly!" Was that Jason's voice? I peered through the foliage.

There he was. He was striding across the camping loop. A woman with long, red hair was following him.

"Jason, wait," said the woman with red hair, very possibly Polly.

Jason didn't wait. He kept going. He walked right past the spot where I was hiding in the woods and down the path to the road out of the camp. He must be late for the battle.

As quietly as I could, I followed him, still staying behind the cover of trees.

When he broke onto the road, he turned on his heel and glared at Polly, who was still behind him. They were out of sight of the encampment at this point. I crept closer, wincing when I crunched on a dead twig.

Jason didn't seem to notice. "I'm late," he said. "They left at least fifteen minutes ago. I do not have time for this."

"I know," said Polly. "I'm sorry." She closed the distance between the two of them in two steps. She put her arms around him. She pressed her lips against his.

I let out a little gasp.

Jason didn't hear that either. He was too busy closing his eyes and crushing Polly against him, pulling her so, so close.

Polly looked an awful lot like my ex-best friend, Lilith. I guess Jason had a soft spot for redheads, no matter what he might have claimed to the contrary. I glowered at the kissing couple.

Why had he begged me to join him, when he already had his little redhead? Why had he nearly assaulted me, pretended that he still wanted me?

My stomach was twisting into knots. It had all been part of Jason's attempt to manipulate me, I realized. He was playing my attraction to him to his own advantage. He knew it threw me off balance. He had never meant any of it. And to think, last night, when I was talking to Kieran, I'd actually half-considered what it would be like to give in to Jason. To think that I'd bought any of his lies. That jerk. Tears were forming in my eyes.

Polly pulled away from Jason, smiling a small, satisfied smile. "That's all I wanted," she said. "Be careful."

He shook his head at her. "Woman," he growled mock-angrily, reaching forward to tickle her.

My stomach twisted over again. Jason used to tease me that way.

Polly darted out of his reach, giggling.

Jason was serious now. "I've got to go."

They kissed again, briefly, before Jason sprinted off after his troops.

I seethed in the woods for a few minutes, watching Polly trudge back up into the encampment.

Somehow, I hadn't thought of Jason finding someone

156

else. Why, I didn't know. And maybe it shouldn't make me angry, but… The tears seeped out of my eyes onto my cheeks.

No. I wasn't crying over Jason. Not again.

I left the woods and emerged onto the road. I walked out the same way Jason had. As I did, I reached inside myself and began uncapping the power that flowed within my body, the way the OF had taught me to do years ago. I liked to keep the power completely tamped down. But today, right now, I didn't much care.

It rushed into me, like lava. I felt aware. Awake. I was a searing force. I searched for the minds of Jason's people. It wasn't hard. There was a huge group of them and they were all single-mindedly focused on one purpose. They wanted revenge. I saw within their collective mind the faces of the guards we'd killed the night before. The names. Andrew. Kevin. David. John. Michael. Nicholas. To the men coming for Hallam's camp, they were just boys. They were beloved children of a town, and we'd snuffed out their lives.

I reached for the burning flood of my power and sent it pouring like a waterfall over the minds of Jason's men. I planted confusion. I burst apart the collectivity of their thoughts. I threw as many distracting thoughts as I could into their brains. They were going the wrong way. They were hungry. They had reasons to hate each other. They didn't like shooting people. They didn't know exactly who killed the boys.

I felt the minds of the men become confused. Perfect.

That should at least give Hallam the time he needed to get organized.

I'd been walking down the path out of Columbus-Belmont Park, but now I began to run. I hurried as fast as I could to find Jason's people and to see what was happening. Green leaves blurred in front of my eyes as I sprinted through the woods. I could hear the voices of Jason's people, who'd begun to question each other.

I rounded a bend in the road, and I spotted them. Instead of marching in the direction of the church, they were now milling about aimlessly. Some were arguing with each other. Jason had caught up to them too, and he was stalking through them, trying to figure out what was going on.

I planted myself in the middle of the road, crossing my arms over my chest. I felt pretty pleased with myself.

Jason's eyes swept his group, who were now more a mob than a small army. Then he saw me. We stared across the expanse of men at each other. At first he looked startled, but then I saw that he understood what had happened to his men. I had taken control of their minds. He gave me a twisted, knowing smile.

I gave him the finger. Dick.

Jason turned his back on me. He lifted his hands above his head. He yelled, "For Andrew! For Kevin! For David! For John! For Michael! For Nicholas!"

I felt it, then. Jason's power. It was different than mine, although also liquid. While my power burned and fizzed, Jason's cooled and soothed. His magic flowed out over the group of men like a refreshing balm, completely undoing my attempt to confuse them. They all stared at Jason adoringly and began to march forward.

I realized then why their minds had felt so focused. It was Jason's magic. His power was the complete opposite of mine. While my power destroyed, his pulled things together. No wonder the men had all had one collective mind. Jason had the ability to focus them.

Well, not on my watch, baby.

I reached out again to the men's minds, and I pulled at them harder this time. Instead of just making them confused, I dug out deeper, darker emotions. I funneled anger and fear into their ranks, and I focused that anger and fear on their neighbors, on the men who they stood and marched next to.

The men scattered almost immediately, pointing their guns at each other.

I fixed an image in my brain of the men all shooting each other. I savored the rage and tasted the sharp metallic bite of blood on my tongue. Some army Jason was going to have if they were all dead.

I poured my power into the men, working each of them up to a fiery rage.

The first shots rang out. I watched one of the men take a shot in the stomach. Another cried out as a bullet tore through his arm.

Jason's arms went up again. He broke down everything I'd done again, pulling the men together. They whipped their guns up against their shoulders and drew their feet together — coming to attention.

But I didn't wait this time. I just pushed back, refueling the men with rage.

Between us, Jason's people danced like flags tied to a rope in our tug-of-war. One second, they faced forward, reading to march. The next second, they dropped into defensive stances, snarling at each other. Shots echoed off the trees. Men clubbed each other with the butts of rifles.

Each time, Jason drew them back together, but with every moment I held their minds, more bodies fell to the ground.

As we continued, I saw Hallam, Kieran and the rest of the people from the church approach, guns in hand. They took advantage of the situation by starting to shoot at Jason's people. Jason's men were helpless to defend themselves. Several more bodies thudded against the ground. Screams rent the air as men doubled over or grabbed at their wounds, staring in disbelief at the blood seeping through their fingers. The air was thick with the smell of discharged guns and sweat. I watched as Jason's army became a chaotic mass, struggling to make any kind of move.

This was the last straw for Jason. He threw his hands down and sent a different message to his men: Retreat.

Immediately, the men scattered, running back for Columbus-Belmont Park.

I took a look at Jason, and I pulled my magic back, bottling it back up inside me. I'd won. Satisfied, I took a deep breath.

Hallam and the OF group chased the men back into the park, their guns raised. Only Jason remained standing, while all his men ran. I approached him, feeling triumphant.

He started for me, his expression dark.

We met in the center, men running around us, parting for us like the Red Sea.

I glared at him. "A redhead, huh?"

He looked startled. He didn't know I knew about that, did he? "Polly?" he said. "Polly's just—"

"A girl you kiss?"

He gritted his teeth and shrugged. "Something like that. Sure."

"Fuck you," I said. "Don't try anymore of that stupid I-still-want-you crap, okay?" I started to push past him.

He stopped me. He leaned close. He whispered in my ear, "I knew you'd use magic again. I knew it."

* * *

Before...

December 2012

It was blowing snow, but none of it was sticking to the ground. Last year, I wouldn't have worried so much about how cold it was, but last year, there was electric heat. Last year, I lived in a house. Last year, warmth was a given.

This year, I was working for the OF, trying to gather as much gasoline as we could. We were in northern Virginia, one of those suburbs of D.C. that's covered with strip malls and cookie cutter housing developments. The power had been out for about three months. I went out with the OF team about a month after it started. We went as far south as we could, hauling empty tanker trucks to store all the gasoline. In the beginning, it had been easy.

Back in early November, people still trusted us. We were the government, and when we said we were coming to help, they believed we could help them. We said we needed fuel to get west and get help. They said that was fine and to take it. Even though I'd been brought along to use my magic, I hadn't had to, not in the beginning.

But it was worse now. People were scared and worried. People were dying. And it was cold. We were finishing our sweep and heading back to D.C. This suburb was our last stop before checking in with headquarters. I had hoped everything would go smoothly. I could still see the river in Tennessee, just a week ago, glutted with bodies. They floated face down in the muddy water, dead. And that had been my fault. I hadn't meant to. Oh God, I hadn't meant to. But when I opened up the container that held my magic, it seemed like I always released the voice too. The whispery one. The one that told me to do awful things. The voice I couldn't seem to resist anymore.

I huddled inside my winter coat, my hands jammed into the pockets. I was watching as the other members of the OF team siphoned gas out of the tanks below an Exxon station. Across six lanes of empty street, a Target store squatted, a remnant of life before the power outage. Its windows were cracked and broken. The parking lot was littered with twisted carts and abandoned cars. The gray sky spit and swirled snow flakes at us. We were alone.

I hoped.

One of the guys on our team emerged from inside the Exxon.

162

The original door was shattered, leaving a gaping dark hole as an entrance. He was holding handfuls of candy bars. I thought his name was Kieran. He loped across the Exxon parking lot to me, offering me a KitKat.

I shook my head.

"You more of a Hershey's Almonds girl?" he asked, sorting through the candy bars to find one.

"Snickers," I said, taking the one I saw peeking out of his jacket pocket.

"Hell, I was saving that for myself," he said. "It was the last one." I offered it back to him, but he shook his head and grinned at me. "You can have it."

The Snickers bar was cold. My hands were numb, and I struggled to open the wrapper. Kieran took it from me and opened it. He handed it back.

"You look cold," he said.

I shivered. "I'm fine."

"I could go across to the Target and look for some gloves or a scarf or something for you," he said.

I took a bite of the Snickers bar. It was nearly frozen and brittle, but still sweet. I chewed and swallowed. "I'm fine, really," I said. "Thanks for the candy bar."

"Your nose is red," said Kieran. "You look like — "

He was interrupted from what I was sure wouldn't have been a flattering comparison by a gun shot.

We both started forward in the direction of the sound. There was a group of about twenty locals marching up the empty street. They were carrying shotguns. Wonderful.

"Damn it," I said.

"Damn it," said Kieran.

We exchanged a look.

Since I was here to be the negotiator, I had to go and talk to the locals. Mournfully, I glanced down at the Snickers bar. I'd only had one bite. However, I didn't think the people with shotguns would take me very seriously if I was chewing on a candy bar. I thrust the Snickers at Kieran and jogged to intercept the mob.

"Stand down!" I called as I approached. "This is an official government squad. We're just following orders."

The locals neither stood down nor stopped walking. I planted myself in front of them, in the center of the road. I'd try logic. Sometimes logic worked. "Our weapons are more sophisticated than yours and we've all been trained," I said. "If you try to engage us, you will lose. Why don't you all just go home?"

There was a man in the front. He stopped and motioned for the others to stop walking. He stared me down. "Who are you, girlie?"

Girlie. Seriously? I clenched my teeth. "I'm the only one in this team whose job it is to be nice to you people. Those guys – " I jerked my head towards the men siphoning gas – "don't talk. They shoot."

"Well, maybe we don't feel like talking either." The man fired another gun shot into the air for emphasis.

Oh. This was perfect. This was really perfect. "For your own safety," I said, "I really must insist that you disband and return to your homes."

"You're stealing our gas," said the man.

"We are taking possession of fuel in order to get west and get help," I said. "The government needs this fuel in order to help the country." No one seemed to believe me anymore when I said things like this. Maybe it was because all the teams we'd sent west thus far had disappeared without a trace. No help had come. Maybe it was because it was winter, and everything seemed gloomier and gloomier with each passing gray day.

"We need the gas," said the man. "What are we going to do while the government steals our fuel?"

"I thought those Order of the Fly assholes were magical, anyway," yelled someone else within the mob of people. "How come they can't just magic up some gasoline?"

"Yeah," chorused several other voices.

Uh oh. This was getting worse. The last thing I need was a bunch of people yelling and complaining. Especially if those people were all holding guns. Things were going to get ugly fast, unless I used my magic. But I didn't want to. In Tennessee, all of those people floating in the river had gotten there because of my magic. Even if these people were planning on shooting all of us, I felt guilty about manipulating their minds.

Maybe I wouldn't hear the voice. Maybe things wouldn't get out of hand. Maybe if I was careful –

But I didn't have more time to think, because the man leading the mob raised his shotgun into the air and yelled, "Charge!"

Before the stampede could start, I reached inside myself and uncapped the container holding my magic. As always, it flowed into my entire body, making my limbs tingle and the back of my head feel like bubbles were rising up my spine. I could feel the hazy focus of the minds of the mob. They were angry and scared. They

165

wanted to hurt us, because they were hurt and there was no one else to blame.

I tried, as I always did, to simply quiet them. I tried to quench their anger and calm their fears. But my power never seemed to work that way. It was as if it fed on anger and fear. As if it could only cause pain and destruction.

Within seconds, I realized it would be easier to simply redirect the mob's fear. I pulled the focus away from our team and placed the focus on the Target. The store was already destroyed. How much worse could they make it?

The mob howled and took off towards the store, guns at the ready. They began to pump bullets into the store's windows. Glass shattered. A hole appeared in the target emblem on the side. Bullseye.

I couldn't help but laugh. It was appropriate, I guessed. They needed a target for their anger, why not Target?

Maybe it was the laughter that brought the voice. Maybe it was just the magic. I didn't know. But it spoke to me in scaly whispers, a voice that came from a deep, dark, musty place. Human targets , it said.

Before I could stop myself, I found myself picturing the people turning on each other, emptying their shotguns into each other's chests. I tried to turn off the image, to think about Target, to refocus them on the store, but the images had taken hold of my brain.

The locals began to snarl at each other.

No. No, stop it. I struggled with the magic. I'd stuff it down, back inside me, if I couldn't control it. I reached out for it, trying

166

to pull it back to my body. It wouldn't budge.

The man who'd been the leader shot one of the local women in the head. Her skull exploded in red gore, and she toppled to the pavement. Another man shrieked and shot at the leader. Two red holes burst through his chest. He fell to his knees, clutching at his wounds before crumpling to the ground.

I yanked as hard as I could on the magic, drawing it back closer to me. But I was too late. The parking lot in front of Target had erupted into a shooting frenzy. Bodies danced as they were riddled with gun fire and thudded on the empty lot.

I bottled the power back up, capping it tightly. I was shaking. This always happened. This always happened. I couldn't use this magic anymore. Not if this was the result.

Grimacing, I took one last look at the carnage across the street. Then I looked away, ashamed.

CHAPTER TEN

I froze, horrified. Jason grinned at me, an awful grin. And then he walked past me, following his men back into the camp. Now that the people had cleared out, I could see the damage I'd caused. There were bodies lying on the ground. Those men were dead, not because of a fight with the people they'd come to fight, but because I'd twisted their brains and forced them to turn on each other. Jason had stopped them from all killing each other, but he hadn't been able to stop everything I'd done.

I stumbled forward, running to the first man I saw. I knelt next to him. His eyes were wide open. Blood stained his slack lips, twisted in an expression of agony. I threw myself to my feet and ran to the next man. He was dead too, lying face down on the ground. His blood spilled out of him, turning the grass crimson. There was a man beside him, his neck twisted unnaturally. No, on closer look, he was hardly a man. He couldn't have been more than fifteen years old. The sparse blonde hairs on his upper lip gave his youth away. I rushed from one body to the next, hoping to find someone alive, someone I could save, but they were all dead. Dead bodies. Dead, because I was jealous of Jason's new girlfriend.

What kind of sick monster was I, anyway?

I stood in the middle of the empty battlefield, my shaking hands pressed to my lips. What had I done? I hadn't wanted to kill anyone else. I hated hurting people. Why hadn't I had one moment of regret, one second to consider these men's lives while I was toying with them? I let out a little gasp. I couldn't handle this.

I stumbled past Hallam, Marlena, Kieran, and the rest of them. I walked all the way back to the church. Kieran had parked the Subaru in front again, where it had been before. I got inside. No keys. Darn it. I sat back against the driver's seat, pulling the door shut after me.

What had I done?

I sat in the car, turning it over and over in my head, the way you do when you can't shake a horrible thought. I tried to make excuses for myself. I was angry. I wasn't thinking clearly. If I hadn't done what I'd done, then Jason's people would have hurt Hallam. But I knew that I hadn't done it for them. Not really. I'd done it only because I was angry at Jason. I'd used those people as my weapon against him. That wasn't the right thing to do. That was clearly the wrong thing to do. Why did I have this kind of power when I was so clearly unable to use it responsibly?

The things I could do...

I could rule the world. Everyone would fear me, because I could make them do things they didn't want to do. And no one would be able to stop me.

I realized it then. It cut through me like ice, chilling me.

The voice. I hadn't heard the voice once today.

Did that mean that I was the source of its perverse orders and visions, not the magic itself? Did it mean that all the horror I caused came directly from my own brain? I shuddered.

The worst thing was that I could have gotten that grimoire, and I could have completely neutralized myself as a threat. But I'd been distracted by my own anger and now the damage was done.

It didn't take long for the others to get back to the church.

Kieran noticed me in the car and came around to the passenger side. He tried the door. I'd locked it, so he just tugged at it.

"Go away," I told him.

He pounded on the window. "Let me in."

Kieran sighed heavily. Hallam and Marlena peered in at me.

"What do you suppose she's upset about?" Hallam wanted to know. "She was fabulous. Without her, we would have been slaughtered."

"Let me talk to her," Kieran said.

Forget it. I wasn't talking to anyone.

After a little more conversation, Hallam and Marlena went inside, leaving me with Kieran. He stood outside the car. "I'm not leaving," he said. "Not until you talk to me."

I scrunched down in the seat. I did not want to talk to Kieran. Why couldn't everyone just leave me alone?

Kieran pulled the keys to the Subaru out of his pocket

with flourish. Great. He opened the passenger door and got in the car next to me.

"I don't want to talk," I said.

"You're mad at yourself because of using magic, right?"

"Did you see all those people who were dead, just lying on the ground there? I did that. I made them shoot each other."

"They were going to shoot us."

"Whenever I do magic, it always leads to destruction and death," I said. "I'm sick of it. I'm sick of hurting people. I don't want anyone else to die because of me."

"Azazel, stop blaming yourself. You did what you had to do," he said.

"I didn't have to do that," I said.

"They were like that mob, in Virginia. You stopped them from hurting anyone."

I flashed on the bodies in the blowing snow, their blood freezing on the parking lot. So many dead men. I didn't want to think about it anymore. I banged my hands against the steering wheel. "I wish you'd just go away."

"I know you do. And I will, if you really want to be alone. But first, tell me why you think your power is so horrible."

I sighed. "It's just always done horrible things," I said.

"I think it's a matter of perspective," said Kieran. "It's horrible to some people, good for others."

"Right," I said. "So what was so great about my baby niece dying then? From what perspective was that a good thing?"

He furrowed his brow. "I don't know what you're talking about. Do you want to tell me about it?"

I didn't. Not really. But maybe if I told him, he'd understand. Maybe he'd let it go and I wouldn't have to explain myself over and over again. Maybe he'd be on my side. "Right after the thing where all the Sons died," I began, "Jason, me, Marlena, Hallam, and my brother and his girlfriend all moved into my grandmother's house. She was dead, and we inherited the house and her money. It was a big enough house for all of us, and it was nice. We were happy there. My brother's girlfriend, Mina, had a baby. A beautiful little girl named Jenna. I loved her more than I've ever loved another being, not even Jason. She was so helpless and perfect and wonderful.

"But," I continued, "she cried a lot."

"Babies do that, or so I understand," said Kieran.

"Right," I said. "None of us thought anything of it. I don't know if anyone would have, though, if anyone had ever really heard her cry for very long. I used my magic a lot to…quiet her down. Just to make her calm. Because, I don't know, I guess I just thought she was more pleasant that way. And it was easier for everyone not to have to deal with a screaming baby.

"But we didn't know that Jenna was crying so much because she was dying. She was very, very sick, and we couldn't tell. She was trying to tell us, but I made her shut up. So, she died, and if I'd never used that fucking magic on her, she wouldn't have."

172

I slammed my hands against the steering wheel of the car again, then I gripped it. I wished I could shake the car apart. No matter what anyone said, there was no way I could forgive myself for what I'd done. I'd killed my baby niece. It just made it worse that no one really blamed me. Everyone had forgiven me. Everyone said it wasn't my fault. Even Mina, before she ran off. She said she didn't blame me. It was no one's fault.

"I know how you feel," said Kieran.

I turned to him sharply. That wasn't what I'd expected him to say. I'd expected more of the same ridiculous drivel, that it wasn't really my fault.

"I should have saved my family," said Kieran, "and I didn't."

I bit my lip. Neither of us said anything to each other for a few minutes. I just reached over and took Kieran's hand. He squeezed it. We sat in the car, holding hands. And, somehow, that was better than any reassuring words that anyone had ever tried to tell me before.

* * *

I spoke to Hallam about the fact that Jason had been using magic that afternoon. I told him that I could feel that our powers were different—mine was destructive and Jason's was cohesive. The powers had different textures. While Hallam was concerned about the fact that Jason had the ability to influence a large group of people's minds, just like I did, he dismissed the idea that our powers were opposite or that my power was evil, like I thought it was. I didn't argue too much with him, because I was beginning to wonder if he was right. Maybe my power wasn't evil. Maybe I was just evil.

Hallam said I had to get over it, because he and his people needed to rely on my magic. I didn't like this. I didn't like killing people or hurting people. After a brief discussion, Hallam convinced me to talk to Lily, who was supposed to convince me that my powers weren't evil.

Lily and I met in the radio room. She perched on a chair elegantly. She was probably somewhere in her early forties, but she was a wiry woman. I could tell she was strong and in shape.

I slouched in my own chair, not really interested in anything she was going to tell me. I'd heard this business from the OF. Power comes from the earth, and everything on the planet is part of the same cycle, therefore nothing could really be all that bad, could it? Stupid.

Sure enough, she started in with natural analogies right away. "Do you know anything about redwood pine cones?"

What did this have to do with anything? I glared at her. I was starting to feel a little sick to my stomach. Had I eaten anything today? "No, I don't know anything about pine cones."

"Redwood pine cones will not release their seeds if they go through a fire. Fire is destructive, you see, but it brings about regeneration."

I rolled my eyes. "You're saying that destruction isn't always bad."

"Precisely. It is, perhaps, a matter of perspective."

"Try to explain to me a perspective where it's better for people to be dead."

"Well…" She stood up and walked over to the radio. "If they were trying to kill you, then the threat to you is neutralized."

That wasn't a good enough reason. "I don't like it," I said. "Ever since I was seventeen years old, I've had to kill people. I don't want to do it anymore. There's got to be a way where I don't have to do it."

Lily picked up a pencil, which was sitting next to the radio, along with a pad of paper. It was for taking notes on orders. She began to gesture with the pencil while she talked. "I don't think anyone enjoys killing people. I certainly don't. But like you, I've been forced to live a life of violence."

"Because of the solar flare."

"Because of who I am and what I choose to do. I work for the OF, and I have always used my abilities to protect others. Protection means neutralizing threats. That's the way things are. I believe that because of what I do, others are able to live lives without violence. It's a sacrifice I make for others."

Right. Okay. Sure. But I'd made all my sacrifices for the sake of Jason, and now he wasn't worth sacrificing for. Now, I wasn't sure why I was doing any of this. Did I even really care about other people? I didn't want them to die, so that must mean something.

"Your connection with Jason makes you the only person who can fight him effectively," said Lily, putting down the pencil. "But your anger towards him rules you. It makes you erratic. It makes you doubt yourself. You need to forgive Jason."

I snorted. Now I got up. I wasn't listening to this. I headed for the door.

Lily intercepted me. "Why does the mere thought of forgiving Jason make you run for the door?"

I tried to duck around her, but she grasped my arm. "I can't forgive him. He doesn't deserve it."

"We forgive for ourselves, not for others."

"If I forgive him, it makes everything okay."

"No. If you forgive him, it means you accept that he is the way he is, and that you don't allow his actions to wound you anymore."

I knitted my eyebrows together. "That's not a way I've heard forgiveness described before."

She released my arm. "It's a good definition, I think." She smiled at me. "Azazel, tell me why you fight Jason?"

I was taken aback. I didn't know if I'd ever thought about it before. "Because he's keeping us from going west," I said finally. "I mean, that's why we're here."

"You think it's important to get west?" she asked.

Of course I did. "We need to get help. We need to restore power. Yes, I think it's important." My stomach was still feeling unsettled. I kind of wanted to get out of there, and not just because she was making me uncomfortable with her

176

questions.

"So," she said, "you do believe what we are doing matters?"

Was she deaf? "Yes."

"We're not just inconsequential flies, easily brushed aside?"

Flies? Like my dreams. "What did you say?"

"I mean, what we do matters, that's all. If you think that, then you have to ask yourself how far you're willing to go to make sure what matters happens. Sometimes we have to do things we find distasteful or uncomfortable in order to accomplish important things."

"The end justifies the means," I muttered. Agh. I was going to throw up. I grimaced. "Um, hold on, I have to get out of here for a second."

I tore out of the door to the radio room, through the hallway, and out the backdoor. Bile was rising in my throat. Lily was yelling after me to come back, but I couldn't.

Kieran was in the yard. He looked up as I streaked out the door. "Azazel?"

I got as far as I could outside before I couldn't keep it back anymore. I threw up all over the lawn. Gross.

Kieran wandered closer, patting my back. "Morning sickness?" he asked.

Damn it.

Marlena appeared at the back door to the church. She looked horrified. "What did you say?"

I wiped my mouth with my hand. Kieran tried to put his

arm around me, but I shoved him off. Marlena descended the stairs slowly. She headed over to us, shaking her head. "What did you say?" she repeated.

"Uh..." said Kieran, "I asked her if it was morning sickness."

"Why would you think that?" asked Marlena. "I mean, don't you think it would be a little soon after last night?"

This was embarrassing. "We, um, before we came here, there was an incident," I said.

Marlena raised her eyebrows. "I see." She sounded annoyed.

"It's going to be okay," said Kieran.

Marlena crossed her arms over her chest. "Oh, you think so?"

Kieran and I exchanged a sheepish look.

"Walk with me," Marlena ordered.

We did. The three of us walked away from the church, along the road. I was beginning to feel like I'd spent too much time having serious conversations on this road. There needed to be a different "serious conversation" spot. On second thought, maybe it would be cool if there was no more need for "serious conversations." Fat chance of that happening, with everyone trying to make me use magic, and Jason trying to keep us from going west, and Kieran and I having a non-relationship.

"How long have you known?" asked Marlena.

"I don't know," I said. "I'm a week late, and I threw up this morning. I don't think it's necessarily conclusive. I mean, Mina didn't have morning sickness until way later than a week."

"Everyone's different," said Marlena. "But I don't really know, myself. I've never been pregnant." She threw her hands up in the air and talked to the sky, "Ridiculous. Hallam and I are in our late twenties and everyone else starts having babies. This is what happens from being responsible, is it?"

Neither Kieran nor I said anything.

"You shouldn't have kept this from us," said Marlena.

"But I'm not even sure yet," I said. "I've been looking all over for a pregnancy test, but I haven't been able to find one."

"Azazel and I are working through this on our own," said Kieran. "It's kind of complicated, but I don't think it's anyone else's business."

"Not our business?" Marlena couldn't believe him. "We're sending a pregnant woman on dangerous missions, places where bullets are flying at her. We can't do that. No, Azazel, you're going to have to go back to D.C., now."

"I thought we needed her magic," said Kieran.

Marlena covered her face with her hands.

"Look," said Kieran, "I'm looking out for her. And she's tough. She can take care of herself. It will be okay."

Marlena shook her head. "No, if something happened to that baby, it would be a disaster."

"Hey," I said, "maybe there's not a baby, huh?"

"But what if there is?" asked Marlena.

"Then we'll deal with it," said Kieran. "We can do that."

"You're going to send her out to fight against Jason when she's nine months pregnant?" said Marlena.

"You think we're going to be here for nine months?" I said. God, I hoped not. All told, this whole pregnancy thing just sounded like a huge pain in the ass. Why me?

"Well, maybe not," said Marlena, "but you definitely won't be coming west with us if you're pregnant."

"I wasn't planning on it," I said. "You guys are the scouting team. I work in suppression of riots, or did you forget?"

"This is a disaster," said Marlena.

"Tell me about it," I said.

"It's not a disaster," said Kieran. "It's good. It's beautiful. Is no one besides me excited about the prospect of there being a baby?"

Marlena and I both looked at him. "No," we both said.

"Jesus," said Kieran, running his hands through his hair. "This is going to be fine. It's going to work out. People have been having babies since the dawn of time. It can't be that big of a deal."

"I still say that we shouldn't freak out until we know for sure," I said.

"But how can we know for sure?" asked Kieran.

"A pregnancy test," said Marlena. "They don't have any in Columbus, but I bet you might find one in Clinton."

"Clinton?" I asked.

"It's not far from here. You and Kieran could drive there

tomorrow. I'm sure they have drug stores there. You should be able to find one, and then we'll know," said Marlena.

Perfect. I nodded. "Yes," I said. "We're going."

"Okay," said Kieran.

"I just have to figure out what to tell Hallam about why you're going," said Marlena. "If he thought you were pregnant, he would flip out."

Like he didn't flip out about everything I did, anyway. But whatever.

* * *

The rest of the day passed without incident. I never finished my conversation with Lily, because I told her I was sick. Since I was sick, everyone thought I should lie down for a while, and I did feel a little tired. I realized that since Kieran and I had been busy the night before, I really hadn't gotten much sleep. I napped away the afternoon.

Kieran came in to wake me up for dinner. It was late afternoon. The inside of my sleeping area was lit up with golden light and shadows. Kieran crawled in next to me and shook me gently. I opened my eyes slowly, and I was happy that he was the first thing I saw.

I reached up to stroke his cheek.

He smiled at me.

This thing between Kieran and me was totally weird, but I kind of liked it.

"It's time for dinner," Kieran said softly.

I yawned and propped myself up on my elbows.

"You were tired, huh?" he asked me.

"Yeah," I said. I felt better now, though. Much more rested. And my stomach didn't feel icky at all anymore. This pregnancy thing was all going to be a scare and then everything was going to be fine.

"Do you think that's a sign?" he asked.

Damn it. I hadn't thought so. But Mina had definitely been tired a lot in the beginning. She'd slept constantly. Crap. "Maybe," I said.

Kieran chuckled. "You really don't want to be pregnant, do you?"

"No," I said, pushing myself up into a sitting position. "You don't want me to be, do you?"

He turned away from me a second, grinning. "I don't know. Sure, it would be inconvenient. It would be hard. But, it would kind of be neat, don't you think?" He looked back at me.

I rolled my eyes, but I was still smiling. "Neat, how?"

He leaned close to me. "Just that it would be parts of us. Both of us. And it would be cool, watching it grow up and learn to talk and walk and stuff."

I shoved him playfully. "It?"

"Him," he said.

I shoved him again, harder. "Him?!"

"Her?" he said, laughing.

"Better," I decided.

"You want a girl?"

I didn't want a baby at all, but Kieran was making me think about it. Here inside the enclave of sheets, in this lazy, warm light, I felt like we were cocooned somewhere away from the world. Here, crazy things were possible. "Maybe a girl," I said. I envisioned it. Baby clothes. Ribbons. A pudgy hand in mind. The weight of a squirming, giggling baby in my arms. Kieran was right. There was something about it that was…neat. I poked him. "But I guess a boy would be okay too."

"Just okay?" he said.

I laughed. "More than okay."

Kieran kissed me.

I was startled.

He looked abashed. "Sorry. I know we never got to have that really long conversation in the car getting to know each other."

"It's okay," I said. I put my hand on his shoulder. He had very nice shoulders, quite broad. Under my fingers, he felt solid and firm. My hand trailed down over his shoulder, onto his arm, where I felt his biceps through his shirt.

Kieran's fingers grazed my throat, sending shivers down my back.

I scooted closer to him, placing my other hand on his other shoulder. I explored his back with my fingers, all the flawless, smooth muscle of him.

Kieran made a noise in the back of his throat.

Our lips met again. He urged my mouth open with his tongue.

I crushed myself against his chest.

His arms went around me, at first lightly dancing over

my hips, then urgently pulling me closer.

I felt it again, the liquid warmth. Kieran made me feel so good, and not in a scary way. My heart wasn't thudding away in my chest. I wasn't hyperventilating or sweating. Instead, he was relaxing and protective. I could stay here in the circle of his arms for a very, very long time.

Eventually, though, our kiss broke.

Our faces lingered close to each other.

"I don't know," I murmured, "I think since it's the apocalypse, we might have to teach our little girl or guy to shoot a gun before they learn to walk."

Kieran laughed. "Come on. Hallam and Marlena will go west and bring back the lights. Everything will be okay after that."

"Yeah," I said. I laid my head on Kieran's shoulder. His arms held me close.

"So," Kieran said into my hair, "what is going on here between the two of us?"

"I don't know," I told his shoulder, "but it's nice."

* * *

When Kieran and I showed up at dinner holding hands, Marlena shot us a murderous look. We stopped holding hands. As we ate, I watched him, talking easily to others around him. I did like Kieran. I really did. I couldn't say it was anything like love, exactly, not yet, but maybe there was hope for that.

In some ways, maybe it was good that I'd seen Jason with that redhead this morning. It had set me free in a way that I hadn't known I needed to be set free. I hadn't really thought there was any part of me that was still attached to Jason, but when I'd seen the two of them together, it had hurt me.

Still, it was good. Because now I knew that Jason was really gone. He'd moved on. Somehow, knowing that, it made it okay for me to do it too. Whatever happened, I wanted to see how things could be with Kieran. I'd never been with someone who was just a nice guy before. It might turn out to be a very nice change.

We grinned at each other over our plates of food, like the two of us shared a secret that no one else could possibly fathom. And that was a nicer feeling than I thought I'd felt in a very long time.

CHAPTER ELEVEN

I was sleeping, a beautiful dreamless sleep like I hadn't had in a long time, when a rough hand shook me awake. It was Gus. "They're here," he said.

I fumbled in the darkness for my gun and was on my feet in minutes.

Everyone in the room was in the same position as me. We crept out into the hallway, where we were met by Hallam and Marlena, both still with mussed hair and bleary eyes.

"We heard shots," said Hallam. "Jason's people are here. They're retaliating against us for what happened today."

Hallam sent us all to the windows first.

I was assigned to one of the busted stained glass windows in the sanctuary. I knelt beside it, and peered out, gun first. Outside, I saw nothing but dark foliage and stillness. There was nothing there. I waited. They must be hiding, waiting to ambush us.

We all waited. Ten minutes went by. Twenty.

Hallam came into the sanctuary. He tagged me, Kieran, and a few others. We were to go out the back door and spread out, looking for intruders.

"Don't engage," Hallam said. "You see them, you get back here immediately. Got it?"

We nodded.

Hallam looked at me. "Azazel, can't you use your magic to find them?"

I shook my head. "It doesn't work quite like that. I have to know where they are before I can touch their minds."

"Fine," he said. He sent us out.

Outside, the stars glittered above us, serene in their stationary positions. They didn't care whether the whole world was at war or not. If all of us were gone, the stars would still shine down. Actually, that wasn't true, was it? Hadn't I heard somewhere that the stars we saw were actually already burned out? It took so many light years for their light to travel to us that by the time we saw them, they were all already dead.

But I wasn't supposed to be thinking about stars. I was supposed to be looking for Jason's people. We divvied up directions and each of us set off in a separate one. I headed down the road in the direction of Columbus-Belmont park. I stayed close to the line of trees on one side of the road, hugging the shadows. I didn't see anyone. At all.

I walked for thirty minutes, past the park entrance, covering as much ground as I could. I still didn't see anyone. I headed back. No one on the way back either.

I could see the church when I heard the sounds of footsteps on the road. I darted behind some trees for cover and watched. At first, I could see nothing more than shadowy figures, but as they approached, I was able to see the people more clearly. They weren't from Jason's camp.

They had packs on their backs like backpackers and they were shrouded in hooded sweatshirts. Two of the figures were smaller, their hands reaching up to hold the hands of their...parents? It was a family. They looked like they'd been traveling for a long time.

A hand came down on my shoulder. I jumped and whirled, surprised.

Jason.

He was wearing a white t-shirt and jeans. He gave a sheepish half grin. "They're coming," he said.

Don't engage , said Hallam's voice in my head.

But I stayed where I was, not moving away from him, like his body was a magnet. Like I couldn't stop myself.

"Azazel," he said. I could see that he was holding a bottle of moonshine. It was nearly empty. Had he drunk the entire thing himself? Surely not. He'd be passed out by now.

But Jason was definitely drunk. He staggered on his feet, weaving in and out. This wasn't an attack. I didn't think it was, anyway. Why would Jason come to our camp drunk?

"I'm a little drunk," Jason slurred.

No shit. I glared at him. "I should shoot you now and be done with it."

Jason sat down hard on the ground. He grunted. He patted the grass next to him. "Sit down with me."

Why did I do it? I don't know. Maybe I was just too curious. Why was Jason here, trashed out of his mind, wanting to talk to me? I sat down.

He smiled at me. His smile seemed soft. I guess he was

just drunk. "Do you remember back in Bramford, when I tried to run away? Sheriff Damon brought me back and you got Toby to help you skip out on school to come see me?"

I remembered. "Yes."

"When you saw me, you ran across the room and you hugged me. I'd never been so close to you before. I still remember what that was like. Smelling you for the first time."

I raised my eyebrows. "Smelling me?"

"I like the way you smell," he said. He took a swig from his bottle. "I can smell you now. It's nice."

I scooted a few inches away from him.

He laughed, hanging his head between his knees. "And she moves away."

"Jason, you're drunk—"

"I know. I shouldn't be. The people are all angry. They want to come after your camp again. I just ran off and got drunk." He shrugged at me, his hands spread wide. All his gestures seemed exaggerated.

I didn't know what to say, so I didn't say anything. I should probably go back inside. I should tell Hallam that Jason was drunk and in our backyard.

"I'm sorry you saw me with Polly," he said.

Oh God. So this is what all of this was about. "Jesus, it's okay that you've moved on. It's fine. We haven't been together in a long time."

"Polly and I are not really together," Jason said.

"You looked together."

"We fuck," he said. "But she's not you."

I snorted. "Right. She's Lilith."

Jason sighed. "Nothing happened between me and Lilith. Why don't you ever believe me about this?"

I did believe him. Sort of. I guess. But it was so long ago. "It doesn't matter anymore."

"If you say so."

"Jason," I said. "You should let me go. You should try to be happy with Polly." Hell, what was I saying? I didn't want Jason to be happy. I wanted Jason to get out of our way west. Sometimes, I was pretty sure I wanted Jason to die. But here, in the darkness, it seemed almost like I was having a normal conversation with an ex. And Jason didn't seem nearly as horrible as he usually did. He was vulnerable. I missed seeing him vulnerable. It was the only thing that used to make me believe he was human.

"That's just it," he said. "I thought I had let you go. But now that I've seen you, I know that it's never going to be over between the two of us. Not really."

He couldn't keep talking like that. "It's over. It's been over since the day I told you to leave."

Jason contemplated his bottle of moonshine. "You really don't feel it? When we're around each other, you don't feel the pull? It's bigger than us. It's bigger than what either of us wants."

I started to say that I didn't feel it, but I knew that would be a lie. Sure, there was a connection between Jason and me. That didn't mean we had to date. "What do you want?" I asked instead.

"You."

"Sure you do. That's why you were making out with that redhead this morning."

"It doesn't mean I don't still want you."

Fine. Whatever. "I want you to let us get past you and go west."

"Listen to me, Azazel. There is something I believe very much, and I think I've always been clear about it. When someone is doing something you don't like, you have two options. Either accept what they're doing or make them stop doing it. I don't like the OF telling everyone what to do. So I'm going to make them stop. And there's no point in going west. You have to trust me on this. It's a worse mess there than it is here."

"You can't convince me of the same lies you tell your people. A fascist government? Please." I rolled my eyes.

He was quiet for a few minutes. "This is what this is about, isn't it? It's not that you don't still want me. You do. I can tell."

"I don't." I hated when he got arrogant like this.

Jason wasn't phased. "It's because I'm not cooperating with the OF."

"That and the fact you're cutting off people's fingers."

"I needed you to know I was serious," he said. "I didn't want to kill them or hurt them too seriously. Besides, the finger cutting off thing is very effective. It really upsets people."

"Because it's seriously fucked up," I said.

"Desperate times..."

Right. The end justifies the means. Wasn't that what Lily had told me earlier? If I believed that, what would separate me from Jason?

Jason took a long drink of his moonshine. "I know you so well. I can see the way you're looking at me. Maybe it won't be tonight, but someday, you'll come back to me."

I stood up. "I'm not ever coming back to you."

He stumbled to his feet as well. "You can tell yourself that, but I know what's between us."

He was making me so angry. "There's nothing between us," I said. "There's something between you and Polly and there's something between me and Kieran. But there's nothing between you and me."

He arched an eyebrow. "Finally committed to that doormat out of pity, huh?"

"No," I said. "Not pity. I *like* him."

He put his hand under my chin. "And you *love* me."

I slapped his hand off me. "And I'm pregnant with Kieran's *child* ."

Jason took a stumbling step back. It was as if I'd punched him in the stomach. "You're what?" he whispered, horrified.

"I'm pregnant," I said again, even though I didn't know for sure if it was true.

Jason dashed the moonshine bottle against the ground, where it thudded on the grass, liquid spilling out. He took an angry step towards me. "You will use your magic again," he said, his finger in my face. "And I don't care how many babies you want to have with however many men you want to sleep with. You will use your power. And you will be mine. You're mine, and you always will be."

Then he turned and ran, disappearing into the woods.

* * *

"Remember that time I scared you in Columbus?" Jason asked. He was sitting across the table from me in our kitchen. The remains of our dinner were on the table. I needed to get up and clear the dishes.

"Which time?" I asked, feeling a little annoyed. After all, Jason had been scary in Columbus. A lot.

He laughed. "Touché." He got up and began to stack up the dishes.

"Jason, you don't have to—"

"No, I'm doing it," he said. "I'm clearing the table for my pregnant wife who slaved over this amazing meal."

I rubbed my hands over my huge stomach and sat back in my chair. "Well, when you put it like that, go ahead then."

He leaned across the table and kissed me lightly on the lips. "I was talking about the time you told me you were pregnant with Kieran's child."

I groaned. "Oh that time. You *were* scary. You screamed at me that I was yours and I'd always be yours."

Jason took a stack of dishes over to the sink. "Well, I was right, wasn't I?"

I twisted in my chair to see him better. "Jason Wodden, I do love you, but you do not *own* me."

He came back to the table and squeezed my shoulder. "I know. I'm sorry I joked about it." He grabbed the skillet and saucepan, which were both sitting on hot pads on the table. To hell with serving platters.

"There a reason you brought this up?"

Jason paused, balancing the dishes on one hand. "I was thinking about it. I'm glad you showed up there."

"I only showed up because you demanded to see me."

He laughed. "Well, yeah, I guess so." He went back to the sink, and turned on the tap, adding soap to the stream of water. "But, while I had to find a way to change myself and I had to do that on my own, I don't know if I would have if it hadn't been for you. You've always motivated me to be a better man."

I smiled. "That's sweet."

"It's true," he said. He turned back to the sink. "But I'm glad you weren't really pregnant with that Kieran guy's kid."

I got up out of my chair. It wasn't easy, with this enormous stomach. It always threw me a little off balance. I waddled over to Jason. "Hey, Kieran was a nice guy."

"No, I know," said Jason. He stopped what he was doing to put his hand on my belly. "I just like it this way better." He grinned. "Besides, you like me because I'm a scoundrel," he said in his best Harrison Ford impression, which really wasn't very good.

"Occasionally," I said. "You were a little too much like a scoundrel in Columbus."

He kissed my forehead. "I'm sorry."

I punched him playfully. "It's okay. You made up for it."

Jason shut off the tap and picked up a scouring pad. "You know that even if there had been a baby with Kieran, it wouldn't have bothered me, right?"

"I know that," I said.

He began scrubbing at one of the plates from dinner. "What are you doing standing up, anyway? Go sit down. I've got this."

I raised my eyebrows. "I'm pregnant, Jason. I'm not an invalid."

He just chuckled and continued with the dishes.

I took careful steps across the room, to the window in the kitchen. I peered outside at the black plastic that surrounded us. There was a huge banana peel outside the window. It was rotting. Living inside a garbage bag had seemed horrible at first, but we'd gotten used to it. "It's just been so much easier to be alive now that I've accepted what we are," I said.

"What are we?" Jason asked me, still scrubbing away.

"Just flies," I said. "Insignificant insects, easily brushed aside. Nothing we do really matters to the grand scheme of things."

"That's right," said Jason. "So there was no point in fighting anymore, was there, baby?"

"No," I said. "Not at all. It's okay just to be happy."

"Are you happy?"

I smiled at him, my heart bursting with joy. "Very, very

happy."

* * *

I woke up in my sleeping area. Kieran was curled around me from behind, his arm wrapped around my waist. He stirred and moaned, pulling me closer.

Flies again.

Did these dreams mean something? Did I care if they did?

I snuggled closer into Kieran. I hadn't told anyone about meeting Jason and talking to him. I felt like no one needed to know. He hadn't hurt me. When we woke up, Kieran and I were going to Clinton to find a pregnancy test. I'd finally know the truth. I squeezed my eyes shut and willed myself to go back to sleep.

* * *

Clinton looked like an old mining town in West Virginia that I'd visited once when I was a kid. All the buildings were tall and brick, but kind of boringly rectangular and blocky. I got the feeling it was one of those towns that had experienced a lot of growth somewhere in the mid-twentieth century and then hadn't had much growth since. It was much bigger than Columbus, which wasn't so much a town as it was a place with a Post Office and a bunch of houses. But as towns go, it wasn't big. It was a little bigger than Bramford.

It kind of reminded me of Bramford, actually. Strangely, even though terrible things had happened to me in Bramford, I felt a twinge of homesickness.

Of course, Clinton was far worse for wear than Bramford had ever looked. Most of the buildings featured broken windows and ripped-off doors. There was a four-car pileup on one of the streets. The cars had just been left there. The stoplights at several of the intersections had been torn down. They lay broken on the road, never to blink again.

We didn't see any people. When we'd spoken to Hallam this morning before leaving, he'd been a little miffed. Marlena had told him we were going to look for supplies in Clinton. He told us that he and a party had been to Clinton when they'd first arrived in Kentucky. "Picked clean," Hallam said. "Bunch of dead people in city hall."

Apparently, there had been a mass suicide in Clinton. Hallam tried to use this as evidence that bad things like mass suicides happened everywhere, whether I intruded with magic or not. I just let him talk, like I always did. What was the point?

Kieran and I creeped up and down the empty streets in our Subaru, searching for a drug store or a pharmacy. Finally, we found one. It squatted on the corner of two streets. Its massive rectangular front had an off-center sign on top: "Parks Pharmacy." There was an awning, crumbling in several places, over the doorway. Kieran parked the car.

We shut the doors, and the sound echoed down the empty street.

"Great place for zombies," Kieran commented.

Which might have been funny if I didn't feel like we lived in a horror movie already. Parks Pharmacy had glass doors

197

and big glass windows. They were all destroyed. Shards of glass glittered on the sidewalk like little gems. Kieran stepped around them and pulled the door open for me. "Ladies first," he said.

We were greeted by empty stretches of metal shelves. Inside the pharmacy, the air felt dank and muggy, like a cellar. There were no windows, and the blackness swallowed us. We could only see the first set of shelves. It seemed Hallam was right, thus far. Picked clean.

Kieran had a flashlight. He flicked it on. Its tiny beam illuminated an aisle reaching into the depths of the store. He shined the light higher.

"What are you doing?" I asked.

"Looking for those things that tell you what's in each aisle," said Kieran. "They hang them from the ceiling."

"Pregnancy tests are usually towards the back," I said. "And they never say pregnancy tests on the signs for the aisle. If you're lucky, it might say family planning."

If Parks Pharmacy used to have signs directing its customers to what was in each aisle, it didn't anymore. We began to walk further into the pharmacy. It felt as if we were being sucked into the darkness. Kieran's flashlight swept the aisles. Most looked empty, but the deeper we got, we began to see a few stray items on shelves. Lightbulbs. (Who would need them anyway?) Greeting cards. Hair dye. Lotions.

Finally, we hit the back wall. From Kieran's flashlight, we could see this was where the pharmacy itself had been, where all the prescription drugs had been dealt out. It was smashed into and looked cleaned out. But in front of the pharmacy, on the walls under the sliding windows, were rows of KY jelly, condoms, home drug tests, and (yes!) pregnancy tests!

"Jackpot!" I said.

There were two different varieties. I grabbed both and held them up for Kieran to see, grinning.

He looked a little nervous. "Whoa. We found some."

"Yup," I said. I didn't know if I'd ever been so happy in my life.

"Look," said Kieran, "I want you to know, that even if the test is negative, it doesn't mean that I don't, you know, like you. I mean, whatever's going on with us, it's not because I think you're pregnant."

I poked him with the pregnancy test box. "You really don't know that, now, do you?"

"You're awesome, Azazel. I do know that."

I hugged him. "Let's just wait and see what it says before we freak out, okay?" I'd had a dream last night which had strongly indicated I wasn't actually pregnant. I really hoped that was true. Of course, the dream had also indicated that I'd marry Jason and live inside a trash bag. It was so hard to separate the prophetic dreams from the regular nightmares.

Kieran nodded. "Okay, we'll just wait it out."

There was a crashing noise from the front of the store.

Kieran shut off the flash light, and we both got quiet. It was probably just an animal or something. It wasn't exactly hard to get inside the pharmacy after all.

Together, we crept up to the last row of metal shelves.

"Nothing here," said a voice, male with an accent I couldn't quite place. Somewhere north.

"Keep looking. There might be something further back," replied a voice in the same accent. It sounded like a cross between a New York accent and Minnesota accent. They turned their hard "th"s into "d"s ("there" was "dere"), but they didn't pronounce the vowels the way someone might on the east coast. One thing was for sure. They definitely didn't sound like they were from Kentucky.

Were they coming back to us? Were they friendly?

Another crashing noise. Apparently, they were knocking the shelves over.

"Why the fuck are we here?"

"We gotta go south. What? You want to swim across the Mississippi?"

The voices were getting closer. They were moving back through the store. I wasn't sure what to do. Should we show ourselves?

Kieran tugged on me. Apparently, he thought we should retreat. I let him lead me as we backed into the darkness, further away from the center aisle.

"Hey, Buck, you want some hand lotion?"

Kieran stopped pulling me backwards.

"Eh, fuck you, Norris, you know you're the one who's got problems jerking off without lube."

Kieran had gone rigid at my side.

I nudged him. "What?" I whispered.

He drew his gun, not answering me.

"Kieran!" I said it as forcefully as I could without making much noise.

"Stay here," Kieran whispered to me. He took off towards the center of the store, moving quickly, not worrying about the noise he made. His shoes crunched against broken glass from the pharmacy window.

Shit! What was he doing?

"You hear something?" one of the guys asked.

"No. Shut up."

"Hello?" called the first guy. "Who's there?"

I could still hear Kieran moving forward, crunching away on the glass. I swore under my breath. What the hell was he doing?

Shoving the pregnancy tests into my pockets as best I could, I drew my own gun and went after him, trying to move a little more stealthily than he was.

The flashlight flicked back on. I could see Kieran, standing dead center in the middle of the aisle, his gun out and aimed. The light flickered wildly over the store. I could barely make out two grizzled men, each wearing ratty flannel. They had unkempt beards and dirty faces. Their hands went over their eyes to protect them from the light.

"Hey!" one exclaimed.

"What the fuck, dude?" the other said.

Kieran opened fire.

Okay, this was insane. "Kieran!" I screamed, not caring that when I did so I gave away my location. "Kieran, what the fuck?"

One of the men shrieked. "Shit, man!"

Kieran's flashlight illuminated him for a second. The man was on the ground, his hand to his stomach. Blood was seeping through his fingers.

Kieran's flashlight snapped back to the other guy who was on his knees with his hands in the air, terror all over his face. "Hey," he said, "we're sorry. We wasn't gonna take anything, man. Hey, calm down, okay?"

Kieran leveled his gun at the man.

I tackled him, but not quick enough. He'd already pulled the trigger. His shot missed, though, ricocheting off the metal shelves.

I pinned him with my knee, my gun on him. "What is going on, Kieran? Have you gone insane?"

"They're from Chicago," he said. "They're the same ones from Chicago."

That made next to no sense to me. Kieran was from Chicago, I thought. I wondered why he didn't have an accent like those guys. I got up off him to retrieve the flashlight. "Don't move, Kieran."

He didn't listen. He rolled onto his feet in a second. Dammit. Why hadn't I gotten his gun? Why had Kieran lost his mind all at once like this?

I aimed the flashlight at the quivering guy and his partner, who was gurgling blood, his eyes rolling back in his head. Great. "Who are you?" I demanded of the man on his knees.

Kieran was behind me, gun out and ready to shoot.

I swung the flashlight back to Kieran, blinding him by shining it directly in his eyes. "Stop!" I ordered him.

"I'm not anyone, ma'am," said the man. "Not nobody. Just tryin' to cross the river like everybody else. We were lookin' for some food. There's more of us outside. They probably heard the shots. They'll be in here in a second."

Oh. Wonderful.

The man continued. "You just leave me alone, and I'll talk to 'em, okay?" The dude was scared out of his mind. "Don't shoot, okay? I'll tell 'em it was all a misunderstanding."

Kieran snatched the flashlight out of my hands. "But it wasn't a misunderstanding," he said. He put the flashlight under his chin, like he was telling a camp fire story. "Don't you recognize me? Or did you kill so many other people's parents and rape so many other people's sisters that I've just faded in your memory?"

Oh. Oh my God. "It's them?" I whispered to Kieran.

"It's them," he said, his voice acid.

"Shoot him," I said.

"No," said the man. Kieran put the flashlight back on him. "You're wrong, man. I never seen you in my life. Don't do it."

Kieran cocked his gun.

"I'm not lyin' about the others. They're outside. There's six of them. If you shoot me —"

Kieran pulled the trigger. The bullet sunk into the man's head. A red trickle appeared between his eyes. His body fell over.

The doors to the pharmacy burst open and several men came in holding guns. They looked from Kieran to the dead man on the floor. Then they started shooting.

Kieran didn't move. He seemed transfixed by the body of the man he'd just killed. I grabbed the fabric of his sleeve and yanked him after me.

We dove behind the final metal shelf, both hitting the concrete hard. I banged my chin, biting my tongue. God! I tasted blood in my mouth. Kieran still had the flashlight on. I took it from him, turning it off.

Bullets ripped through the flimsy metal of the shelf. This was not a good cover. How were we going to get out of here?

I pulled Kieran with me as we crawled backwards on the floor. I crawled over some of the broken glass Kieran had been crunching earlier. It bit into my skin like tiny needle pricks. Ouch! Jesus.

"Come on out of there," the men yelled at us. They were getting closer.

Kieran and I backed into the wall of the pharmacy. I scrabbled behind me, reaching over the partition to open the door. It was stuck.

"Azazel," said Kieran.

"Help me," I told him, wrenching at the door.

The first of the men cleared the last of the shelves. He couldn't see us in the dark, but he sprayed bullets across the back of the store.

The door came open in my hands. I pushed Kieran inside and scrambled in after him. At least we had a barrier between us and them.

We crawled behind a row of cabinets. Even more barriers. I peered up for a second, squeezed off a few shots at the approaching men. More of them were back there now. I don't think I hit anything. It was hard to aim when you couldn't see.

"Azazel," said Kieran. "Use your magic."

My magic? They were bad men, weren't they? We were about to die. *Desperate times call for desperate measures. The end justifies the means.* It shouldn't be too hard. I could just make them all—

But then I saw a sliver of light against the floor. It was just ahead of us. I nudged Kieran. "A back door," I whispered.

We crawled for the door. Once there, I reached up to grab the knob. Locked!

But we were inside. I twisted the lock on the knob and tried the door again.

Sunlight streamed into the pharmacy.

Kieran and I tumbled out into the street, bullets chasing us.

Kieran slammed the door after us. Several bullet holes splintered through the door.

We struggled to our feet and were off, dashing around the building as quickly as we could.

As we rounded the corner, we were greeted by more shots. They'd beat us?

No, I realized, looking up at the entrance to the pharmacy. They'd left someone on the door. A lookout.

I paused for one second, fixing him in my sights. I pulled the trigger twice, and both of my shots hit home. The man grabbed at his chest and fell his knees.

Kieran was already at the car, flinging open the door. I went after him, opening my door. As soon as I was in the seat, Kieran peeled down the street. I pulled my door shut as the wind rushed by.

We raced down the streets of Clinton wordlessly.

Kieran stared straight ahead, stony faced. I didn't know what to say to him. Even though I'd seen my parents killed, I hadn't had the same experience as Kieran. Jason had shot all the men who'd killed my parents right in front of me. I guess I'd always had more closure than Kieran had. And anyway, I suppose if you looked at it another way, I'd taken revenge on the Sons by convincing them all to shoot themselves.

I reached over for Kieran, touching his leg.

He pushed my hand off without looking at me.

"Are you okay?" I asked.

"Why didn't you do it?" he said.

"Do what?" What was he talking about?

"You had a chance to use magic against them, and you didn't do it," said Kieran. "Why not?"

Jesus. Was he mad at me? He couldn't be. Not really. This must be some kind of transference thing. Since he was so upset over seeing his family's killers, he needed someone to lash out at. I guess, since I was the only one around, that was going to be me. "Well, I didn't have to," I said. "I saw that door. It was a better option."

"How do you figure that?" Kieran said. He glared out at the road, driving much faster than he had on the way into Clinton.

By this time, we were out of the Clinton city limits, and back on country roads heading towards Columbus. I watched as the trees and grass flew past us. "It was just less complicated to go out the door," I said.

"But they're still alive," said Kieran. "If you'd used magic, they'd all be dead now."

Huh. Jason had killed my parents' killers, but I hadn't killed Kieran's. Was that what he was looking for? Closure? "I'm sorry," I said.

"I just don't get it," he said. "You had no problem shooting that guy in the front. You didn't even think. You just pumped bullets into his chest. But when it comes to magic, you balk. You can give me all that crap about destruction and everything else. But if you really cared about human life, you would have thought twice about killing that guy."

I flinched. When he put it like that, it didn't make much sense, did it? I traced patterns on the door handle with my forefinger, trying to figure out how to explain it to him. "It's different," I finally said.

"It's not different," Kieran said.

"It is," I said, "because when I shoot someone who's got a gun and who's shooting at me, we're on a level playing

207

field. Whoever has the better skills will shoot the other person. When I use magic, I take away another person's will. I make them do what I want them to do. It's just more wrong."

"That's bullshit," Kieran said.

Fine. I sunk down in my seat a little and looked out the window. It was pretty in the spring in Kentucky. I wished there was more time in my life to look at pretty things.

"Don't you think it's bullshit?" Kieran said.

I snapped my head away from the window. "Obviously I don't if I said it."

"Who cares whether or not you impose your will on those guys?" Kieran asked. "They deserve it. They're worthless. They should be dead. Do you agree with that?"

I nodded slowly. "I don't see any reason to keep them alive."

"So, then, why wouldn't you kill them?"

"Because I don't want to get in the habit of remaking the world to my liking!" I said. "Because it would be too easy to use magic like that, whenever I wanted. How would you feel if I started messing with your head? What if I just made it so you never wanted to be angry with me? I could do that, right now, you realize that? I could make your entire argument disappear."

Kieran's knuckles were white from gripping the steering wheel. Now he released them a little. "You wouldn't do that," he muttered.

"Not now," I said. "But the more I use the magic, the

easier it gets. If I start doing it all the time, if everything gets easier all the time, who knows what I'll start doing."

"Azazel, you're a good person," said Kieran.

"Am I?" I said. Because I wasn't so sure about that.

"Yes," he said. He sounded so certain.

I just shook my head. I turned away again, and I didn't answer.

We were quiet again, for a long time.

Finally, Kieran said, "I can't let them live."

I sighed. "Are you going to go looking for them?"

"Sure," said Kieran. "And then I'm going to kill them all."

"How did they even get here?" I asked.

"Chicago's not that far. You just head south on I-57. It won't bring you right here, but it's close."

"Did you hear what he said about trying to get across the river, like everybody else?" I said.

"Maybe," said Kieran. "What does that matter?"

"If they were trying to get west, why would they come this far south? Isn't there a bridge across the river closer to Chicago?"

"Yeah, I guess so. I still don't see why it matters," said Kieran.

"It's just weird, don't you think?" I said. "Besides, I didn't know that it was common knowledge that they had power out west. I didn't think the government was advertising that fact until we were sure."

"This is interesting," said Kieran, "but all I'm saying is

that I want to kill those men. Not try to figure out where they're going and why."

"Kieran, you can't kill them. You'll never even find them again."

"If I got help from the others back at camp, we could canvas the area—"

"In cars? You want to waste gasoline on these guys?"

"They killed my family!"

"I realize that, Kieran, but lots of people have lost loved ones since the lights went out. And if we all ran around trying to get revenge, we'd never make any progress."

Kieran glanced at me, disbelief written all over his face. "That has to be the most inconsiderate thing you've ever said to me. Seriously? Everyone's in pain, so my pain means nothing?"

What?! "That's not what I said."

"Whatever," he said.

"It's not!"

"Just don't talk to me, okay? Just shut up."

Wow. Okay, then. Kieran was in a great mood. Apparently, he was on my side about the magic and stuff whenever it didn't personally affect him, but whenever he wanted to use me for his own reasons, then it was open season. I folded my arms over my chest and glowered at the foliage. And to think, yesterday, I'd thought he was so great. I'd thought there was really something going on between us. I couldn't be in a relationship with someone like this. No way.

We still weren't speaking when we got back to the church in Columbus. Kieran parked the car. We both got out and slammed the doors. The Subaru quaked, as if shuddering from our anger.

I didn't wait for Kieran. Instead, I stalked into the church. The sanctuary was still and quiet. Everyone must be in the back rooms or out in the yard behind the church. Did I want to see anyone? Well, it would beat being alone or being stuck with Kieran. I went through the sanctuary into the back rooms. No one was in the room with the guns and the sleeping pallets. No one was in the room with the radio. No one was in Kieran's office. No one was even in the room where Jason had been kept prisoner. This was odd.

I threw open the back door and looked out into the yard. Empty. The grill was knocked over.

Oh my God. I tore back through the church, nearly colliding with Kieran in the sanctuary.

He saw the look on my face. "What?"

"Everyone's gone," I said.

CHAPTER TWELVE

Kieran and I grabbed guns and ammunition from the weapons room. Then we climbed back in the Subaru and took off. I was convinced they were all in Columbus-Belmont park. Jason had all of them. They could be dead by now. Jesus. What had I expected when I told him last night that I was pregnant with another man's child? He'd been angry. Now he was out of control. What was I going to do?

I raked the nearby area with my eyes as we drove by, looking for bodies. Would Jason keep them all prisoner, sending us fingers and toes? Or had they all been slaughtered and their bodies strewn across the town? Maybe he was planning on hanging them. Maybe the townspeople were thirsty for blood, since we'd killed those boys. Maybe—

But then we saw them. They were all standing beside the road in a huge clump. Hallam was running his hands through his hair and swearing loudly enough for us to hear it inside the car.

Kieran pulled over next to them. I nearly started sobbing in relief.

"Hey," said Kieran, reaching across the car and folding me into his arms. "It's okay."

"I thought they were dead," I said.

He pulled me close, patting my back. Hadn't we just been fighting? Why, then, did it still feel so nice to be in his arms? Kieran and I got out of the car. We didn't slam the doors so hard this time.

"What the hell?" I yelled at Hallam. "We had no idea where you were! I thought Jason had killed you all."

"We're fine," said Hallam. "The motorboat, however…" He stepped aside from the clump of people, and I could see what they were all gathered around.

The motorboat that Kieran and I had dragged here from Georgia had been destroyed. It was riddled with bullet holes. The motor was ripped out and twisted, a deformed hunk of metal. The boat itself had been chopped up. It was in pieces. Holey pieces. It lay on the grass like an animal ripped to shreds by a predator. There was nothing left. It was irreparable damage.

"They must have done it last night," said Hallam. "It was the noise I heard when I sent everyone out on alert to look for them. When we were searching the area, we must have missed the boat."

I didn't know. I hadn't walked this way. I looked at the ruined boat, feeling glum. We'd never make it across the river now.

Some of the others were trying to pick up the pieces of the motorboat and take it back with them. Hallam waved a hand at them. "Leave it," he said. "It's hopeless." He started trudging back towards the church.

The others dropped the pieces they were holding and fell in behind Hallam. They were a pathetic procession, heads hung. They looked utterly defeated. Kieran and I got back in the Subaru and drove back to the church. We beat them there by a few minutes. When Hallam and the others arrived, Kieran and I were sitting on the front steps of the church.

They all walked by us and into the church. Hallam stopped to ask, "You guys find anything in Clinton?"

I hadn't been expecting that question, but Kieran saved me.

"No," he said. "It was like you said. Picked clean."

"Told you," said Hallam as he went into the church.

Marlena lingered behind. Once Hallam was inside the church and out of earshot, she said, "Well? Did you find anything?"

"Yeah," said Kieran, "the assholes that killed my family."

Marlena looked confused. "The pregnancy tests?"

Crap. I'd almost forgotten about those. I'd shoved two in my pockets, one on each side. I checked. I came up with one severely smashed cardboard box. "I have one," I said. "The other must have fallen out in the scuffle."

"Scuffle?" said Marlena.

* * *

The instructions that came with the pregnancy test said that after I peed on it, I had to wait three minutes. It also said that it was 99% accurate, and that if I tested too early, that the negative result might only be because there wasn't enough pregnancy hormone in my body. But I was over a week late, so I hoped it wasn't too early. It said that a negative result shouldn't be read after ten minutes. I didn't know what that meant.

Two lines meant pregnant. One meant not pregnant. One strong pink line and one faint pink line was still a positive, no matter how faint the pink line.

I hadn't told anyone I was going to take the test. We'd eaten dinner, which had been a somber affair. Ruining the motorboat was quite a blow. We couldn't get across the river without it. To get to the nearest bridge we had to cross the Ohio River, which fed the Mississippi and cut across Kentucky. No one seemed in much mood for happiness. Really, it was annoying. Why had the OF sent us all the way out here and then told us to maintain our position? We weren't moving forward. We were a moored ship. If we didn't move on soon, we were going to run out of resources. There was only so much we could steal from this area. Things looked bleak.

After dinner, I'd shoved the pregnancy test in my pocket, taken a kerosene lantern, and snuck off to go to the bathroom.

We had a makeshift outhouse that someone had set up near the church, which was basically a toilet seat over a hole in the ground. The thing smelled horrible, and I had this image of dropping the pregnancy test in the hole while I was trying to pee on it. I wasn't going to go digging for it if that happened. Instead, I was just going to go squat in the woods.

I'd sat for minutes, my bladder begging for release, reading every single word of the instructions twice. Then I'd just gone for it. The whole experience was super gross. I mean, seriously, who wants to hold a little plastic thing in her own urine stream?

But it was done now. I'd recapped the test. It was sitting on the ground. I was pacing and waiting for three minutes to be up.

The sun was going down and the inside of the forest was all bright streams of light and shadows. I surveyed the trunks of the trees, thinking about how trees reproduced. They didn't have to have messy sex, oh no. There were no weird relationships and wondering if you actually cared about someone. Just wait for the wind to knock your seeds off into the ground. Some of them would take, maybe, if they got buried or if a squirrel ate them and pooped them out somewhere. It was much easier. Trees never even had to worry about being pregnant.

I didn't want to be pregnant. I stared down at the test, willing it to be negative. I checked my watch. One minute had passed. Wonderful. These three minutes were going to last longer than the car ride from Georgia.

Thinking about the interminable car ride here made me think about Kieran. He wanted a baby. Why? Was he crazy? Wasn't it supposed to be the other way around? Wasn't the girl supposed to want a baby and the boy supposed to want his freedom?

Was that what I wanted? Freedom?

Not really. I didn't feel very free right now. I didn't want to be pregnant because it would make my life miserable. I remembered the dream, waddling around with my enormous belly. How would I function if I was so impaired by my own body? I wouldn't be able to shoot. Of course, only really fucked up people shot at pregnant women.

Maybe I'd be sort of safe if I was pregnant. At least once I started showing, I would be, I guessed. God. It couldn't be. Kieran and I had used a condom. We'd been safe. Things like this were only supposed to happen to stupid girls who didn't pay attention to what was going on. They were not supposed to happen to me, because I wasn't ready.

Forget shooting at people with a big belly. How was I supposed to shoot at people with a baby in my arms, screaming to be fed? What was I going to do? I was going to be helpless, wasn't I? I guess I'd have Kieran. Jesus. Maybe that's why he liked the entire idea. He'd be important. He'd have to protect us. I'd be worthless, nothing more than dead weight.

And I'd be fat. Overall, there seemed to be nothing particularly good about the idea of being pregnant. God knew that when Mina had been complaining about being pregnant, I'd suggested she get an abortion. She'd been horrified. I didn't think it was particularly nice to get an abortion. I wasn't sure whether it was actually a baby or a blob of tissue. But I did know that if the option existed for me right now —

But wait. If the option existed for me right now, I'd be in my senior year of college. I'd be almost ready to have a degree. Would I still choose to have an abortion?

It wasn't like I hated babies.

I didn't know. And anyway, it didn't matter. I didn't have a choice, thanks to the apocalypse. Nothing like all the lights going out to set the women's movement back a few hundred years, right?

I checked my watch again. Two minutes. Really? It had only been two minutes? This last minute was going to be torture, wasn't it? I bet that it would feel like it lasted longer than the first two minutes combined.

I couldn't help it. I snuck a look at the test. Oh goody. Only one line. That was a good sign, wasn't it? I probably wasn't pregnant.

I looked at my watch again. Wait. Wait. Okay, I'd wait.

I heard a rustling behind me. I pulled my gun, scanning the area with my eyes. "Hello?"

Maybe it was an animal. Maybe Kieran had followed me, because he'd somehow known I was going to take the pregnancy test.

"Kieran?" I called.

But instead, a girl emerged from the woods, looking sheepish. She had red hair, and she was wearing a long skirt. It was Polly, Jason's new girlfriend.

CHAPTER THIRTEEN

"I'm sorry," Polly said. "Put down your gun."

"No fucking way," I said, cocking it.

She put her hands up, her eyes widening in fear. "I'm really sorry. I wanted to find you alone. I swear, I looked away while you were…you know…"

Jesus Christ, was she serious? I just glared at her.

"I wanted to talk to you," she said. "I don't have a gun. I promise I won't hurt you." She had a teeny, high voice, kind of like Minnie Mouse. *This* was what Jason was screwing?

I looked her over. She probably didn't have a gun. She was one of those petite, girly types. She probably did the damsel-in-distress bit a lot. "Are you alone?" I asked.

"I swear," she said, "it's just me. If Jason found out I came to talk to you, he'd be really angry."

I put the gun away. "What do you want?"

"Can I come closer?"

I considered. "Whatever."

She took several timid steps forward, but eventually stopped out of my reach. She clasped her hands in front of her, twisting them nervously like a five-year-old. In that moment, she disgusted me. I hated her.

Sometimes weakness does that to me. I see it, and I sneer

at it. I know that I was weak once, and if Jason hadn't trained me, I'd still be weak. It doesn't matter, though. I still can't stand it.

"You're different than I expected," she said to me in her tinny voice.

"So are you," I said. I'd expected Jason would want someone with more of a spine.

"You're like him."

I was so not like him. But she could say what she wanted. "Is there something I can do for you?"

"I've known Jason for a while," she said.

Not as long as I had. But I didn't say that. It sounded petty. "Okay."

"I met him when he used to do the street fights."

"Street fights?"

"You didn't know about that? They were on youtube. Lots of people knew about them. Jason was like a celebrity."

Somehow, the fact that Jason had run around beating people up on youtube after we broke up did not surprise me.

"Anyway," she said, "I really liked him. He seemed so strong and masculine, you know, but he was also kind of...haunted. I thought it was sexy."

Yeah, okay. I guess she'd pegged that right. I nodded. "I get that."

"Well, he's just, he's getting different," she said.

"No," I said. "He's not getting different. He was always like that. You just wanted to see something else."

She twisted her hands harder, getting them caught up in her skirt. "Maybe so," she said softly.

Damn it. Despite myself, I felt a little bad for this girl. I kind of knew how she felt.

"Sometimes he scares me," she said.

"Leave him," I said. "Get the hell away from him."

She laughed kind of helplessly. "I wish I could."

"You can," I said. "You could stay with us. We'd find someplace for you. Someplace safe." I didn't really know how we'd do that. I didn't like this girl much, but I did feel sorry for her. Maybe if someone just helped her out a little bit, she'd be stronger, and she wouldn't need to be with dickwads like Jason.

She shook her head. "No, that's not really an option. I can't do that."

I wasn't going to force her. "So you just wanted to have girl talk, then? Did you think I'd tell you that underneath all that violence and anger, Jason's really just a fuzzy puppy? Because he's not. He's deeply disturbed. And he still flirts with me all the time, so—"

"No, I know that," she said. "He's still in love with you. He's never lied to me about that. I didn't come to complain about him." She looked embarrassed, like she'd brought the wrong thing to a dinner party. "He's scary sometimes, and I think he's losing it, and that's why I came to talk to you. You're looking for that book he has, aren't you?"

The grimoire? "Yes," I said.

"I thought so. If you had it, he says you could make it so

he can't, you know, make everyone listen to him."

I nodded. "I could."

"I think that would be better," she said. "He didn't used to do that all that time, but now, it's like he's controlling everybody. Maybe if that went away, he'd be more like he used to be."

I smiled sadly at her. "Sweetie, I don't think he's going to change. I waited for years, and he never did. He just got worse."

She unclasped her hands and rubbed the tops of her thighs, still looking incredibly nervous. Was it me? But I was being nice now. "I have to try, though, you know? Everyone else has given up on him. If I give up on him too, I'm afraid he'll lose it completely."

My heart went out to her. "You can't help him," I said. "You can't stop him." Maybe only I could do that. And I resisted doing it all the time, too. How messed up were we both?

"I'll help you get the book," she said. "I'll get it for you, and I'll bring it you. It's really all I can do, okay?"

"Okay," I said. "But I don't want you to get hurt."

"He won't hurt me," she said. "He never hurts me."

I'd said that before.

But as much as I didn't want Polly to be in danger, I wasn't going to look a gift horse in the mouth. If she wanted to help, I'd let her. We set up a time to meet again, in two days, dusk, in this same spot.

We didn't talk much more. I couldn't help but repeat my

offer to her. She could leave Jason and stay with us. She was firm, if quiet, in her response. She wouldn't leave him.

After she walked off, her small body disappearing into the trees and the growing darkness, I couldn't help but think a little about her. What was the difference between Polly now and me at seventeen? At that age, I'd been just as devoted to Jason, and just as sure of his internal goodness, hidden in there amongst all his complexity and danger.

If I were honest with myself, what she said was true. Jason wasn't one to hurt women he dated. When it came to other women, like his mother for instance, he didn't seem to care too much about gender. But he'd never hurt me. No. Jason's violence had always been directed towards people who threatened our safety. He'd protected us. If he hadn't done a lot of the things that he'd done, we'd be dead. And it wasn't like I was a saint either.

Well. Jason's violence hadn't always been directed against threats to our safety. Maybe he thought of them as that, but sometimes, he was motivated by jealousy, pure and simple. It made him ugly. Hell, I guess I wasn't immune to it either. Hadn't I let loose with my magic because I'd seen him making out with Polly? If only, back in New Jersey, things hadn't gotten so out of hand. If only, when I thought about Jason, I didn't remember a motionless body on the floor, and Jason's wide eyes as he claimed, "I didn't mean to hurt him."

And I guess it wasn't strictly true that he'd never tried to hurt me. There had only been the time in the Sons' stronghold, when he'd shot at me. That was the only time he'd ever threatened to hurt me. When he'd done it, he'd had that look in his eyes. That empty look, full of rage.

Afterwards, I remembered him sobbing on his knees, forcing me to hold a gun to his head, and begging me to shoot him, to end all of the darkness within him. He'd known what he was capable of. I'd discarded it. I hadn't believed it was there. Did that make me stupid? He'd sobbed like that in New Jersey too, but it hadn't mattered anymore. He'd crossed a line, and he could never make it right. Never.

Back then, Jason was all I had. I didn't believe I could count on anyone else. I guess, back then, I felt like I needed someone to count on. Now…well, now, I was used to being on my own. Maybe that was why it was so hard to let Kieran in. Because Kieran wanted to take care of me. And I didn't know if I wanted to let anyone do that for me ever again. It was scary for one thing. And it was unnecessary. I didn't need help. I'd been through so much. I was what I was. Trying to be vulnerable for someone like that wasn't something I really wanted to do. But if I was going to have a baby, I was going to be vulnerable, and I was going to have to get used to—

Crap. The pregnancy test! I checked my watch. Fifteen minutes?!

That was too long, wasn't it? But what happened if you read the test too late?

I raced over to the test and snatched it up off the ground.

It was too dark. I could hardly see anything. I sat down hard on the ground and held it up to the kerosene lantern. I could see one strong pink line. My heart thudded.

Negative.

But no. There was another line there. It was faint, very faint, but I could see it. And the test said that even a faint line was a positive.

No. No, no, no. Please, no.

Why had I lost that other test? If I had it, I could test again.

Two lines. I was pregnant. Oh, God. I was pregnant.

* * *

As I got back towards the church, I could hear angry voices, talking over each other. Great. This was all I needed. I was pregnant, and now I was coming back to an argument. I trudged up from the woods. Everyone was still sitting outside around the grill, where I'd seen them last. Kieran was on his feet, gesturing wildly. Hallam was standing too. He was pointing his finger at Kieran. They were both talking at once. I couldn't make out what either of them were saying.

I sat down in an empty chair. No one seemed to notice that I'd arrived. Maybe no one had noticed that I'd left.

"You'd risk the lives of these people on some kind of revenge errand?" Hallam was saying.

"They're dangerous people," Kieran said. "And they're in this area. I think they need to be dealt with." Oh, okay, I got what this was about. Kieran wanted to rally everyone into going after the people who'd murdered his family. Hadn't I told him that Hallam wouldn't go for it?

"We have neither the resources nor the time—" Hallam started.

"Time?" said Kieran. "What are we so busy doing here, huh? I don't think we're doing anything. We're sitting around waiting while Jason's people attack us and ruin our boat."

"You're not taking anyone with you to find these people, and that's final," said Hallam.

"Well, can I ask them?" Kieran said. His eyes swept the group. Everyone turned away from him, not meeting his eyes. "Maybe they want to help."

Hallam gritted his teeth. "It's not their decision. I'm in charge here, and I say that no one's going anywhere."

Kieran's nostrils flared.

"Sit down," Hallam said.

Kieran did, but he didn't look like he liked it.

"Now," said Hallam. "If that madness is over, perhaps I could get back to what I was trying to discuss, which was that—"

He was interrupted by Gus, who'd been inside. He stuck his head out the back door. "Radio transmission!" Gus yelled.

Everyone stood up at once and started for the church. We got a little bottlenecked at the doorways, but within a minute, we were all inside the radio room. We crowded inside, not bothering to sit down. Hallam squeezed between our bodies to get to the radio.

Hallam seized the radio's microphone and pushed the button to talk. "Wakefield team here. Wakefield speaking. Over."

"Copy that, Wakefield. Sit tight while I put on Phillips. Over," said the crackling radio.

We waited. The radio hissed and sputtered for a few seconds, and then Phillips came on.

He didn't waste any time on pleasantries. "We've been trying to reach Junkin's team up north for the past three days with no answer. We can only assume the worst. Teams to the south aren't making near the progress you've made. Right now, you're our best shot. Over."

"You're saying you want us to try to get across the river? Over," said Hallam.

"Affirmative, Wakefield team. Your orders are to get across that river as soon as possible. Over."

"Well," said Hallam. "There's a slight problem. We don't have a boat anymore. Over."

"What happened to the one we sent you? Over."

"It was sort of destroyed. Over."

"Good God. You'll have to find another boat somewhere. We need your team on the move as soon as possible. Over."

"Copy that, HQ," sighed Hallam. "Over and out." He looked around at everyone who'd gathered inside. "I need to think. Everyone out except Marlena and Lily."

We all trickled out of the room with the radio. Most people headed back outside to talk about this new turn of events, but I didn't feel much like company. I started back for the sanctuary. I thought maybe I'd go out the front of the church and take a walk, maybe look for a coat hanger or some stairs to throw myself down.

But Kieran caught up with me in the sanctuary. "Hey," he said. "Where were you? I could have used your help with Hallam earlier."

I was amazed. "Kieran, I was on Hallam's side. I don't think we need to go after those guys."

"Well, now, it's impossible anyway, considering we have orders to get across the river."

"They have orders, Kieran. Not us," I said. "I think we should go back to D.C., like we're supposed to." I hadn't realized I thought this. But I guessed I did. I wanted to wait until I saw Polly again, but if she delivered the grimoire, then everything would work out. I'd strip Jason and me of our powers. Hallam and Marlena could get past Jason easily then, I hoped. And Kieran and I could go back and...what? Play house? Except for the baby part, everything would work out, I guessed.

"You do?" He considered. "I guess you're right. We were only hanging around to try to stop Jason. Now that they're going to go west for sure, I guess they'll sneak around him or something, like you suggested earlier."

I nodded. "Right."

"So when do you want to go?"

"A few days, I guess. They still need another boat. I'm sure Hallam and Marlena are in there deciding who's going to go looking for one."

"Okay," said Kieran. "Sounds good." He sat down heavily on one of the pews. "I guess it was crazy of me to try to get everyone to help me go after those guys. It just drives me nuts knowing they're still out there. I wish I'd killed them before."

I sat down next to him. "Sorry," I said, taking his hand. "Maybe I should have used my powers."

He shrugged. "Well, it's done now. There's no point dwelling on the past." He squeezed my hand. "Where were you anyway? You disappeared after dinner."

There wasn't much point in keeping it from him, I guess. I got the pregnancy test out of my pocket and handed it to him.

He made a face. "What is this?"

"It's a pregnancy test, moron. Two lines are positive. One's negative."

"Oh," he said. "I can't read it in this light."

I took it back from him. "It's positive."

He sat up straight, taking my other hand. "It is?" He sounded excited.

"Yes," I said, doing my best not to sound excited at all.

"Wow," Kieran breathed. He hugged me.

I let him, but I didn't hug back.

"Hey," said Kieran. "What's wrong?"

Was he an idiot? "What do you think is wrong? I told you I didn't want to be pregnant. I'm glad you think it's so wonderful, but I don't."

Kieran let go of my hands and got out of the pew. He stood in the aisle, not facing me. "Damn it, Azazel."

I let my head fall back and stared at the ceiling. "What?"

"You're so hot and cold," he said. "Yesterday, I thought you were into it, and now you're not. I don't know what to think."

"It was just an idea yesterday," I said. "Now it's a reality."

"I want you to be happy about it. I feel like an asshole if I'm happy about it and you're not."

"Sorry that the fact that I'm going to gain tons of weight, get stretch marks, and go through hours of painful labor doesn't make me thrilled. Sorry that makes you feel like an asshole." How could he possibly make this all about him?

"Forget it," Kieran mumbled. He trudged back through the church, out the front door, the way I'd planned to go. Now I couldn't even go for a walk.

Instead of following him, I lay down on my side and curled up in a little ball on the pew.

* * *

I dreamed of honey. Just outside Columbus-Belmont park, the river was made entirely of honey. It was thick and amber colored, and it oozed over the rocks and the grass on the banks. It smelled cloyingly sweet. The scent drifted up to the lookout house where we'd rescued Lily and the others. I was standing outside the lookout house, gazing down on the river of honey, wondering if it was tainted, or if it would still taste good.

A fly alighted on my shoulder. It spoke to me in a teeny voice, not unlike Polly's. "You can't go across the river, or you'll get stuck in it," it said in my ear.

I brushed the fly off of me, annoyed.

Above me, the sky abruptly convulsed into storm clouds. The blue sky was obliterated with gray. Lightning flashed behind them, illuminating the wispy edges of the clouds. The clouds shifted, moving in and out of each other, and then solidifying into a shape. I cocked my head to stare. The shape became clearer and clearer as the clouds knitted themselves into each other. It was a face.

I shuddered as I recognized the face. Liam Sutherland, the most evil man I'd ever met. We'd never been enemies, not quite. But he'd never really been on my side either. Sutherland's idea of fun was raping and killing teenage girls. Sutherland made his living by selling information to the highest bidder. Sutherland had dirt on everyone, and no one could touch him. He bought his immunity from every government. He worked with high officials in churches and pagan organizations alike. Why was I dreaming about Liam Sutherland?

Sutherland's cloud face looked down on me. His angry eyes bored into mine. "Azazel," he said, delighted. He'd always found me a little too creepily attractive for my taste. I'd hoped that these days, I'd be too old for his taste. I'd hoped that he'd died when the solar flare happened. Why was he in the clouds? "There are things you don't know about what's happening out west."

Ah. It was the same song and dance all over again. "What do you want for your information, Sutherland?" I asked. He always had a price. He always wanted to trade. And if I had no money and no information, he always suggested we trade by him raping me. I'd never let that happen. If Sutherland didn't always turn out to be so damned useful, I would kill him.

"Why, my safety, of course," said Sutherland. "You don't think I don't know that you and your boyfriend are trying to spoil all my fun, do you? Promise to leave me alone, and I'll tell you all about it."

Leave him alone? "You afraid of me, Sutherland?"

"Terrified," said Sutherland, grinning widely. Then the clouds that made up his face dispersed as rain began to fall.

Drops of it fell on my hands and head. It wasn't water. It was honey.

Sticky, warm honey was coating my hair and clothing and sliding all over my skin. I dove for the lookout house, the only shelter around. Jason was inside. He was holding a baby. It was swaddled inside blankets. I couldn't make out its head.

"It's raining honey," I said.

Jason just shrugged. He made cooing noises at the baby. "I don't know how much longer I can wait for you, Azazel. He's getting stronger."

I wanted to get away from Jason, but the sky was still spitting out large gobs of honey. I could hear them splat against the roof of the lookout house.

"They're coming," said Jason. "I've held off as long as I could, waiting for you, but soon I'll have to do it without you." He sighed. "It won't be easy. I can make them want to work together, but I can't make them want to destroy. They have to want that themselves already. But you can do that. You can make them want to kill him. If we were together..."

Even in my dreams, Jason was trying to get back together? Jesus. "Give me the baby," I said.

"Why?" said Jason. "It's not yours. You don't have babies. You never have babies."

"I'm pregnant now."

He shook his head. "This baby isn't yours. You remember what kind of babies you have." He pointed into the fireplace in the lookout house. In the corner was a twisted piece of blackness, a worm-shaped thing with rows and rows of sharp teeth. My dream in Italy at the Sol Solis school. My dream of having a baby with Jason. That monster thing. But you couldn't remember other dreams in dreams. Could you?

"Stop worrying about babies and worry about what family you've got left," said Jason.

I turned away from the fireplace. There, standing behind Jason, tied to the poles holding up the lookout house, were Hallam and Marlena. They were bleeding.

I rushed to them, working at the knots that held them fast to the poles with honey covered fingers. I couldn't untie them.

Hallam moaned.

I looked at Jason furiously. "If they're my family, they're

233

your family too. Why are you doing this?"

Jason laughed. "Because it's fun," he said.

"Untie them."

Jason turned back to the baby. "Baby's going to learn how to torture people today, aren't you?" He tickled the baby's tummy. "Yes, you are, little man. Yes, you are."

"Stop it!" I screamed, and—

—woke myself up on the pew where I'd been sleeping. It was morning. Light streamed in through the shattered windows. I'd slept out here all night, apparently.

CHAPTER FOURTEEN

Hallam and Marlena had decided that they'd be going to look for another boat to get across the river. I didn't think this was a good idea. I wasn't crazy about my dreams, and I didn't always know what they meant, but I was pretty sure that the dream I'd had last night was warning me that Jason intended to capture Hallam and Marlena and torture them. What the raining honey, cloud face of Sutherland, and baby had to do with anything I didn't know. Possibly they were just things my subconscious was trying to work out. My dreams were confusing at best, but I had a feeling about this.

Hallam and Marlena grilled me about everything that happened in the dream and concluded that since it contained so many weird and irrelevant things, they shouldn't take it seriously.

I tried a different tactic. Why were they the ones who were going to find the boat? Hallam was the person in charge of the team. If he left, we would all be bereft of leadership.

Hallam explained that he wasn't going to send any of the people who'd been captured by Jason out alone again. He didn't think it was fair to them after their ordeal, and he didn't think they'd be able to do the job quite as well, because they might be overly cautious. He didn't want to send people who hadn't been captured by Jason because there were reasons they hadn't been part of scouting parties in the first place. It could only be him and Marlena, in other words. They were going. As for who would be in charge, he was leaving me in charge, but I had express directions not to do anything crazy like go after those nut jobs Kieran wanted to go after.

I volunteered Kieran and myself to go after the boat instead. I thought that made more sense.

Marlena wasn't into that. I demanded to know why, and Hallam was a little curious too. Marlena got kind of quiet, and asked me if I'd had a chance to take the test we'd talked about.

Hallam wanted to know what test.

I got mad. I told her that yes, I'd taken the pregnancy test, and yes, it was positive, but that was no reason to keep Kieran and I from going after the boat.

Hallam freaked out. He was unintelligible for several seconds, just stringing together swears. His face got really, really red. Finally, all he could yell at me was, "How could you be so stupid, Azazel? How could you be so stupid?"

I tried to tell him that I'd been as careful as was possible these days. It wasn't like I could pop into a pharmacy and get my birth control prescription refilled. It had been an accident, the way these things usually were, and I wasn't any happier about it than he was.

It didn't matter, though. Hallam wasn't about to let "a

pregnant lady" put herself in that much danger. I needed to sit tight until he and Marlena got back and then hightail my butt back to D.C., where they would hopefully assign me someplace less dangerous.

There wasn't anything else I could say. I begged them to be careful. I begged them to watch out for Jason or Jason's people. I made them promise to be back by a certain day or we'd go looking for them. They agreed.

Later that morning, they left.

Kieran wasn't speaking to me. He was really pissed off about not getting revenge for his family and my not wanting to have a baby. I kind of thought he was being stupid about it, but telling him that didn't seem to make him any less angry with me.

I was in charge, so I considered ordering him to get over it. I decided that wouldn't work either.

Instead, I just kind of moped around. I didn't offer to help with food preparation, which I probably should have done. I sat on the steps in front of the church, staring at the empty road, the trees and their new leaves, and the abandoned buildings of Columbus. I sat there for hours. I tried not to think. I'd been over and over everything in my head so many times, there wasn't much point in going through it again.

There was a baby. Damn it.

Sometimes it seemed like there was no end of people who needed my protection. With my powers, I felt that responsibility keenly. Personally, there was Chance, Hallam,

Marlena, and now Kieran. I used to feel like I had to take care of Jason. I didn't have to protect him from danger, because he was pretty good at doing that himself, but he was always getting himself into trouble, and I had to comfort him and be there for him. Overall, it just felt exhausting. I had to make sure people were safe all the time. And here I was, with some other little being growing inside me, some other being that I'd have to keep safe.

So, who was it that took care of me, huh?

Certainly wasn't going to be a baby, that was for sure. I wasn't an idiot. I knew that babies were tons of work, and that they didn't love you back. You loved them and they took, took, took. And since you loved them, you didn't mind that they took everything away from you. Hell, you liked it.

I was going to be a terrible mother.

Maybe I could just have the baby and pawn it off on Kieran. He wanted the baby so bad, he could have it.

But I knew that wasn't going to work, either. If I was going to have this baby, I'd want it when all was said and done. You didn't carry a little being around inside you for nine months, and not want to hold it when you were done. Your body released all these weird bonding hormones and stuff, and it was only natural to want to take care of it. And beyond all that biology, I knew that I kind of wanted the baby anyway. I wouldn't have chosen to become pregnant, but if I was, I'd do the best I could. It would turn out okay.

Maybe if I went and said something like that to Kieran, he'd snap out of whatever funk he was in. I stood up, ready to try to reconcile, when I heard the sound of a car motor.

What? There were never any cars. Most people hadn't been able to figure out how to get gasoline out of the ground without electric pumps. And a lot of the gasoline had been taken and stockpiled by the government. So why was I hearing a car?

The sound got louder, and then an old gray Volkswagen bus chugged around a bend in the road and pulled up to the church. Who was this?

The side door slid open and inside, I saw a man sitting in a wheelchair.

Chance?

I rushed forward. Chance was holding a remote which controlled an electric ramp. It was lowering him and his wheelchair to the ground.

"Chance," I said.

He grinned at me. "Pretty sweet, right? Someone converted this thing into a wheelchair accessible vehicle."

"What are you doing here?" I asked.

Chance wheeled himself off the ramp and hit a button on the remote. Everything folded back up on itself, going back into the interior of the bus. He wheeled himself around to the back of the bus. "The best part," he said, "is that I can work on the engine myself." He pulled open a hatch on the back of the bus. "See. The engine's right here in the back. I can sit in my chair and fiddle with it when stuff breaks." He beamed at me.

"What are you doing here?" I repeated. "You're

supposed to be in D.C. You're supposed to be safe."

"I'm glad to see you too, sis," he said.

"Chance!" Had my brother always been this annoying?

"D.C. was boring," he said. "I'm missing all the action there."

"You should be missing the action," I said. "I want you out of the action. You're...handicapped for God's sake."'

"We prefer wheely people these days, actually," he said, wheeling past me to look at the church. "I heard Hallam and Marlena were here too. I came to see you guys. I think I can help." He looked at me. "You know, with Jason."

I clenched my teeth. "You never have to see him again. I made sure of that."

"Are Hallam and Marlena here?" Chance asked.

"You missed them. They're away, looking for a boat."

Chance shrugged. "Cool. I'll see them when they get back."

"No, you won't. You'll get back in your little magic bus and drive back to D.C."

"Geez, Zaza, come on."

"Zaza?" said Kieran. He was standing at the door to the church, hands in pockets. "Now why didn't I think to use that nickname for you?"

I glared at Kieran. "No one calls me that except Chance," I said. It always made me think of my family, and most of my memories of my family were pretty unpleasant.

"Hi!" said Chance, waving. "I'm Azazel's brother, Chance. I'm here to help with Jason."

Kieran raised his eyebrows.

Good. Kieran was on my side, at least.

"No, wait," said Chance. "I know I'm in a wheelchair. I'm not going to fight him. I'm going to talk to him."

"Chance, we've all talked to him. He's completely gone off the deep end," I said.

"But, Zaza, he's like this because of me. I know you don't forgive him, but I do. I don't mind, really. I mean, I was pissed for a while, but now, I just think —"

"You're not talking to him," I said.

Chance started around me and began to wheel himself up the ramp outside the church.

"Chance you can't stay here," I said.

"I drove all this way, and you're not going to offer me dinner?" he said. "I think mom taught you better manners than that."

I groaned. This was a disaster.

Once Chance reached Kieran at the church door, they shook hands. I tromped up after Chance. Kieran put his arm around me. "Zaza," he said, "you didn't tell me you had a brother."

"Please don't call me that, Kieran." I rolled my eyes.

We all entered the sanctuary. Chance looked around. "This is cool," he said. "I can sleep here on the pews. It will be much easier than trying to get out of the chair and onto the ground." He turned back to Kieran and I. "You two look chummy," said Chance.

"Yeah, well, I'm having his baby," I said.

"Really?" said Chance.

"She's always full of surprises, isn't she?" Kieran said.

They laughed, like they were old friends. Wonderful. Perfect.

"I wish you'd told me you had a new boyfriend," said Chance. "I really think I should know about these things, being your brother. I mean, it's great, don't get me wrong. I'm glad you moved on, but—"

"He's not my boyfriend," I said. "We're just having a baby. Okay?"

Chance put up his hands. "Okay," he said.

I crossed my arms over my chest.

"So, about me talking to Jason," said Chance.

"Jesus Christ, no!" I said. "What if he decides to finish the job?"

"Finish the job?" said Kieran.

"Why do you think Chance is in a wheelchair?" I said.

"I think it was an accident, really," said Chance.

"Yeah," I said. "He accidentally shot you and severed your spinal cord. Sure."

"Jason shot your brother?" Kieran asked.

"Why do you think we broke up?" I snarled.

CHAPTER FIFTEEN

Before...

April 2011

Jason's birthday was right around the corner. The previous year, we hadn't made too big of a deal about it, but this year, Chance and I wanted to throw Jason a huge party. We were pretty sure he'd never had a really big birthday party, and he was turning twenty. I wanted it to be awesome. Chance's friend Mitch was in school for event planning, and we'd been able to rope him into our scheme by bribing him with some of Grandma Hoyt's money. Chance and I were pretty rich. Our grandmother had left everything to the two of us, and she'd been absolutely loaded.

I guess I'd been avoiding Jason. We had a rocky two years. At first, things had been idyllic. We'd been completely happy together. It was the first time we'd been able to live together and share a room and openly be a couple (okay, have sex). We started college together in the fall of 2009. We commuted from our house and took classes. I loved it.

Then the thing with Jenna happened in June of 2010. I took it pretty hard. Well, everyone did, but I took it the worst, because I thought it was my fault. For a few months, I'd started drinking really heavily again, which had been a problem for me for a while as a teenager. I started hanging out with some friends from school and getting smashed a lot. Jason got pissed, and I got resentful. We worked it out for the most part, and I cooled it on the drinking. Jason made me make up a bunch of rules for myself, like not to go above four drinks in a night unless I took an hour-long break and had a full stomach. It was all ridiculous, but sticking to it did help.

It didn't keep Jason from getting jealous, though.

Hell, maybe it was me. I was jealous too.

I don't know why we didn't trust each other, but we were always checking up on the other person. I didn't like it if Jason studied with a group of girls. He didn't like it if I went to parties without him.

My therapist said that I was just insecure, and that Jason was too. Jason's therapist didn't say anything because Jason had stopped going to therapy after about a year. He said that he'd had enough, and that he was fine. Which was rich, I thought, because Jason had been raised in a really screwed up atmosphere, and I thought he needed years and years of therapy.

We argued about that too.

We also argued about Jason's beating people up. Jason always had a temper, and now that we weren't on the run, it didn't go away. There weren't many of them. Maybe three. But they always ended the same way. With Jason injuring the other guy so badly that the guy needed an ambulance. I kept telling him he was lucky that these guys weren't pressing charges. I kept telling him he was lucky he didn't kill someone.

Anyway, even though everything was royally screwed half the time, I still thought this birthday party for Jason would help things. If nothing else, he'd know how much I cared about him.

And I was so focused on that, I guess I didn't pay much attention to him for a few weeks.

What Jason saw was me spending a lot of time with Mitch, sometimes with Chance, and sometimes without Chance. Mitch and I would meet at restaurants and coffee shops and plan the party. We'd hang out in the kitchen at our house and call places to set up catering and decorations and guests. And whenever Jason showed up in the kitchen, we acted like we were hiding something. Because we were. A surprise party. And whenever Jason asked if he could come along, I said no. Maybe I was an idiot not to realize that this would drive Jason nuts.

No. I guess I knew it would drive him nuts, but that was part of the game. When he found out about the party, everything would be okay. I could picture myself in his position and knew he must feel frustrated. Any normal person would. But I forgot that Jason wasn't a normal person. So, yeah, I expected him to be frustrated. I didn't expect him to get a gun.

I don't know if I'll ever be able to forget that night. Mitch, Chance, and I were at a restaurant in town. Mitch and Chance had driven together. I'd come separately. So we split up to get to our cars. I don't know exactly what happened then. I was getting in my car when I got the phone call from Chance. He was screaming, saying they were getting mugged, and they needed my help. "Call 911," he yelled at me. "Call 911!"

I started to hang up and do what he said, but he stopped me. "No," he said. "No, it's Jason."

I didn't call 911. I raced to the parking garage where Chance and Mitch had been headed. When I got there, the parking garage was nearly empty, except for a few cars which skulked in the yellow light of the garage. The concrete was covered in oil stains and graffiti. I hurried over it, my footfalls echoing throughout the garage, which was otherwise silent.

I nearly tripped over Mitch's body. He'd been shot in the head, but Jason had taken the time to rough him up first. His face was smashed in. If he'd been alive, his nose would never have healed straight. Blood was everywhere, smeared all over the concrete, gushing from the wound in Mitch's head.

That would have been enough. I don't know if I could ever have felt the same way about him after that. But two feet away from Mitch lay my baby brother. He was lying face down against the concrete, and he wasn't moving.

At first I thought he was dead. I rushed to him, turning him over. He looked up at me, his eyes frightened. "I can't move, Zaza," he whispered.

And Jason? Was he still there, or had he run like a coward?

Jason was in a corner, curled up in a ball. He had his arms over his head, including the one that held a gun. He was crying.

I advanced on him. "What the fuck, Jason?" I said. I stopped when I stood over him. He didn't look up. "What did you do?"

"I didn't mean to hurt Chance," he said, looking up at me. His eyes were red-rimmed. "It was an accident, I swear."

"And Mitch?" I said. "I guess you meant to do that."

"Why couldn't you just break up with me?" he said, his voice wracked with sobs. "Why did you have to do in front of my face like that? I couldn't take it, Azazel. I just couldn't." His nose was running. He rubbed it with the back of his hand.

246

He disgusted me. I was appalled and horrified. I despised him. "Mitch and Chance and I have been planning a fucking surprise birthday for you, Jason," I said. "I didn't break up with you because I was in love with you."

The shock in his eyes was intense. He'd really thought I was cheating on him. I could see that he'd never even considered another option.

"Even if I'd been screwing him behind your back," I said, "that doesn't give you the right to kill him."

Jason started to sob again. "I told you," he said. "I told you to do it in England. I said to kill me, and you wouldn't."

I snatched the gun out of his hand. "You want me to kill you?" I said. My voice was shaking. So were my hands as I aimed the gun at him.

"Zaza," said Chance weakly. "What are you doing to Jason? He didn't mean to shoot me."

"You shot my brother?" I said. I hadn't been able to tell before. I hadn't been able to see the blood. The whole situation was a nightmare, but all I felt was rage. Jason had hurt my brother. He'd shot Chance. My Chance.

Jason swallowed his tears. He nodded, staring me square in the eye. "Do it. Shoot me. I don't work right, Azazel. You have to do it."

I think I might have. I struggled to steady my arms, pointing the gun in his face.

"Zaza?" said Chance.

Oh, God. I closed my eyes. I dropped the gun to my side. I was shaking all over.

"Don't shoot him," said Chance. "Please don't."

I opened my eyes. I looked over at my brother. "You don't want me to kill this asshole?"

"He didn't mean it."

I snapped my head back to Jason. "You get out of here," I growled. "Get away from me. Get away from my family."

Jason stood up. He started to walk away, his head down. He got to Mitch's body. He stopped and looked at me. "Azazel – "

"Chance and I will lie for you," I said. "We'll say it was a mugger. But this is the last time, Jason Wodden. I never want to see you ever, ever again."

He nodded. "Yeah," he said. He slunk off into the night.

I wouldn't have come here to see him if it hadn't been for that damned grimoire. I meant it when I said it. I never wanted to see him again.

* * *

The whole story came spilling out, with various interruptions from Chance, helpfully pointing out that I'd ignored Jason almost completely for a month and that Jason had probably felt abandoned. I didn't let Chance snag the forward motion of my recounting the events. When I was done, I was seething mad at Jason again. I thought I'd been mad at him before, but I'd forgotten the force of my fury.

Kieran absorbed the entire thing. By this time, he was sitting on one of the pews in the sanctuary. Chance was parked next to him in his wheelchair. I was on my feet. The anger had made it impossible to sit down.

"You were too harsh on him," said Chance. "If I can talk

to him, then he'll see that everything's okay, and then he'll stop being horrible."

I spun to face Chance. "Too harsh on him?"

Kieran held up a hand. "Wait," he said to me. He turned to Chance. "She wasn't too harsh on him. She wasn't harsh enough."

Chance furrowed his brow.

"Jason had killed someone. He should have gone to jail," Kieran said. He looked back at me. "I gotta say I wish you had called the police."

I sat down heavily, relieved that Kieran had taken my side. I should have known he would. Kieran didn't have any love for Jason. After Kieran and I had argued so much the past two days, I had just expected him to take the opposite side as me. "I couldn't do that," I said. "After all, I've killed people too."

"You've killed people in self-defense," said Kieran. "It's not the same thing. Jason killed out of jealousy." He turned back to Chance. "I guess you and Jason were friends, huh?"

Chance laughed. "Well, I'm not going to lie. I was pretty angry with him for a while. I mean, I can't walk anymore." He considered ruefully for several seconds. "There are actually a lot of things I can't do anymore." He brightened. "But I'm not angry with him anymore. And maybe you guys are right that Jason really screwed up, but maybe what he needs right now is a friend."

"We can't let you talk to him," said Kieran. "I'm sorry. It's too dangerous."

"He won't hurt me," said Chance.

Kieran raised an eyebrow. "Five minutes after I met the guy, he had a gun to your sister's head."

Chance looked shocked. He didn't say anything.

"He's different than he was, Chance," I said as gently as I could. "He's a lot different."

Chance shook his head. "Well, then, I have to see for myself."

"No," I said.

Kieran shook his head.

"I still can't believe they let you leave D.C.," I muttered.

"Hey, give me some credit," said Chance. "They didn't let me do anything. I decided to leave, so I did. They couldn't stop me. And you guys won't be able to stop me from going to see Jason either."

"Chance," I said.

"Just because you and Jason aren't together anymore doesn't mean that I have to hate him too," said Chance.

"He *shot* you, Chance. I'll never forgive him for that."

"Why not?" said Chance. "I have."

* * *

I was stunned. I shambled back up to the church from the outhouse, not really sure how to react. I didn't look at anyone, I just went back to my pack and dug through it for what I needed. Armed, I headed back to the outhouse. Kieran stopped me on my way there. "Where are you going?" he asked.

In response, I simply held up the tampon.

I hurried away before he could say anything.

I'd gotten my period. It was a week and a half late, and I'd just tested positive for pregnancy, and here I was, getting my period. I didn't know what that meant. My period wasn't accompanied by any kind of relentlessly painful cramps or gushes of blood. It seemed like my normal period. Was this a miscarriage? If you miscarried this early, did it not hurt?

I guessed it didn't matter, one way or the other. After all, if I was bleeding I wasn't pregnant. I repeated that in my thoughts. I *wasn't* pregnant. This was good news. So why did I feel so sad?

If it was a miscarriage, I could blame biology again. Weren't there all kinds of hormonal imbalances that happened when you lost a baby? On the other hand, your regular menstrual cycle threw a cocktail of hormones at you. I could just blame my period.

Thing was, I didn't really believe my period made me think or feel things I wouldn't normally. Sometimes, I guessed, it just made the reactions stronger. So, maybe I wasn't really as sad as I felt. But I was sad.

I didn't know why. I didn't want to have a baby. Thinking I was going to have a baby had been depressing. I'd been through over and over the litany of reasons why having a baby was a bad idea. But somehow, in the course of waiting for my period, I'd gotten kind of used to the idea. And that positive pregnancy test—

That was the worst. They were supposed to be so

accurate. How could it have screwed up? Of course, I had kind of left it for longer than I was supposed to. It had said something about not reading the results past ten minutes. Had that caused me to read a false positive?

However it had happened, I had adjusted to the idea that I was going to have a baby. Now I wasn't. I had to readjust back. Which should be easy, because I'd never wanted a baby in the first place. Had I? I thought about my conversation with Kieran in the afternoon that day, when the light was streaming through the sheets. I remembered my image of the little baby girl. I bit my lip. Okay. Well. Maybe I had wanted a baby. Maybe just a little bit.

I left the outhouse and trudged back to the church. Kieran was standing on the lawn, waiting for me. God. Kieran was going to be so upset.

I couldn't help it. The sight of Kieran for some reason made it worse. I started crying.

Kieran jogged over to me. "Azazel?" he said softly.

I threw my arms around him, buried my face in his chest, and cried.

Kieran held me and let me cry, which he was really good at doing. He was so comforting. He was like some kind of enormous stuffed animal. When I was done, I backed away, scrubbing at my face with my hands.

"I thought the test was positive," said Kieran.

"I did too," I said.

"Do you think you lost it?" Kieran said. It was an it now that it didn't exist. It wasn't a him or a her.

I shrugged.

"I thought you'd be happy," he said.

"I thought so too," I said.

He touched my face. I closed my eyes.

"I *am* happy," I said. "I'm relieved."

"Me too," Kieran said.

My eyes snapped open. "Really? I thought you'd be upset. I thought you wanted the baby a whole lot."

"I did," he said. "But it's relieving. It was going to make things complicated."

I nodded. We were quiet for a little bit. Kieran put his arm around me. It was late evening, and the sun was drooping in the sky. We looked at it together, watching the darkening sky and the heavy sun.

"I feel like something's missing," I said. "Like I lost something that I didn't really get a chance to understand or know."

"Yeah, I get that," said Kieran. "It will be okay, though. I mean, all the arguments you made about why it would be hard to have a baby right now were true. And so now, things are just easier again."

"Right." Why didn't easier seem better?

"And it would have made our relationship even more complicated to sort out," said Kieran.

I looked up at his face. "We have a relationship?"

He smiled at me. "Don't you think so?"

"I don't know, Kieran. We seem to argue a lot."

"Mostly, we've argued about the baby. And there isn't a

baby. So that should help to make things smoother."

Maybe he was right. I leaned in against his body, enjoying his warmth and his closeness.

"Here's what I think," Kieran continued. "I think I should run back to the church and get a sleeping bag and we should talk. And sleep outside tonight, away from everyone."

I gave him a look, remembering what happened last time we slept outside in a sleeping bag. "You realize I'm having my period, right?"

He just grinned. "I wasn't propositioning you, Zaza. But if the opportunity arose, you don't really think that would bother me, do you?"

"I really don't like that nickname," I said.

"Well I like it a lot," he said. He kissed my forehead. "Yes to the sleeping bag?"

I nodded. "Yes. But while you're there, get Lily or Gus or someone to watch out for Chance. I don't want him trying to sneak out to see Jason."

* * *

Kieran's body was pressed tight against mine. I clutched at him, arching my back and gasping. His lips met mine. His breath was labored too. I was focused completely on him and on nothing else. I no longer heard the insects singing in the trees or felt the faint sting of the cool night air. All I felt or thought now was Kieran and me.

It must have been how they managed to get so close to us. They made a racket in the church before they got to us, and if Kieran and I hadn't been so distracted, maybe we would have heard it. I'd feel guilty later. Very guilty. I should have been in the church. Hallam had left me in charge. He hadn't left me to get freaked out about my personal problems and run off to be alone with my boyfriend. If that was even what Kieran was.

They were surrounding us before we knew they were there.

I heard the laughter first. It took a moment, because, as I said, I was focused on Kieran and what we were doing. Not much sound was cutting through. But then I did hear it. Jeering laughter.

I went rigid against Kieran. "Stop," I whispered.

He didn't listen. I dug my nails into his shoulders. "Stop," I repeated, still a whisper, but a more forceful one. He stopped. "Listen."

There were voices now. I recognized the same accent from before. "Hey, I think I found them." A snicker.

Kieran's eyes widened. He made a flailing grab for his pants, which were outside the sleeping bag. Under my breath, I swore. I didn't have a gun. How had I been so sloppy to come out here without a gun?

They had kerosene lanterns, and I peered around Kieran who was trying to get dressed inside the sleeping bag. I could see them gathering close to us, five lanterns. Five men. The same men who'd been in the pharmacy in Clinton. The same men who'd murdered Kieran's parents and raped his sister. And now they were all standing in a circle around our sleeping bag. We didn't have any guns, and we weren't wearing our clothes.

This wasn't good.

"It's them, all right," said one of the men. "The ones who killed Norris, Jeff, and Buck." He had a rifle slung over his shoulder, and he shifted it now, so that it was in his hands, and it was pointed at us.

They had guns, and we didn't. And they outnumbered us. I tried to think. Was there any way to get one of their guns? Could I knock one out of their hands if I kicked?

"Pretty stupid of them to park that car right out on the road, wasn't it?" said another of the men.

The sleeping bag was in my way. I'd have to wriggle out of it before I could kick, and I'd lose my advantage. For all I knew, they'd shoot the minute I moved.

One of the men leaned down over us. "Buck was my brother," he said, anger and hurt in his voice. "You shot him down like a dog."

A dog? Their legs were close. Maybe I could reach out and bite one of their ankles. Maybe he'd be so surprised he'd drop his gun.

Kieran's voice next to me, ragged: "You killed my family too, you bastards."

The other men rearranged their guns. There were five barrels pointing at us. The biting thing was a long shot. And I wished Kieran hadn't antagonized them like that.

"Killed your what?" sneered one of them.

"Chicago," said Kieran. "You took our TV. You raped my sister. She bled to death later."

One of the men turned to another. "You remember this fuckface?"

"Sure as fuck don't," said the man. He looked down at Kieran over the barrel of his gun. "If it was us, your sister was asking for it."

One of the men prodded me with the barrel of his rifle. "What about this one? She looks like *she's* asking for it."

"What kind of slut takes it outdoors, anyway?" said another man. "You don't got a stitch on under that sleeping bag, do you, sweetheart?"

Great. This was turning out well. Kieran started to sit up. His fists were clenched, his jaw set in a firm line. The men stopped him with their guns.

"No, no," said one. "You're gonna watch."

Oh forget that. Well. I didn't really have any options here, did I? I might care a lot about the good of mankind and my own psychological health, but there was a line. Sometimes, the end really did justify the means.

"Let us see what you've got on," said a man, pushing the sleeping bag aside with his gun, nearly exposing me.

"I don't think so," I said, gritting my teeth. Which would screw me up more? Forcing a bunch of men to kill each other or being gang raped? That was a pretty easy answer wasn't it?

"Besides, you dicks, I'm on the rag."

I unleashed the magic in my head, funneling the hatred I felt for each of them into their brains. I felt their initial confusion, then I felt it fade as the destruction washed out their thoughts. They were easy targets, their minds already focused on violence. It was too easy to push them in another direction, to make them hate each other.

They began to hit each other with the butts of their guns. One man smashed the man next to him in the face over and over again. There was a crunch when the man's nose broke. Blood spattered down on Kieran and I. The other man kept smashing him in the face with the butt of the rifle until he crumpled to the ground.

Next to him, the other two men were engaged in a fist fight. The final man had a knife and he was going after the guy who'd just killed his companion by beating him to death. He lunged over Kieran and I, slashing the air with the knife. Showing no fear, the other man lunged for him. We watched as, over our bodies, the man with a knife stabbed the other in the stomach, in the chest, in the throat. There was seemingly no end to the stabbing.

It reminded me of watching the musical *Chicago* in high school for chorus class. "And then he ran into my knife. He ran into it ten times." I giggled.

Kieran turned to me. His face was splattered with blood. The expression on his face was distorted, almost cartoonish. It made me laugh harder. I doubled over in the sleeping bag from the force of my laughter. Tears sprang to my eyes.

The man being stabbed fell lifeless on our legs. I didn't bother to push him off. Instead, I twisted around to look behind us. The man with a knife was going after the other two men. No, there was only one guy left. The other one was thudding against the ground, his eyes bulging. He'd been strangled.

The man who strangled him had dropped him. His arms were wide. He went towards the man with a knife as if he were going in for a hug. The man with a knife slashed his throat. The man gurgled, blood spilling out of his mouth as he dropped to his knees. His eyes fixed on mine for a second, then went blank as he toppled over.

For some reason, this was even funnier, and I laughed harder.

There was only one left. What should he do? Should he commit hari kari? Disembowel himself? I'd never disemboweled someone. I cocked my head, sizing him up and still giggling.

The man punched his knife into his gut and began to drag it through his flesh. I didn't know if his knife was going to be long enough to actually disembowel him. He might have to dig inside his rib cage with his knife, cutting through the meat of himself —

There was a gunshot and a bullet blew up the man's face. He fell down. I stopped laughing.

Kieran set down the rifle. He must have picked it up after one of the men dropped it. "Jesus," he said, swallowing.

"Hey," I said. "I was in the middle of something there."

"Yeah," said Kieran. "I could see that."

I shrugged, and got out of the sleeping bag. My clothes were lying on the grass, all bloody and covered with dead guys. Gross. "You wanted me to use my magic," I said.

Kieran looked around at the bodies. "You went a little overboard, don't you think? I mean, they could have all just shot each other."

"Sure, if you want it to be *boring* ," I said. Whatever. He and I could have died. I could have been raped. I pulled my shirt out from beneath the strangled dude. It wasn't too bloody. I guessed I could put it back on.

As I shrugged into my shirt, I realized I hadn't heard the voice this time either. Something about that should bother me, shouldn't it? I tried to remember why. It was silly, wasn't it? I hated the voice. If it was gone, it was good. I got to my feet and looked down at Kieran, who was still sitting in the blood-smeared sleeping bag. "By the way, you're welcome. I just saved your life."

CHAPTER SIXTEEN

When we got back to the church, we were astonished to find it in bad shape. Two of our people had been shot, and one was dead. I realized that when the men found the Subaru, they must have gone through the church looking for us. If we'd been there, I could have stopped them earlier. Several of the others were wounded, including Gus.

Mercifully, they'd left the Subaru intact. I didn't for the life of me know why. It seemed like they would have smashed it to bits. Maybe they'd planned on taking it after they killed us. Kieran and I changed our clothes, and I sent him for Nancy. We needed her to heal those that were left.

I checked everyone out, and then I realized something. Chance was gone!

Damn it. I asked Lily if she knew where he was. She told me that she hadn't seen him since the men had broken into the church. It had simply been too confusing after that. I couldn't blame her for losing track of Chance. But I knew exactly where he'd gone.

I'd have to go to Jason's camp and retrieve my stupid little brother. Good God. I really did have to take care of everyone, all the goddamned time. Why was it my responsibility?

I made sure Lily had things under control and that everyone was at least bandaged or in the process of getting bandaged. I stopped to pick up my gun and headed for the door.

I heard a car pull up. Its engine was loud. Shit. Were there more of the men? What the hell?

I sprinted through the sanctuary, gun cocked and loaded. I'd head them all off myself if I had to. Hell, I'd use magic. It had worked fine just a few minutes ago. It would work again.

The door of the sanctuary burst open and men dressed in black t-shirts and black jeans poured in, their guns out. Then Jason came in, with Chance trailing behind him in the wheelchair.

"Chance, stay back," Jason threw over his shoulder.

Chance didn't listen. Jason swore at him, but scoured the room with his eyes. He saw me. "Azazel? Are you okay?"

Why was he asking, anyway? "Fine," I said.

Jason eyes swept the sanctuary. "Chance said you were being attacked."

"So you came to rescue me?"

"Well, whatever our differences, Azazel, I don't want you to die," he said.

"I took care of it," I said.

He nodded, holstering his gun. He signaled to the other men to do the same. "I think the men that attacked you might have been some of mine. I'm sorry about that."

"They weren't yours," I said. "We ran into them in

Clinton. They came after us because we shot some of them. It had nothing to do with you."

He considered. "I hope so. I don't know what I would have done with men like that." He took a deep breath. "They're coming, Azazel. I've held them off for as long as I could, waiting for you, but I can't wait any longer."

They're coming. That was what Jason had said in my dream. What did he mean? "Who's coming?"

"There's so much I need to tell you," said Jason. "I wanted to tell you that night I came here, but when you said that stuff about being pregnant, I lost it."

"Well, you've always had a temper," I said. I wished he'd leave.

Jason hung his head. "Yeah," he said. "I'm sorry about Chance. I'm sorry about Mitch. I was out of control."

"You're always out of control."

He looked up at me. "I'm not. Not now. Not as long as I have something to fight. Something worth fighting."

"The Order of the Fly is not worth fighting," I said.

"It's more than that now. I need to tell you about it. Come back with me. Talk to me. I'm sorry I got so weirded out about your pregnancy. I was an idiot. Congratulations and all of that."

"I'm not pregnant," I muttered. "Not anymore. And I don't want to talk to you."

"It's important. Please."

"No." I swung my gun in a circle, sighting each of his men in turn. "Get out. I'll start shooting if you don't."

"For Christ's sake, Azazel—"

" *Get out* ."

And then the door opened, and Kieran and Nancy came inside the sanctuary. They looked at all of the people there and at me with my gun.

"What's going on?" said Kieran.

"Chance went and got Jason to help with the guys who attacked us. Jason came, but he was too late. And now he's leaving. Right, Jason?"

Jason shook his head in disgust. "Yes."

"I'll give you guys a ride since I drove you over here," said Chance.

I waited silently, my gun still trained on them, as they all filed out of the sanctuary. Kieran and Nancy moved forward as they left. They'd gotten here fast.

Nancy had met Kieran halfway, as it turned out. She'd known he was coming and had gone out to wait for him. She asked me to take her to the wounded right away. I did. While Nancy did what she could for the wounded, Kieran asked me to fill him in on what had happened with Jason. I told him as best I could.

Within an hour, everyone was patched up and feeling better. Kieran and I were sprawled on pews in the sanctuary. Nancy came in and threw herself down in a pew next to us. "What I wouldn't give for a beer," she said.

Of all the stuff that people raided, they raided the alcohol first. Go figure. I hadn't seen an alcoholic beverage in at least three months, if you didn't count the moonshine Jason had.

It was just as well, I guess. I didn't do well with alcohol. But that didn't stop me from saying, "Guess that's another good thing about not being pregnant. I can still drink beer."

"You thought you were pregnant?" asked Nancy.

Oh right. Nancy hadn't known about my pregnancy scare. I told her all about the false positive and getting my period that day.

"Doesn't sound like a miscarriage to me. You just read the result too late. Happened to Carol and I when we were trying too. I wanted a positive so bad, I think I willed myself to see it," said Nancy.

"So I was never pregnant," I said. Somehow this made it even worse.

"Probably not," said Nancy. "But I did have an odd dream about you the other night. You were in a gazebo thing with the Wodden guy. What do you call him? Jason? It was raining honey."

"You had that dream too?" I asked.

"He was holding a baby in that dream."

Kieran sat up in his pew. "Did you tell me about this dream, Azazel?"

"I told Hallam and Marlena. You weren't speaking to me at the time," I said. I turned back to Nancy. "Did you dream the part where I was talking to a face in the clouds too?"

She shook her head.

"What do you think it means?" I asked.

Nancy shook her head. "There's something between you and him. Something powerful. But that dream was so

265

convoluted, I couldn't say what any of it meant." She frowned. "It's late. I need to get back to Carol and Guy. Can you drive me, Kieran?"

Kieran nodded. "Sure."

Chance came back into the sanctuary, wheeling himself up to the three of us as Kieran and Nancy stood up. He looked tired. "You're right, Zaza," he said. "He is different. But you're different too."

* * *

I met Polly in the woods on the day we had picked to meet. She was there when I arrived at the spot we'd talked before. Her red hair was tied back in a sloppy bun, and she looked pale and frightened.

"Polly," I said. "Are you okay? Did you find the grimoire?"

She shook her head. "I don't know where he keeps it. And he hasn't been talking to me so much lately. Or coming near me. After your brother showed up the other night, he's been ignoring me completely. I can't get close to him to look for it without him being suspicious."

The grimoire was not such a big deal anymore. I'd spent some time thinking about it, and I'd concluded that I wanted to keep my magic. If I hadn't had magic, the situation with the men, Kieran, and me the other night might have turned out quite differently. Kieran and I could be dead. I wanted to be able to protect myself in the future. Still, if Polly brought it to me, then I could use it against Jason. That would work out well. But I didn't need the grimoire as much as I'd originally thought. "Polly, you don't have to get stressed about it," I said. "If you can't get it, you can't get it."

She shook her head. "But he's getting so much worse. You don't understand. And I don't think he cares about me anymore. All he thinks about anymore is you." She glared at me. "I wish you'd never come back into his life. Before you showed back up, I thought there was a chance that someday he'd get over you. But now, he's obsessed with you again. Why you?"

Great. Now Polly was angry with me. "I don't want him. I'm not interested in him. I'm not trying to get in the way of your relationship with him."

She laughed bitterly. "It doesn't matter if you try or not. He'll always only love you and no one else."

"He's not capable of love," I said. "All he's capable of is a twisted attempt at it. It's all jealousy and anger and violence in him. There's nothing else."

Polly shook her head. "No, you're wrong."

"I used to want to think so, too, Polly, but eventually, I had to face it. Jason was bad for me. He's bad for you. Get away from him before he hurts you more than he already has."

"I'm finding you that grimoire. Maybe if we can take away his magic, he'll be like he was."

"Was he ever really that much better?"

She was angry now. "You're just trying to get me away from him so you can have him back again. You want him for yourself."

267

"I *don't* want him," I said.

There was a noise, the crunch of footfalls on dead leaves. Instinctively, I grabbed Polly and pulled her down to the ground. It was probably a deer, but I didn't feel like taking any chances after what had happened the other night. Other people might be threats. We peered through the leaves and bushes to see a group of maybe ten people making their way through the woods. I'd never seen them before. They wore jeans or coveralls and cotton t-shirts. They had guns strapped to their backs. They dragged toy wagons stocked with food and water. Clearly, they were going somewhere.

"More of them," whispered Polly.

More? I waited for the group to pass through the woods, and then I asked her what she meant.

"They've been showing up every day," said Polly. "More and more of them keep arriving at our camp. I think Jason's calling them somehow."

They're coming. That's what Jason had said in my dream and what Jason had said when he came to "rescue" me. And hadn't he said something like that when he was drunk on moonshine as well? Right after I'd seen the family walking down the road? Had that family been headed to Columbus-Belmont park like these folks were? If I thought hard, the men in Clinton might have said something about going to the river... Jason had said they were some of his. Was that what he meant? Was he using his power to draw people to him?

"They come from all over," said Polly. "They travel from

all the way up in the northeast. They all seem to know who Jason is when they see him."

This startled and disturbed me. "Polly, what do you think he's doing with them?"

"I think he's building an army," she said.

An army? Oh God. "But why? Is he going up against the OF? Why does he want an army?"

She shook her head. "I don't know."

This wasn't good. If Jason had an army, then he would be far more difficult to deal with than he had been. We'd had issues tangling with the size of the force he had already. If he had a large army, we'd never be able to make it across the river, boat or no boat. My heart sank. I hadn't realized how dedicated he was to this. I definitely couldn't get rid of my magic. I'd have to fight him with it. It would be a repeat of the battle we'd had before. This was bad. This was very, very bad.

I turned to Polly. We were both sitting down on the ground now, and I reached for her hand. "You can't stay with him if he's gone this far off the deep end," I said. "Who knows what he might do."

She squeezed my hand. "I know you're only trying to help. I know you don't really want him back."

"Good," I said. "Then you'll leave. You'll come stay with us. I can protect you. I have power that rivals Jason's. I can turn his army against themselves."

"No," she said. "I can't do that."

"You can," I said.

"I can't leave him." She looked like she might cry. "I'm pregnant."

The words stung me. I dropped her hand and looked away from her. *She* was going to have a baby. Her? I felt abruptly hollow, wishing again that I had actually been pregnant. Wishing for it, when all I'd wanted was for it not to be true. How could I have changed how I felt? How was it that something I'd hated was something I now wished for?

"Does Jason know?" I asked.

"I haven't had a chance to tell him. He's been so distracted."

"Don't tell him yet," I said. "Wait and see if you can find the grimoire. If we can remove his magic, maybe he will change. Maybe he'll be a better father."

She promised me she would. But as I watched her go back to Jason's camp, I wondered if my reasoning for urging her to not to tell him was really the truth. Maybe I just didn't want Jason to know. Maybe I just didn't want him to have something that I couldn't have. Maybe I was just being horrible.

* * *

Hallam and Marlena hadn't come back, and the time frame we'd agreed on for them to return had passed. I had to assume something bad had happened to them. I didn't want to worry the entire camp, who were still reeling from the attack by the men from Clinton. So I spoke to Kieran about it. I told him that they weren't back, and I told him about the dream I'd had before they'd left.

I also told him about my suspicions that Jason was forming an army, but I had to leave out the part about Polly. I didn't think Kieran would be too keen on my trying to get my hands on the grimoire. Instead, I just told him about seeing the people in the woods. I said it was possible that Jason's power to influence people could call them to him from far distances. If Jason was so set on the idea of keeping people from crossing the river, then it stood to reason that he'd try to stop Hallam and Marlena. In my dream, he'd been about to torture them. Jason had to have Marlena and Hallam.

Kieran said he didn't know how to interpret my dreams, so I was on my own there. He also said that Hallam had left me in charge, so if there were decisions to be made, I was going to have to make them. That was a little nerve wracking, because I guessed I'd kind of hoped Kieran would just tell me what to do. Once he put it like that, though, I realized that I had to go to Jason's camp.

Kieran wanted to come along, but I told him not to. I said it would be easier if I went by myself. If I got in trouble, I had magic, and I'd just convince people to leave me alone. I was pretty sure that once I found Hallam and Marlena, I could get them out myself.

Kieran didn't like that.

I reminded him that I wasn't pregnant, and that I could take care of myself.

He still protested.

I told him that if he came along, he'd be in my way.

I think that hurt his feelings, because he got quiet after that and said that I was in charge, so, as he'd pointed out, I could do as I pleased.

I left at night, after everyone had gone to sleep. I headed for the lookout house. I'd seen it in my dream, and it was the place Jason had kept the prisoners before. It seemed like the right place to go.

I emerged from the woods by the lookout house. The moon was bright tonight, and everything glowed silvery under its light. Everything was still. The lookout house wasn't guarded. I didn't see anyone around at all.

I crept along the edge of the trees, careful to stay out of the full light of the moon, and got closer to the lookout house. After checking again to make sure no one was visible, I darted into the lookout house.

Empty.

Okay. I should have realized it wouldn't be this easy. Jason would know that this would be the first place I'd go to check for Hallam and Marlena. He must have them somewhere else.

Columbus-Belmont Park was pretty big. Jason could have put them anywhere. There was no way I could scour the entire thing. Last time, Jason had kept the prisoners away from the camp. Had he done the same thing this time? Or were the townspeople out for blood after what we'd done? Would they now be okay with torturing prisoners from our camp?

I didn't know. But it was probably the best place to check

first.

I took off for the encampment. I followed the path, even though it probably wasn't the safest idea. It was the most direct route. Besides, unless it was Jason, anyone I met would be no match for me. I was capable of turning people's minds against them. I was unstoppable.

I was surprised at how soon I ran into pitched tents and campers. Polly was right. The camp had grown exponentially. Why hadn't we seen these people arrive? Jason must have guided them in around our camp in Columbus, so that we wouldn't notice the arrival of all of them. This was an army all right. Jesus.

I skirted the edge of the tents, keeping to the shadows. After a little while, though, I realized it wasn't necessary. The tents were empty. No one was there. They must all be gathered somewhere. Probably the camping loop near the entrance. Could I get there without going through the tents?

Maybe. But I'd have to go the long way around. Screw it. Hadn't I just decided I was unstoppable? I started for the camping loop, making my way between pitched tents and campers, and the smoking remains of campfires. These people seemed quite settled. They'd set up lawn chairs in circles so they could visit. They'd tied strings up between tree branches. Their clothes hung there to dry. It was like a little village. What was Jason doing? Why were all these people following him? What did he want them for?

I was so caught up in my wonderings, I didn't notice one of Jason's elite guards standing at attention behind a camper. In his black clothes, he blended into the night until he moved suddenly, whipping his shotgun forward and pointing it at me.

"Stop," he said, his voice deep and gritty.

I stopped.

"What are you doing here?" he asked.

"I'm going to ask the questions," I said. "You're going to answer, or I'm going to make you blow your head off. I assume Jason's told you about my abilities?" I took a step forward.

"Stop," he said again.

Fine. Whatever. I unleashed my magic and the man whipped the gun under his own chin. I pulled the magic back. The man had control of himself again.

He looked confused. He resituated the gun, so it was pointing at me.

"Jason's got prisoners from my camp," I said. "I need to know where they are."

"No, we don't have anyone from your camp," he said.

I let him have it again. He jammed the gun against himself once more. I made him tense his finger on the trigger. I released him again.

The man looked even more confused. Shaking, he lowered the gun completely.

"Where are they?" I repeated.

"There's no one here," he said again.

This was getting frustrating. I forced him to point the gun at himself again.

"Where are they?" I said.

I meant to release him so that he could answer, but I wasn't quite quick enough. He pulled the trigger and his throat blasted out in a shower of blood and gore. Some of it got on me. Annoyed, I wiped it off as best I could. Dammit.

I started off again, but the gunshot brought more men in black. They surrounded me, their guns aimed at my head. I was about to let loose with my magic again and let them all slaughter each other, but before I could, I felt Jason's power entering their brains. They were all suddenly one mind, focused and disciplined.

Jason sprinted into the area. He was shirtless. "Don't shoot her!" he screamed.

The men put down their guns.

"I felt your magic," said Jason. He was out of breath and unarmed. If I really wanted to, I could make his own men shoot him now. I'd only have to override Jason's magic for a minute, and then he'd be permanently out of the picture. "What are you doing here?"

"You've captured Hallam and Marlena," I said.

Jason looked at me like I was crazy. "No, I haven't."

"Don't lie to me, Jason. I could have your men shoot you right now. I know I could break through your magic with mine long enough to get the shots off."

He laughed. "Whatever, Azazel. You're the only one who can kill me. Or did you forget that?"

Certainly I remembered Michaela Weem saying that. And I remembered the time Jason had sort of died and come back. But that was all just ridiculous. Although... I guess we never really did figure out why Jason didn't die from that gunshot wound to the head. And if Hallam's theory was right, that whatever had been believed about us before had come true for real, then maybe Jason couldn't die except from my hand.

Jason held out his hand and one of the men handed him a gun. Jason put his hand over the barrel and pulled the trigger.

In spite of myself I winced at the loud crack of the shot and at the way Jason's hand splattered blood into the air.

Jason pulled his hand back, clenching it hard. Then he opened it up, palm first. He wiped the blood away and offered it to me.

Perfect. Not harmed. Not even a scar.

I gasped.

He grinned. "I'm indestructible. It comes in handy."

"In Shiloh, you didn't heal so fast," I said in a small voice.

"My powers have gotten stronger just like yours," said Jason. "But I'm guessing you didn't come here for show and tell. I've got things I want to talk to you about. Come with me?"

Should I go with him? Should I listen to him? If he'd found me now, surrounded me with his men with his guns, how likely was it that I'd be able to find Marlena and Hallam on my own? Maybe if we talked, I'd be able to get their location out of him. I sighed. "Fine."

Jason waved the men to put their guns down and they

did. He turned and started back the way he'd come.

I followed him.

Jason led me past the camping loop, where an enormous bonfire raged. Several hundred people were gathered around it, and the sounds of drumming, guitars, and singing drifted through the air to us. That's where everyone was? Hanging out and having a massive sing-a-long? Weird.

Jason took me to the edge of the camp, where a lone RV was set up. He motioned for his guards not to follow him any further, and they stopped where they were. He and I continued alone to the RV. It was a relatively new model and a little on the large side. It was white, with an extended awning on the side and a bed loft above the driving area. Jason swung open the door and called inside. "Polly, I need you to get lost for a while."

"Well, that's polite," I said to him.

"I didn't know you cared about Polly's feelings," he muttered.

"It doesn't look like you care either," I said.

Polly scrambled out of the RV, her clothes a little rumpled. When she saw me, she started.

I noted again that Jason wasn't wearing a shirt. Great. Guess I'd interrupted something.

"I'm sorry," I said to her. "It's not—" I broke off and looked at Jason. "Can't she stay?"

He shook his head. "No. I notice you didn't bring your lap dog boyfriend along either?"

I shut up.

Polly darted off into the darkness like a chastised dog with its tail between its legs. Jason swung into the RV, and I got in after him. Inside, the RV was lit by several kerosene lamps. I could see that it was relatively clean. Its kitchen, with its sink and stove, had clearly never been used. No electricity, after all. Jason walked past the kitchen, barely giving it a look, and into the back of the RV. Behind him, there was a bed, its covers crumpled. He sat down on a couch and motioned for me to sit opposite him on a chair. Beside us, a table jutted out of the wall.

"I don't have Hallam and Marlena," he said. "But I know who does." He gestured to the table. A digital camera was sitting on it. I hadn't seen one in a while. It was hard to find batteries these days. "Go ahead. Pick it up."

I did.

"Turn it on," Jason said. "That was sitting outside my RV a few days ago. I don't know how exactly it got here. Whoever left it got past my guard, and they aren't easy to get past."

I turned on the camera. The screen filled with a digital image of the RV. I could snap a picture if I wanted. Jesus. I hadn't realized how much I missed technology like this.

Jason reached for the camera, and I gave it to him. He hit a few buttons and handed it back to me. Now the camera was playing a video, which must have been stored inside it.

The video took place inside a basement of some kind, where there was—Oh dear God—electric light. I could see exposed light bulbs attached to the ceiling. And I could see

Marlena and Hallam. They were tied up and gagged in a corner. They both looked pretty beat up, with multiple wounds on their faces and arms. That made sense. It would take a lot to take them down. They were tough as nails. Crap.

"Hello, Jason," said a voice on the video. "I thought we could trade."

CHAPTER SEVENTEEN

The view of the video switched, careening around the basement until it faced the owner of the voice. Sutherland.

"What the hell?!" I said.

Sutherland was smiling. "We've had some mutually satisfying transactions in the past, and I thought that you and Azazel might want to do business with me again."

I'd dreamed about Sutherland, and now he'd appeared in my life. Did this mean it was going to start raining honey?

On the video, Sutherland kept talking. "I know your people have been doing surveillance on me. I've noticed your spies. I've left them alone thus far, because I wasn't ready. This side of the United States has been a little bit unruly. Too many loners out west, you know. If the power had gone down on this side, I would have had the east coast in half the time. But, at any rate, I've got everyone under control now. And now I find out about you and your little girlfriend playing games with magic in Kentucky. So, let me put this as succinctly as I can, okay? Here's the deal. You don't cause problems for me and my men, and I don't hurt your friends. Deal?"

Sutherland smiled.

Jason snatched the camera back from me.

"What the hell is Sutherland doing with Hallam and Marlena?" I said.

"This is why I didn't want you to go west," said Jason. "Sutherland's in the west. He's freaking taken over the whole other side of the country, and he's calling himself the emperor of America or something."

"The dictator?" I said in understanding. "The fascist government? That was true?"

"Absolutely."

I was quiet for a few moments, trying to put this together. There actually was a dictator in the west. That was why no one had come to help us. And this dictator was Sutherland? That made no sense. I shook my head. "How did Sutherland become the emperor of America?"

"I don't know exactly," said Jason. "I didn't find out until after I was actively trying to stop the OF from getting west."

"So, it really isn't all just about trying to keep us away from Sutherland, is it?" I said. "You don't want the OF to bring back any kind of order."

Jason glowered at me. "I haven't lied to you about that, Azazel. I want to save everyone from the tyranny of government. Using my powers, I can bring everyone together. You see what I've done here, what this encampment is like. I've got them all around a campfire singing together. Instead of destroying everything, I can—"

"You're forcing people to come here," I said. "Twisting their minds. And maybe you're even building an army."

"For Sutherland!" said Jason. "Well, for the OF too,

281

unfortunately, but it doesn't have to be that way. If you'd join me, we wouldn't need armies. The two of us together, with our power, we could do amazing things."

I wasn't in the mood to hear Jason's psychotic ramblings. "How did you find out about Sutherland?"

"I was curious," he said, "as to why no one had sent help from the west, so I decided to do some checking. It turned out to be harder than I imagined. All the bridges across the Mississippi had been blown up, from the looks of it, on the western side. But I was able to get a scouting party together, and we got a boat, and we made it over there. It didn't take long to figure it out. Sutherland's face was plastered all over banners and billboards. He was on the TVs inside store windows. 'Emperor of America,' was written underneath his face. The few people we talked to made it clear that Sutherland was ruling the country and that he had no intention of coming east."

"Until now," I said.

Jason nodded. "I guess the western half of the country wasn't good enough for him. Now he wants the whole thing."

"But I don't get it," I said. "How did he do this? Sutherland never struck me as the kind of person with political leanings. And he was always more subtle, working to manipulate people, not to outright control them."

"I don't know," said Jason. "Maybe this is what he always wanted, though. This much control."

Maybe. Sutherland had always been one step ahead of

everyone. Maybe it should have been obvious he was capable of this. "Why didn't you tell me about Sutherland?" If Jason had explained all of this better, maybe I wouldn't have thought he was just being a total dick head.

"You didn't need to know," said Jason. "I liked things the way they were. I thought maybe Sutherland would stay on that side of the river. I thought I could stay here. I liked it like that. If it weren't for the pesky Order of the Fly, then it would have been *perfect* here."

"If you'd explained yourself, certain people might not be dead," I said.

"Right," said Jason. "Because the OF would have just believed me. They wouldn't have kept trying to send their little groups across the river to ask for help."

He was right, I guess. "You captured people and cut off their fingers."

"Yeah. Well, if they'd gotten across the river, Sutherland would have killed them. He's killed every other group that has."

The group to the north that we'd lost contact with. Sutherland had killed them. But... "You cut off their fingers to save their lives?"

"To save Hallam and Marlena," said Jason. "When I knew it was them, I couldn't let them get across the river. I had to stop them. I wish I'd known they'd gone off on their own, but recently, I've been a little busy with all the people who've been showing up here."

"Right," I said. "Your army."

"I've got to stop Sutherland," said Jason. "Even if he brings back electricity, he's not really going to make things better. He's going to take over and rule everything like... well, you know what kind of guy Sutherland is."

I did. This kind of made sense. Kind of. I rubbed my face. "So this army is to fight Sutherland, not to obliterate the OF?"

Jason smiled grimly. "I can't obliterate much with you countering my powers, can I? Let's stick to Sutherland for a minute, shall we? Sutherland knows what I can do. How I can focus large groups of people and make them all work together like one being. He knows what you can do too. That you can create destruction and confusion. Sutherland assumes we're working together. He knows that together, we stand a chance of annihilating his army, even though he outnumbers us. He's trying to make us back down by capturing Marlena and Hallam."

I let out a disgusted sigh. "Sutherland likes his trades, doesn't he?"

"The video goes on to outline his deal. He'll give us back Marlena and Hallam when we let him across the river."

"Well, we're not making a deal with Sutherland," I said. "There's got to be another way."

"We go in together," said Jason. "Just you and me, like old times. I think we can find where Sutherland is hiding Hallam and Marlena. We get them out and we kill Sutherland. Case closed."

I considered. It might work. If Jason and I combined our

powers, there was very little anyone could do to stop us. We would absolutely destroy any obstacle. But then what? "What happens to the other side of the U.S. then?" I asked. "Will you stand aside and let the OF go in to restore order and reestablish the government?"

Jason sighed. "You know I can't do that."

"So we stop Sutherland and then it's you against the OF again? You won't let us west, will you?"

"Jesus, Azazel, is that important right now?"

"I think it is."

Jason stood up. "I thought you cared about Hallam and Marlena."

I stood up too. "I do."

"Well, then, how can you let Sutherland kill them? We have to rescue them."

I crossed my arms. "Look, it's news to me that you care about them so much."

"I'm not a monster, Azazel."

I laughed. "Sure. You're a fluffy bunny who can make people care about things they didn't care about before. Who's indestructible, I might add."

"And you? You make people kill themselves or each other."

"Maybe we're both monsters," I said. "But unless I can count on the fact that you'll stop with this crazy power trip you're on, I can't work with you."

Jason sat down heavily. "I might not be able to get Hallam and Marlena out without you. I won't risk that. I'll have to use my army. I'll have to wait for Sutherland to attack. He may kill them both before I get to them."

He was right. I might very well be throwing their lives away. I felt a lump grow in my throat for the only people who had been anything like parents to me since my own parents died. "If rescuing Hallam and Marlena means unleashing you on the world, then I can't risk that."

Jason covered his face with his hands. "What do you think I'm going to do, exactly? Why am I so horrible?"

I gaped at him. "You torture people, Jason. You cut off pieces of their bodies. You manipulate people to coming to you so you can force them to fight against Sutherland. And this is only your behavior in the past couple of weeks. This isn't saying anything about everything you've done your entire life. Even without magical powers you were dangerous."

"You aren't any better than me."

"That doesn't change who you are."

Jason picked up a pillow off the couch and hurled it across the room. "Dammit, Azazel."

I went for the door of the RV. "I'm sorry. But I can't work with you, Jason. I spent too many years of my life lying to myself that there was some wonderful piece of good inside you. Eventually, though, I just had to wake up and smell the psycho."

"I'm not a psycho," he said.

"Psychos never think they're psycho," I replied, opening the door.

He came after me and wedged himself between me and the door. "I'm not," he said. "In England, you said that I wasn't evil. You told me you believed in me."

"I was wrong," I said.

"Fuck you," he said. "Don't say that." He looked desperate. His eyes were wide, and I remembered that I used to feel like I could get lost in them. I remembered how much, how goddamned much, I'd loved this boy.

"Jason, I can't do this for you anymore," I said. "We dated in high school. We lost our virginity to each other. Big deal. That's it. I can't be whatever it is you want me to be for you anymore. I just can't. So if you don't want to feel like an evil psychotic fuckhead, then stop acting like one."

He sagged against the door, and it swung open. Jason tumbled backwards out the door, swearing.

I stepped over him. Looking down at him, I said, "You might want to start with Polly. She loves you, you know. Stop being an asshole to her."

* * *

Jason's guards didn't bother me on my walk back to the church, which was a good thing, because I didn't feel like dealing with anyone right now. I was angry. At Hallam and Marlena for getting themselves captured. At Jason for not telling me about Sutherland until now. At Sutherland for even existing. At myself for not being sure what to do, and for not being able to save everyone. People were going to get hurt no matter what I did. Either Sutherland would hurt them or Jason would hurt them or I would hurt them.

Possibly, all three of us were going to hurt people. Sometimes, I really wished that this was not my life.

I was almost back to the church when a dark figure stepped into my path. I called out, but the person didn't answer. It looked like a woman, and she didn't appear armed, so I got closer. As I did, the light of the moon lit up her face. It was Nancy, but she didn't look quite like herself.

She was staring out at me with unblinking eyes. Her body was stiff. She was expressionless.

"Nancy?" I said.

"Not Nancy," said Nancy in a voice that wasn't hers. She had an accent. It was European. "I'm using Nancy as a conduit to talk to you. It's important."

"Who are you?" I said.

"Agnes."

Agnes was a woman who I'd met in a dream in Italy. She was powerful, with the ability to see the future, and wise, with the ability to calm me down about everything. For months after I'd met her the first time, I'd called her long distance in Italy, looking for advice on how to use my magic. After Jenna had died, I hadn't wanted to talk to her anymore. Now Agnes had taken over Nancy's body to give me a message. I guess I had to listen to her.

"Agnes," I said. "It's been a while. I'm sorry I haven't called or anything, but you know, the phones have been down—"

"There's no time," said Agnes, and her voice was severe, not the sweet old lady voice I remembered. "I read my cards today. The reading was about you, Azazel. Terrible portents are afoot. Things are not looking good for you."

When did things ever look good for me, anyway? "I thought the future was what I made it," I said. Hadn't she given me some Yoda spiel in Italy? *Always in motion is the future. This isn't Oedipus Rex.*

"Darkness," said Agnes/Nancy. "Death. Flies feeding on carrion. Needless slaughter. You are on a path to destruction."

Okay. "Is this because I wouldn't partner up with Jason just now, because —"

"It doesn't matter whether you are with him or against him," said Agnes. "Either way, you descend to the depths."

"I thought I had choices," I said. "I thought my choices were all I had against the forces I couldn't control."

"You have a choice," said Agnes. "You remember the reading I showed you before. The Hanged Man. The sacrifice. It is the only choice you have left."

"I don't understand."

"You are going to do things, Azazel. You have already begun. The power will overtake you. The power will consume you. The power will eat you alive. Vinegar. Honey. It's all the same. The flies all drown."

"Agnes, you aren't making sense," I said. But she was talking about flies. And I kept dreaming about flies. What did it all mean?

"You will lie dead while he feasts on your guts," Agnes/Nancy growled.

I recoiled. Michaela Weems' words.

"Or maybe," said Agnes/Nancy, "you will feast on the guts of your enemies together. Or perhaps, the world explodes while the two of you are trying to work out your differences. It doesn't matter. It all comes to the same thing. The two of you are the problem, not the solution. There is only one thing you can do, Azazel. Make the sacrifice. Kill him. Kill yourself. Both of you must die. Both of you *must* die. *Both of you must die* !"

Nancy's eyes rolled back in her head, and she convulsed. Her shoulders hunched up and her head fell backwards, listless. She gurgled, her tongue falling out of her mouth, drool dripping onto her chin. She swayed unsteadily on her feet and then shrieked at the top of her lungs.

"Nancy?" I murmured.

Nancy's head flopped forward and her eyes rolled forward, fixating on me. Stiffly, her arms came forward. She reached for me. "Kill you myself. I will." She took a shambling step forward. "I will kill you myself."

I backed away. "Nancy," I said, fear shooting through me.

Nancy flopped forward, landing face down on the ground. She didn't move.

I started shaking. "Nancy," I said again, but I was afraid to touch her. " *Nancy* !" I yelled.

The door to the church opened, and Kieran stepped outside. "I heard screaming," he said.

Nancy sat up, rubbing her eyes with the heels of her

hand. "What happened?" she asked. "How did I get here?"

Kieran helped her to her feet and put his arm around me, drawing me close. "Are you okay?" he asked me.

"That wasn't Agnes," I said into his shirt. "That wasn't Agnes." The Agnes I knew would never tell me to kill myself. The Agnes I knew would never try to kill me. Would she?

* * *

I explained the situation as best I could to Kieran as soon as I calmed down, but I didn't go into much details about what Nancy had said to me. Nancy had no memory of any of it. I was going to keep it to myself. I had bigger things to worry about.

Kieran and I got to the radio room as soon as we could and started trying to get in touch with Headquarters.

"Wakefield team to HQ, do you read?" I said. "Over."

Nothing. I repeated myself. Nothing. Crackles. Hiss. Static.

This could take a while. I sent Kieran to round up the team and fill them in on what was going on. Then I returned to the radio. I said it again and again and again, until finally, someone responded.

"This is HQ, Wakefield team. What can we do for you? Over."

I began explaining again, spilling everything I could, from the captured Hallam and Marlena, to Jason's army, to Sutherland, to the deal Jason had offered me and the fact I'd refused. When I finished talking, the person at the other end went to rouse Phillips, and I had to tell the story one more time. Phillips interrupted me with occasional questions, wanting to know if Sutherland was capable of what he threatened and how powerful Jason was exactly. When I was finished, Phillips was quiet.

"Phillips, do you read me? Over," I said. A pause. "Phillips?"

"Loud and clear, Wakefield team," said Phillips finally. "I'm going to authorize every unit I can to get out to you ASAP. I'll alert the President. We'll get you every man we've got. Within forty-eight hours, you should have every member of the U.S. army we can get you. Over."

"Thank you, sir," I said. "Over."

I held a brief conference with the rest of the team at the church, discussing what we were going to do. We'd have to engage Sutherland. We'd have to stop him. And then we'd have to be ready to engage Jason immediately afterward. Things were going to be pretty hairy for quite some time. No one was pleased. Everyone was frightened. I wanted to calm them down, but I was scared too.

Eventually, I was left with Kieran, which was all I wanted. I threw myself into his arms, and he stroked my hair. We sat in the radio room on two metal folding chairs, clinging to each other.

"Did I do the right thing, not saying I'd work with Jason?" I asked. I was terrified that I was screwing everything up.

"You were perfect," Kieran assured me. "You know we

can't trust him. You can't ally yourself with him."

"He's crazy," I said.

"He's absolutely crazy," said Kieran. "You did the right thing."

But when we went to bed, even with Kieran's arms wrapped tight around me, the dreams still found me. And Agnes was in the dreams. She was wrapped in a long, black robe, the hood hanging low over her face. She floated in a pool of red light. She cackled like a wicked witch.

I ran from her, but she followed, arms outstretched. "Kill you myself, I will," she said in a Yoda voice.

"No," I screamed, running away from her down a crooked hallway lit with red lights. I threw open a doorway at the end, and I was sucked outside into the river, which was filled with honey.

Agnes flew out of the door and hovered over me. "You can catch more flies with honey than vinegar," she said, "but vinegar does the trick just fine."

I realized I was surrounded by dead flies, stuck in the river. More were flying through the air. Storm clouds gathered overhead, and the air smelled of vinegar. It began to pour from the sky. When it touched the flies, they sizzled and dropped to the ground dead. The river was filled with dead flies, glutted, just like the bodies in Tennessee after I'd used my power to try to help them.

Agnes was by my side. "The Devil Card," she hissed. "It will come into play."

I put my hand on her head and shoved her down into the

river of honey, holding her face under as she struggled. And struggled.

And struggled.

Finally, she was still.

And I was standing inside the lookout house with Jason. He wasn't wearing a shirt. He came for me, his hands wrapping around my waist, pulling me tight against his body. "You feel so good," he whispered into my shoulder. My bare shoulder.

Suddenly, neither of us was wearing clothes.

"It's never going to be like it was with me with him," Jason whispered in my ear. "Why don't you give up? After all, we're only flies. It doesn't matter what we do."

I struggled, trying to push Jason away from me. "I'm with Kieran now," I told him.

"You're mine," he countered.

"No," I said.

"Yes," he said, and he was inside me, and it was suddenly so, so good, like flowers opening up or a sweet crescendo of thunder across the sky, like the first time he made me come, and I clung to him and moaned into his skin.

Beneath us, I could see armies of flies, marching towards each other, marching towards their doom, but we couldn't let them stop, because it felt so good. It always felt so good with Jason.

I pointed to the flies. "They'll die," I said.

"They're only flies," said Jason. "You and me, Azazel?

We're gods."

He made me come again. I couldn't think for the pleasure.

Agnes hovered behind my head, and she handed me a gun. I gave it to Jason and reached back for another gun, which Agnes supplied for me. I guided my gun to Jason's temple lovingly. He placed his against my temple, a soft caress.

"No more killing," he said.

"No more," I agreed.

He put his lips on mine, sweet like honey, and I fingered the trigger of my gun. His tongue pushed into my mouth. I squeezed my trigger. I heard the thunder of a gunshot, and an echo, louder, closer to my own ear. And then...

Nothing.

* * *

I sat up straight, pushing the tangle of Kieran's limbs off me. I felt like I couldn't breathe. I had to get out of this room.

I stumbled into the hallway and tore into the sanctuary. The sun was just coming up and the light was streaming in through the busted windows, making jagged patterns on the pews. What had the dream meant? It had meant something, hadn't it? The honey imagery made sense now, I guessed. Jason was drawing people to him to make an army. The flies. People seemed to be flies a lot in my dreams these days.

There was a saying, "You can catch more flies with honey than vinegar." Literally, it meant that flies were drawn to

295

sweet things more than destructive things. Figuratively, it referred to people. It was easier to persuade people if you used flattery and compliments than it was if you were confrontational and mean. I'd known for some time that the flies in my dreams represented people. The honey in my dreams represented Jason's power. He drew people with his sweet power, the kind that made people sing campfire songs. My power was like vinegar. I didn't attract people. But the truth was that both of us, no matter the nature of our powers, were killing people.

You could attract more flies with honey than vinegar. But both of them killed flies.

And Agnes had said that we both had to die. She'd referred to a tarot card reading she'd done years ago, before Jason's birth. She'd drawn The Hanged Man — sacrifice.

But she couldn't really mean that she thought I should kill both Jason and myself, could she? Agnes would never tell me to kill myself. I couldn't believe it.

I brushed through the pews, gazing at members of the team who were sleeping. The morning light illuminated their faces. They looked so peaceful.

Maybe I could kill Jason. Maybe. But to put an end to my own life...That was madness.

I spotted Chance's wheelchair just ahead of me. I could never leave Chance.

Chance. I didn't see him. He should be sleeping on one of the pews, shouldn't he? Where was he?

I ran to the wheelchair. "Chance?" I yelled.

Wait. No. What was that on the wheelchair?

It couldn't be.

I picked up the digital camera. No. No. NO!

CHAPTER EIGHTEEN

Jason and Polly were asleep in the RV, spooning. Polly was the big spoon and Jason was the little spoon. Her tiny arms were wrapped around his body, pulling him as tightly close to her as she could manage. Even in his sleep, Jason looked like he was trying to pull away from her.

I flung the digital camera at his head.

Jason was instantly awake, the way I knew he'd be. He sat straight up in bed, picking up the camera.

"He's got Chance," I said.

I stalked out of the RV, slamming the door behind me.

Jason was outside in three minutes, buttoning his pants as he closed the door behind him. "You woke up Polly," he said.

I didn't say anything.

He turned on the camera, and the sounds of Sutherland's voice wafted out of it. I put my fingers in my ears. I didn't even want to hear it again. Seeing it and hearing it once had been enough. Sutherland had Chance, and Sutherland was hurting Chance. Hurting Chance very badly. And Chance wasn't Hallam or Marlena. He'd never been trained by the Sons of the Rising Sun. He wasn't the daughter of a con man who knew her way around a rifle. He was my little brother, and he couldn't even walk anymore.

I could hear the screaming through my plugged ears. I started humming, aware that I might look like a crazy person or a five-year-old. But I didn't want to hear Sutherland saying it again, even though it echoed in my ears. *And if I even suspect that the two of you are trying to rescue them, especially if you're using your powers, I will slit all of their throats.*

In several seconds, Jason tapped me on the shoulder. I stopped humming. I took my fingers away from my ears.

"After you left, I got more intel," said Jason. "Sutherland's already on the move. He and his army will be here in two days. Now maybe you and I can take on his entire army, and maybe we can't. But I know with my army, and the two of us, we can stop him."

I took three shuddering breaths, trying to steady myself. "My baby brother," I said. That was all I got out before a sob stuck in my throat. I swallowed hard.

"I know," said Jason. "Sutherland's a motherfucking bastard."

"Jason, we can't risk going after Sutherland now. Not if he's going to kill them."

"His army's moving every second, Azazel. They are coming for us."

"But—" And this time I couldn't help it. I started sobbing for real. I just broke completely down. Wails. Shaking shoulders. Sniffling. The whole bit. I was a badass, all right. How many times had I cried in the past few days?

Of course, I guess I was on my period.

Jason's arms came around me. I stiffened for a second, but I didn't have the energy to fight him. I relaxed against him, sobbing into his bare chest. I hated to admit it, but it felt nice. Familiar. Maybe I liked the way Jason smelled too. "He's all I have. He's the only one left."

"I know," Jason whispered. "I know."

"I couldn't handle it if I lost him. I'd fall apart," I said between sobs.

Jason pushed me back and held me at arms' length. His face had gotten fierce. "You want to go after Sutherland? We'll do it. Now. We'll get weapons. We'll go. We'll get Chance back."

Yes. That was what I wanted. To go after Sutherland now. I started to nod, but... I shook my head, sniffing back tears and rubbing my eyes. "No," I said. "I don't want to risk their lives. If he's coming to fight us, we'll fight. The OF is sending every man they can spare. They should be here in two days. We'll pool our resources. Between your army and my army, we'll have enough men to give Sutherland a run for his money."

"You're sure?" Jason said. "Because there's a chance if you and I go, that we could just nail Sutherland."

I shook my head. "With the armies, we're guaranteed victory. You make our men unstoppable, a unified force. I make Sutherland's men confused and crazy."

Jason grinned. "You make our men bloodthirsty and ready to slaughter anyone who opposes them. I make

Sutherland's men want to fight for our side."

I took a deep breath. "Yeah. We could do that."

"Fucking A, we could. We can. We will."

I smiled too. And then I hiccupped. Crying sucked sometimes.

Jason took both my hands and stared deep into my eyes. "I'm sorry Sutherland took Chance. But I'm glad you're going to work with me. We make a good team."

"This is temporary, Jason. After the Sutherland business, I don't know where we'll stand."

"I guess we'll see then," he said.

I nodded, gazing at him.

That was when Polly came out of the camper and saw us. Jason and I dropped hands immediately and looked away from each other.

Polly stalked over to me. Her little Minnie Mouse voice sounded more forceful than I'd ever heard it. "I don't know what kind of game you're playing here," she said to me.

"Her brother got captured by Sutherland, that's all," said Jason. "We're going to work together to get him back."

"Oh," said Polly, sounding less than happy about this turn of events, "you're working together, huh? Well, that's just wonderful."

She turned on her heel and walked away from me. I looked at Jason. He shrugged. I started after Polly.

"Polly," I called. "I'm not trying to—"

She whirled. "I'm going to find a bathroom," she said. "I'd appreciate it if you didn't follow me."

* * *

It took the better part of a day to get everything at the church packed up and over to Columbus-Belmont park. It didn't make much sense to have our camps divided if we were working together, and Jason's camp was closer to the river, where Sutherland's forces would attack. We had the provisions and equipment to set up camp in Columbus-Belmont Park, so I relocated Hallam's team there. While we were setting up our tents and getting settled in, the first of the OF forces arrived. I spoke to the commanding officer and got them set up. I also left him in charge of organizing the other troops as they arrived.

Later, I got word that Jason wanted to talk strategy with me, and I brought Kieran along. He wasn't particularly happy about my working with Jason, so I wanted to include him. Plus, Kieran could help with strategy. I was sure of that. We met in Jason's RV. Jason had a few of his elite guard guys there. Fitting Kieran and I both inside was a little bit of a squeeze.

When Jason saw Kieran, he made a face. "You brought him?" he asked.

"Shut up, Jason," I said.

Jason looked Kieran up and down. "I don't like him."

"Feeling's mutual," said Kieran.

Jason shrugged. This seemed to satisfy him. "Your ribs healed awfully fast."

Should I tell Jason about Nancy?

"Maybe you didn't hurt me as badly as you thought,"

302

Kieran said before I could say anything. I guessed Nancy would stay our secret.

Jason shrugged again. He turned to the table, where a map was spread out. I guessed we were going to get down to business and Jason and Kieran were going to stop arguing. Fine with me.

Jason gestured to one of his guards. "Luke here has been doing recon on Sutherland. He reported in this morning with Sutherland's position."

"So, wait," I said. "All this time, you've been going across the river to check things out?"

Jason nodded, looking impatient.

I decided to drop it, even though it pissed me off. If Jason wasn't such an idiot, maybe we wouldn't be in this situation. If only he would have shared his information with the OF.

Jason pointed to the map. "We think Sutherland's army is going to come in here, by boat. They'll probably do it at night, because they know we've got the advantage. If we line up people on the bank of the river, we can pick them off as they come across."

"So we're alert at night, then, and we engage the minute we see them?" said Kieran.

"What about Hallam, Marlena, and Chance?" I said. "Sutherland said he would kill them if we engaged his army. Isn't there some way to trick him?"

Jason grinned at me. "Exactly what I was thinking, Azazel. So, instead, when Sutherland's forces come across, we'll all be completely peaceful. We'll wait for him, you and me—" he pointed to himself and me "—and then we'll get him alone with his prisoners. Azazel, you'll make him kill himself. We'll get Chance, Marlena, and Hallam back, and then we'll give the signal to open fire."

I nodded. "And then we destroy Sutherland's army, which will no longer have a leader."

Jason smiled. "Exactly. It's a good plan?"

"It's a great plan," I said, looking at Kieran for support.

"How do you know Sutherland's army won't start blowing ours up while you guys are negotiating with him to get the prisoners back?" Kieran asked. "Do you really think he trusts you?"

"He doesn't trust us," said Jason, "but he thinks he's got us by the balls. He's very arrogant. He'll go along with it if it's following his plan. We just have to play into his hands."

Kieran was quiet for a second. Then he said, "If you can make Sutherland kill himself Azazel, why don't you just do it now?"

"I can't do that," I said. "I sort of have to know where he is to do it."

"No you don't," said Kieran. "When all those members of the Sons killed themselves, you didn't know where they were."

I spread my hands. "Yeah, but I'm still not really sure how I did that."

"It wouldn't matter if she could anyway," said Jason. "Even with Sutherland dead, his men might kill Hallam, Marlena, or Chance. We can't take the risk."

"Okay," said Kieran. "I guess this will work."

"Of course it will," said Jason, dismissing Kieran with a wave of his hand. "But we've got to have all our soldiers ready to move when we want them to. So they'll all have to wait in tents, dressed and armed. Then once Sutherland's out of the way, Azazel and I will get them out there."

"You mean you'll control their minds," said Kieran.

"Yeah," I said. "We'll also take over Sutherland's army. It should be relatively easy."

"I thought you didn't like doing that," Kieran said to me. "I thought you hated using magic."

"This is important, Kieran," I said. "Besides, I didn't hear you complaining when you wanted me to make the guys from Clinton kill themselves."

"That's just it," said Kieran. "After you did that, I saw why you didn't want to do it, Zaza. It makes you...different."

Jason raised his eyebrows. "You let him call you Zaza?"

"I don't let him. He just does it," I said.

Jason snickered. "It doesn't make her any different than she already is," he said to Kieran. "Maybe you just don't really know her."

"Jason," I sighed. I didn't need him and Kieran at each other's throats.

"Or," said Kieran, "maybe you want her to be just like you, and she's not."

"Guys!" I said. "Stop it, now."

Jason opened his mouth, but I held up a finger in his face,

and he shut it again. Kieran rolled his eyes, but he didn't say anything else.

"Okay," I said. "It's a solid plan, and it's the plan we're going with. Got it, Kieran?"

"Sure," he said.

I promised to relay information to my people, and Jason would take care of his. We'd all be ready tomorrow night, when we thought Sutherland would arrive. We all shook hands, and Kieran and I left the RV.

As we were walking back, Kieran asked me, "How can you stand that guy? He's so full of himself."

I shrugged. "Usually, I can't stand him, I said. "But he's actually on his best behavior right now. I guess I'm just happy to take what I can get."

Kieran glowered. "If things were different, I would have punched him this evening."

Great. I sighed.

* * *

We were gathered around a camp fire in our camp at the park. I had all of the members of Hallam's team in addition to the commanding officers from the OF who'd shown up. I was debriefing everyone on the situation and explaining the plan for the following evening. The glow from the fire flickered against their serious faces.

"More and more troops are going to be showing up," I said. "We've got to get them set up and ready and get them all in the loop. I'm going to put Lily and Gus in charge of coordinating everyone. Is everyone clear on what's going to happen?"

Gus spoke up. "I guess I'm clear, but I'm not sure I agree."

Mutiny? Wonderful. "I don't think I asked that question, Gus."

Gus stood up, and the fire lit his face from beneath, turning him into sinister shadows and hollows. "I don't know why Hallam left you in charge," he said. "By all rights, it should have been Lily. She ranked next highest to Hallam."

"I don't know why Hallam left me in charge either," I said. "But I am, and if we want to stand a chance against Sutherland, you've got to do what I say."

"Hallam would never have done this," said Gus. "He'd never have allied us with Wodden. He'd never have us move camp. We are working with the enemy, and no one else seems to think it's that big of a deal."

"Hallam's not here," I said. I was starting to feel angry. If Gus' feelings spread throughout the camp, I was going to have problems. I needed everyone to work together. "I'm here."

"I don't see why we have to listen to you," said Gus.

"Oh, you don't?" I said. I stood up too, facing Gus across the fire. "I'll tell you why you have to listen to me. You have to, because if you don't, I will make you."

Kieran, who was sitting beside me, touched my arm. I shook him off.

"Your threats don't scare me," said Gus. "You're nothing

307

more than a crazy girl, and ever since you showed up, things around here have gotten worse."

"This isn't a threat," I said. "This is a promise. Shut up now, or I will make you shut up."

"You gonna shoot me?" Gus asked, sneering at me over the fire.

"No," I said. "Last chance, Gus. Sit down and cooperate."

"Absolutely not," said Gus.

It was a lot like what I'd done with Jenna. When she screamed, I'd just reached into her mind and...shut her up. I knew it might have disastrous consequences, but there was too much at stake now. I couldn't have Gus questioning me every three seconds. I touched his mind briefly.

Gus sat down. He looked confused. "Of course," he said. "We'll do as you say. You're in charge."

"Thank you," I said. I looked around the fire. "Does anyone else need clarification?"

No one did.

* * *

I ran into Polly on my way back from using the bathroom before bed. I waved, but I didn't have any intention of engaging her in conversation. She stopped me, though, looking furious.

"Why did you tell me not to tell Jason I was pregnant?" she demanded.

Oh, God. I'd forgotten all about that. Jason was having a baby. Dammit. I felt ambushed. "I just think you should wait. He's distracted right now."

"I think it's because you're still in love with him," said Polly.

"That's ridiculous," I said. I was tired. Did we really have to do this right now?

"No, it's not," she said. "I see the way you look at him. He wants you, and you want him. You can both pretend that you don't have it bad for each other, but I know better."

"Polly, I'm with Kieran." I thought of Kieran then, already snug in our tent. I wanted to be close to him right now, not standing here arguing with Jason's girlfriend.

"Right," she said. "Just like Jason's with me." She snorted. "No wonder you kept telling me to leave him. You didn't want him to be with anyone else."

"I don't care who Jason's with," I said. That wasn't entirely true, I guessed. I'd been jealous, sure, but I was over it now. Maybe I was kind of jealous of the pregnancy thing, but all things considered, I was glad I hadn't actually turned out to be pregnant.

"You're lying," she said.

"I'm..." What was I supposed to say? She was convinced.

"Well," she said, "whatever you did, it worked. I can't get in to see Jason at all anymore. He's too distracted by the battle and by you. So I definitely can't tell him about his baby, and I can't get the grimoire either."

"Forget about the grimoire, Polly. I don't need it." I didn't think I'd be getting rid of my magic any time soon. I needed it. The world needed it. That was just the way things were.

"Forget about the grimoire," she repeated. "And forget

about Jason, too, I guess. Keep me out of the way so that you can take him from me."

"I don't want his psychotic ass," I said. "I mean it. I don't. Take him and welcome. Seriously."

I walked past her. I wasn't going to listen to that anymore. It was interesting that Polly seemed to have grown a spine when it came to someone taking Jason from her. I hadn't thought she had one in the first place.

She was wrong, of course, wasn't she? I'd let Jason hold me when I was upset about Chance, but that hadn't been romantic in any way. I was with Kieran. There was no part of me that still wanted to be with Jason. No part at all.

I shoved myself into the tent with Kieran and curled into his body. His arms came around me, and he kissed me feather soft on the neck.

I snuggled close. Good. Here I could relax and sleep.

Kieran whispered in my ear. "You used magic on Gus today, didn't you?"

No. I didn't want to talk. I just wanted to feel secure in the circle of his arms and drift off to sleep. "Yes," I said.

"Why?"

I thought for a second. "It was just easier."

"You aren't worried about something happening to him? You were worried about that all the time before. You never wanted to use your powers."

What was this? Before, Kieran had wanted me to use magic. Now, he was against it? "I thought you wanted me to use magic."

310

"I'm just trying to figure out why you're using it now," said Kieran. "What changed your mind?"

I considered. I had been against using magic for a long time, but now it didn't seem nearly as bad as I thought it had been. "It must have been when the men from Clinton attacked us in the sleeping bag," I said. "If I hadn't done what I did, we'd both be dead."

He didn't say anything for a few minutes. All I could hear was his steady breath. Then he said, "I'm not going to lie, Zaza. That freaked me out."

"What? Why?"

"It was so bloody and violent. You had those guys mutilate each other. And you...you seemed to enjoy it."

I stiffened next to him. "I didn't enjoy it," I said.

"You were laughing."

"Kieran, I was just thinking about this line in the musical *Chicago* , and I started giggling. It wasn't like I was laughing at them all dying."

"Are you sure?"

"Of course I'm sure."

He was quiet again. Finally, "If you were right before, about the nature of your magic being destructive, is it possible that it could destroy you?"

"Kieran, please. It's a tool, like everyone's been saying all along. What we're fighting for now is important. And sometimes, it is true that the ends justify the means." Hadn't Lily tried to tell me this before? I'd simply been too confused to listen. Things were clearer now.

He pulled me tight against him. "I just worry about you. That's all."

"I'm fine," I said.

But as I fell asleep, I saw the faces of the men I'd forced to kill each other. I saw all the blood. I remembered that there was something about the voice that I used to hear when I used my magic. There was something... I put it from my mind. I was very tired.

CHAPTER NINETEEN

The next day was full of the arrival of more men. OF forces swarmed into the camp, and Gus and Lily got them set up. Jason's army was arriving too. People were appearing from all over, ready to help fight against Sutherland. Our numbers were growing.

I spent as much time as I could helping to organize everyone, supervising Gus and Lily, and lending a hand with Jason's new arrivals as well. Gus didn't challenge me again. Whether it was because the magic I'd used on him was still working or because he was afraid of my messing with his mind, I didn't know. But I was glad. It made things much easier.

Nancy and Carol showed up with baby Guy in the afternoon. Nancy had had some dreams and was concerned about what was going to happen. They wanted to know if they could help.

I was sure that we could use Nancy's healing skills, but I didn't think I wanted her close to the fighting. I did think there were ways they could be of service, however.

We sat at a picnic table in the park. It was a warm day, and I was glad the fight this evening would take place in the dark, when it was cooler. "I don't want the two of you to be harmed," I said. "There are probably going to be a lot of casualties, and I can't risk Nancy being hurt. Her healing powers will probably be needed later."

"We can't just sit back and do nothing," said Nancy.

"Sure we can," said Carol. "Are you forgetting we have a baby to take care of these days?"

Nancy rolled her eyes. "I'll be safe. I just need to know what I can do."

"Well," I said. "There is something that could be done. There are a lot of small children and their mothers in this camp. Jason's call has reached out to entire families. I hate the fact that they're in harm's way. If you two could take them further out, away from the fighting, that would be really helpful."

"That wasn't what I meant," said Nancy.

"Absolutely," said Carol. "We'd be happy to do that."

"Great," I said.

"A lot of these people are from Columbus, aren't they?" asked Nancy. "I don't think they're going to want to be around Carol and me. At best, they're afraid of us because they think we're witches. At worst, they hate us because we're lesbians."

"They'll have to get over it," I said.

We went to round up the mothers and children. As Nancy predicted, there was a bit of resistance from some of the people from Columbus who remembered Nancy and Carol. But it wasn't much, and I was able to convince them easily. They knew they were in danger, and they wanted to go someplace safe.

It took time for them to pack up and say goodbye to their families, but eventually, we got all of them to follow Nancy and Carol, who were going to take them back to their farmhouse. I promised Nancy that we would send for her when we needed her healing services.

"If I have any important dreams," she told me, "I'm coming to find you."

I smiled. "Okay." It wasn't as if I could stop her, was it?

The atmosphere seemed more focused and less worried with the children gone. Squadrons were being formed, points of attack being explained, guns loaded, hiding places for snipers scouted out. I walked among our army, which was larger than I'd imagined it could be. When Sutherland arrived, we'd be ready for him. He wouldn't be able to get past us. And soon, very soon, I'd have Chance back. But until then, I had to be patient.

There was nothing to do at this point but wait.

* * *

It wasn't even dusk when one of Jason's personal guards came running up from the river bank. He was out of breath and sweaty, and his clothes were ripped and dirty. There was a gaping wound on his forehead. Blood and sweat were smeared on his face and hands.

Jason went to intercept him immediately, and I followed.

The guard stopped when he reached Jason and bent over, his hands on his knees. He struggled to catch his breath. "They're here," he wheezed.

Here? I sprinted away from the both of them to look out over the river. It was full of black boats, crammed with soldiers in uniforms. The boats had heavy artillery, and they were coming across the river in full force. Behind the boats on the water were more boats on the shore and more squadrons of men. The mass of bodies stretched over the horizon. I couldn't see the end of Sutherland's army. There were just swarms and swarms of people as far as I could see. My breath caught in my throat. We'd thought we would have hours yet. Were we even ready?

Kieran was behind me. "They're early," he said.

Jason yelled for me to come to him, and I did. Kieran was right behind me.

"He's in the cemetery," Jason said as soon I was within earshot.

The cemetery? "Who is?"

"Sutherland. He's got Marlena, Chance, and Hallam, and he says if we wait with him while his army passes, he'll give them back once he's clear of our camp," said Jason.

"What cemetery? And how do you know this?" I said.

"He told me to give Jason the message," said the guard, who was still out of breath. "His boat docked maybe five minutes ago. We were under orders not to engage, so we let him pass."

"You did the right thing," said Jason to the guard. To me, "The cemetery is just outside the park. It's an old civil war cemetery. There are bunches of graves from the 1800s."

Jason barked out orders for his men to hold their ground

and stick to the plan. I did the same. Then Jason took me by the arm and we were running for the cemetery, with Kieran just a few steps behind us.

The cemetery was overgrown. No one had cut the grass in months. The graves were obscured by high grass and leafy trees. The sun was setting and the whole area seemed quiet, abandoned, and spooky, like in a horror movie. We stopped short at the edge of the cemetery and looked around for Sutherland.

At this point, Jason noticed Kieran. "What's he doing here?" he demanded.

I grabbed Kieran's hand. "He's with me," I said.

Jason clenched his jaw, but didn't comment further. Instead, he pointed. Sutherland was standing next to an iron fence that surrounded a group of maybe twenty elaborate gravestones. Seeing him reminded me of the time Lilith and I had run from him outside the church in Shiloh. His feline grin was exactly the same. It gave me chills. He had five or six soldiers with him. Chance, Hallam, and Marlena were sitting on the ground, tied and gagged. They had scabbed-over wounds, stringy hair, and wild eyes.

At the sight of Chance, I took off towards him, screaming his name. I collapsed on my knees in front of him, reaching out to touch him, to make sure he was okay.

"Uh uh," said Sutherland, and one of his soldiers put a machine gun in my face. I dropped my hands.

"He better be okay," I said to Sutherland.

"He'll be fine," said Sutherland. "As long as you stick to

317

the deal."

Jason and Kieran came up behind me. Kieran helped me to my feet.

"I know you wouldn't have any stupid ideas about trying to double-cross me, would you?" asked Sutherland.

Jason crossed his arms over his chest. "Of course not," he said. "But I think it's fair for us to make sure you haven't hurt our friends. Un-gag them. Let them talk to us."

Sutherland laughed. "I don't think so. You can see them. There's no reason for them to talk."

"Why?" said Jason. "If you remove their gags, will they tell us that this is a trap, and you're planning to slaughter all our people anyway?"

"Why would I do that?" asked Sutherland. "I know that if I open fire on your troops, you'll use your little mind tricks to turn them into super soldiers. No thank you."

"Then why can't we talk to them?" asked Jason.

Sutherland sighed heavily. "Fine, fine." He waved carelessly at his soldiers. "Remove the gags."

The soldiers untied the gags in their mouths. Hallam began to swear as soon as his was off. He threatened to do all kinds of foul things to Sutherland. Good. So Hallam was all right.

Marlena seemed only concerned about me. "What are you doing here?" she asked me. "You shouldn't be running around like this. It's dangerous for your baby."

"There's no baby," I said. "It was a false alarm."

"Thank heaven for that," she said.

And Chance just seemed out of it. "Zaza?" he whispered.

I turned angrily on Sutherland. This man was pure evil. I hated him. "What did you do to him?"

"He's fine," said Sutherland, inspecting his fingernails.

"He doesn't seem fine," I said. "He's a paraplegic, for God's sake. Have you been taking care of him? He needs —"

"Shut up," said Sutherland. He gestured to one of the soldiers, who put a gun against Chance's head.

I balled my hands up in fists. I wished I could just kill Sutherland. Wait. I could. That was the plan, wasn't it? Why were we wasting time chatting when I could be forcing Sutherland to commit suicide?

I reached out with my mind and let my power brush Sutherland's mind. I tried to implant anger and hatred and the desire to do himself in. But it was different, somehow. Generally, I just reached inside and there was something that I sort of...I don't know...flooded.

With Sutherland, when I tried to pour my power into him, I couldn't. There was a resistance.

Sutherland laughed. "Trying to use your magic on me, Azazel?"

"No," I said.

"I think you'll find me a bit hard to influence," he said. "I don't have an impressionable mind."

When my grandmother had told me about her power, which was also the power I'd inherited, she'd told me that it only worked on people with impressionable minds. She couldn't manipulate everyone. My power was much stronger than hers, and I'd never really encountered someone I couldn't influence. But if there was anyone with an iron will, it was Sutherland.

Dammit. What were we going to do now?

CHAPTER TWENTY

I tried not to convey my panic as I surveyed Sutherland, my tied up brother and friends, and his armed guards. This whole plan had hinged on my being able to take Sutherland out. What did we do now? If Jason and I got our armies to fight Sutherland's, he'd kill Marlena, Hallam, and Chance.

If we stood by and did nothing, Sutherland would have won his first battle in taking over the whole country.

I looked at Jason, whose face was stone. No help there.

I didn't want to sacrifice Chance in order to save the rest of the country. He was my little brother, and I didn't have any family left besides him. Everyone was dead. If I let Chance die, I'd be all alone. How would I live with myself if I did that?

I couldn't do that. I looked down at him. His eyes were wide and glassy. He looked terrified. He looked sick, possibly feverish. Oh God. My little brother. I couldn't help him. I was going to —

Wait, what was I thinking?

I reached into the minds of the soldiers Sutherland had with him and forced them to point their guns at Sutherland. Well. I forced all except one. The one who had a gun against Chance's head. He must not have had an impressionable mind either, wouldn't you know it.

It all happened extremely fast. They fired on Sutherland, under my influence.

Sutherland hit the ground, evading their bullets.

Kieran darted forward and grabbed Hallam and Marlena. He yanked them to their feet.

Sutherland tangled his arms in the legs of one of his soldiers and the soldier went down.

Jason dove for Chance.

The soldier covering Chance shot Jason. Jason swore.

I made my men shoot again at Sutherland. Sutherland rolled out of the way.

Kieran dragged Hallam and Marlena away. The three scrambled across the cemetery.

Jason was bleeding, but recovering fast. He drew his gun.

Sutherland wrenched a gun away from the soldier he'd tripped. He shot that soldier in the head.

The soldiers I was controlling fired again. One shot grazed Sutherland's cheekbone and blood spattered onto the grass.

Jason aimed his gun.

A soldier shot Chance in the head.

Sutherland shot the soldiers I was controlling.

I didn't move for several seconds. I looked at the bodies on the grass. The soldiers. And Chance. My Chance.

Then I wrested Jason's gun out of his hand and shot the soldier who'd shot Chance. I shot him in the forehead. I shot him in the stomach. I shot him in the chest. I shot him in the mouth. I shot him and shot him and shot him.

Jason pulled me away. "Stop, Azazel. He's dead," he was saying. "Stop. He's dead."

I turned on Jason, rage coursing through my veins. "Chance."

There he was. Dead on the grass, blood spurting out of his forehead, his eyes still wide open.

But I had forgotten about Sutherland, and now he had *his* gun to my head. "Deal breaker," rasped Sutherland.

I didn't care at that moment. I really didn't care. "You killed my brother," I spat at him. "And right now, your entire army is coming for *you* ."

I wasn't lying. I didn't know how many minds it was. Thousands. But I'd filled them all with my rage for Sutherland, and I'd let them all know where he was. And now they were changing course, and they were all marching toward Sutherland. When they got to him, I would make them rip him into little pieces.

"That's supposed to keep me from shooting you in the head?" Sutherland said. He cocked his gun. There was blood trickling down his face from the place where the bullet had grazed him.

"Don't shoot her," Jason said. "She'll back off."

"I most certainly will not," I snarled.

Suddenly, I felt the minds wrenched away from me. Jason. He was focusing them all someplace else, and not on killing Sutherland.

"Their minds aren't on you anymore," said Jason. "Lower

the gun."

Sutherland didn't listen. "I knew you'd be easy to control if I was going to kill her," he said. "You were always too soft when it came to her, Jason. She's your weakness."

"Okay," said Jason. "Sure, fine. I'm weak. But put the gun down."

Sutherland jammed the gun against my cheek. I glared at him.

"Turn around, Azazel," said Sutherland.

"Fuck you," I said.

"Turn her around," Sutherland said to Jason. "And I'll let you say goodbye to her before I shoot her."

Jason took me by the shoulders and turned me so that my back was to Sutherland. He mouthed to me, *I have an idea* .

I'd had an idea too. It was to make Sutherland's army kill him. I'd really liked that idea.

"Good," said Sutherland. "Now say goodbye."

Jason kissed me.

I struggled in his arms, against his tongue that was pushing into my mouth. I pushed ineffectually at his shoulders. I suppose I should have been worrying that Sutherland was going to shoot me. I should have been thinking about how to stop him. But right then, not much mattered. Chance was dead. I was alone. I didn't care about anything. I could die. Fine.

But I didn't want my last kiss on earth to be with Jason. I hated Jason.

"Don't fight me," Jason said against my mouth. "It's not

going to work if you fight."

Work? What?

Then it came to me. Our theory that kissing made people do what we wanted them to. It had confused the Sons, brought Jason back to life, and made the Sons commit suicide. I opened my mouth to Jason, and I felt like I'd been kicked into warp speed, stars streaming past me so fast I could hardly breathe.

I was everywhere at once, inside the minds of each and every person on earth. I could feel them all and control them all, for good or evil, destruction or creation. It was too easy then. I could break the flimsy bit of resistance that Sutherland had in his mind. There was no reason not to. And likewise, there was no reason to make him die in such a messy way by making him shoot himself. It was easy to find the parts of the body that were keeping him alive and convince them just to stop. Shut down his brain. Stop his heart from beating.

Sutherland fell to the ground behind us. He was a bag of bones. His gun discharged when it hit the ground.

Jason and I kept kissing.

We worked together like one being. Our power spread out into the armies that were gathered to fight. We could push our army against Sutherland's army, annihilate them. But that suddenly seemed like too much effort for something that was now so simple. We could brush the minds of each of the soldiers in Sutherland's army. If we wanted, we could switch all of them off, kill them like we'd killed Sutherland.

Or we could just scramble their minds, like we'd done so long ago in the church in Shiloh to a group of the Sons. Back then, our power hadn't been so all-encompassing, and we hadn't understood it the way we did now. The easiest thing to do though, was the least intrusive. We just made them stop. They all lay their weapons down, sat down on the ground, and we made each and every one of them think of home.

There would be no battle. There would be no struggle. Everything would be done simply. There would be Jason and me and our bodies and our lips, and we could make the world over into a beautiful place, where no one ever wanted to hurt anyone else. Paradise.

Our kiss grew fiercer as we envisioned it. Our power reached out with hungry fingers, touching the minds of the planet, pulling them up into it, gathering them to us. They were ours to manipulate. Ours to use. Soon—

But there was a closer mind. A familiar one. We probed it. It stood outside us. It hurt. We wanted to turn off the hurt.

No. We were divided. I wanted to turn off the hurt. Jason wanted to snuff it out. He thought the mind was a barrier between us, a divisive force and he wanted to kill it the way we'd killed Sutherland.

Kieran.

I broke away from Jason, shoving him away from me with all the strength in my body.

Searing pain shot through me, as if I'd just cut off half of my limbs. And all the power and connection I'd just felt, my ability to see the world and manipulate everyone's mind and change everything, shut off, like I'd just blown a breaker in my brain.

I screamed, clutching my temples. Jason was yelling too.

I opened my eyes. Jason and I were both sprawled on the grass of the cemetery, both holding our heads because they hurt.

Kieran was standing next to us. He looked stricken and sad. "You were kissing him," he said.

"We had to," I said. The pain was fading. I squeezed my eyes shut and opened them again. It was a little better.

"Why did you push me away?" Jason asked, agony in his voice. "Couldn't you see what we were doing? Couldn't you see what we're capable of?"

"You wanted to kill Kieran," I said.

Jason got to his feet, wincing. "He's in the way, Azazel. You belong with me."

"Even if that were true," I said, "it wouldn't mean you could kill him."

"What do they matter, really?" Jason asked me. He walked closer, his eyes bright. "You must have felt it. Compared to us, they're nothing. They're like flies, easy to brush away, easy to kill. Who cares if one of them dies?"

I did know what he meant. Two seconds ago, with that heady, beautiful power rushing through me, it was difficult to distinguish one person from another. They had seemed insignificant, like insects or pests. But I'd wanted to help people. I still wanted to help people. "I care," I said. "I don't want to hurt people anymore. I'm sick of hurting people."

"But that's what we could do," said Jason. "You saw it. A world without pain. We wouldn't let them hurt each other."

I shook my head. "No, we shouldn't do that," I said.

"Why not?"

"It's wrong. People need to be able to make their own decisions. We can't just control them."

"We do that all the time. Every time we use our magic. We just did."

"But that was different," I said. It was, wasn't it?

"No it wasn't," said Jason. "It's who we are, Azazel. We are meant for something huge and exciting and important. We are meant to change the world. Join me. Kiss me again. With you by my side, I can —"

"No," I said. I looked at Kieran, who still looked sad, but now also confused. "No." I reached out for Kieran, and he slowly put his hand in mine.

"Fuck you," said Jason. "I'll make you change your mind. I'll take everything away from you. Every one. You'll have no choice."

"Jason," I said. "Please stop —"

"You're mine," Jason said. "You'll always be mine. And if I have to kill every last person that tries to convince you otherwise, so help me, I will."

Jason's guards appeared suddenly, sprinting into the cemetery with their guns drawn. They were aiming at Kieran.

CHAPTER TWENTY-ONE

I let my power loose on the guards, confusing them, making them doubt their purpose. They lowered their guns and looked around, as if they didn't remember where they were. But Jason fought my power, strengthening their resolve. They lifted their guns again.

Jason and I went back and forth for fifteen minutes. He tried to force the men to fight. I tried to make them confused. Eventually, I realized this was stupid. Jason and I were evenly matched. We could fight over the minds of these guards for eons, but neither of us would get the upper hand.

While still keeping my focus on clashing with Jason's attempt to focus the men, I branched out, searching for other nearby minds to control. There were many to choose from. I didn't care whose they were. Jason's people, OF army, remnants of Sutherland's forces. Armed bodies were all that mattered. I brushed the minds of forty or fifty men and filled them with the desire to shoot Jason's guards.

They flooded the cemetery, their guns ready. Jason's guards were mowed down with gunfire in a matter of seconds. Bullets ripped into their flesh and blood spurted onto the tall grass of the cemetery. They fell, screaming.

But that wasn't the end of it, because Jason had also taken control of the minds of a group of soldiers as well. They charged across the cemetery heading directly for Kieran.

Kieran turned to me. "What the hell?" he said. "What is going on?"

I shook my head. "Get behind me."

Kieran wouldn't, so I redirected my army against Jason's new group of soldiers. The firefight began. It was loud, messy, and relentless. Our soldiers moved without fear or hesitation, because Jason and I had both taken that away from them. His soldiers moved with a single purpose. Mine moved with the desire to destroy. They shot at each other. Bullets shredded men's arms and guts. They tumbled to the ground. The ones left behind scrambled over them and kept heading for the other side.

As my forces were depleted, I called for more. There were enough men that I could do this for quite some time. The air smelled of discharged firearms and dead men. I fueled my soldiers with rage, and the carnage continued.

Kieran said to me, "You're killing all these men."

"Jason is trying to kill you," I said. "I won't let him."

"Fine," said Kiernan. "Let's run away or something. You don't need to send all these soldiers to their death."

Was it bad that they were dying? They'd come here to fight Sutherland, hadn't they? I felt confused suddenly. Should I feel bad about the dead soldiers?

But while I was distracted, Jason surprised me by sending in a squadron behind me. I heard their gunfire before I saw them. I only had time to glance at them over my shoulder. There were twenty of them, and they were coming at Kieran and me, guns blazing. I hit the ground, pulling Kieran with me.

Using my mind, I urged some of my forces to engage the squadron attacking us. They turned away from Jason's other men and dove over us. More shooting.

I couldn't tell who was winning or losing. It was only important that I kept Kieran safe. My men were taking a bit of a beating from Jason's men, so I called in more. Kieran and I were sprawled on the grass of the cemetery, the ground around us soaked in blood. I reached for him, and he put his hand in mine. I saw movement out of the corner of my eye. I turned towards it. Jason's men were closing in on us, forming a circle around Kieran and I. Their faces were blank as they moved forward, like blind men.

I had enough men within the circle of Jason's forces to hold them back, but the rest of my guys had been cut off. I called them in to attack Jason's men from behind.

Jason strode across the grass to us, his men parting to let him through. He was holding a gun. His face looked darkly intent on his purpose. I got to my feet, putting my body between the approaching Jason and Kieran.

Jason had one of his men run over and toss me out of the way. I had one of my men shoot the man in the forehead, and I dove for Kieran.

Jason was two feet from him. He tossed his gun aside. "I think I want to do this with my bare hands."

"Don't you touch him," I said, sending three of my men at Jason. Their bullets tore into him, but he barely reacted to them. He just laughed and kept going for Kieran.

Right. Jason was indestructible. Only I could kill him. Maybe. Michaela Weem had told us that. We'd never tried to test that theory. I thought it was about time we did.

I lunged for the gun Jason had dropped, picking it up and rolling onto my knees. I leveled it at Jason and pulled the trigger.

But at that moment, one of Jason's soldiers slammed into me, and my shot went wide.

It caught Jason in the shoulder. I watched it burst through his shirt, blood gushing.

Jason screamed. He clutched the gunshot and fell to his knees. And he lost control over his men. They all stopped what they were doing and surveyed the bloody battlefield, strewn with hundreds of corpses.

I was on my feet. I was next to Jason in three steps, my gun against his back, right behind his heart. Jason looked at me. "You," he said. "You shot me. It's not healing."

"I want you out of my life," I said.

"I can't believe you shot me," said Jason. "I love you."

"No, you don't," I said.

A high-pitched shriek echoed across the cemetery. "Stop!" And then Polly streaked in front of us, her arms going around Jason. She looked at me over his shoulder, her eyes full of tears. "Don't shoot him."

"He's trying to kill my boyfriend," I said. "He's caused all of this." I waved my hand around at the dead bodies.

"I know, I know," she said. "He scares me. But you can't kill him."

Jason shoved Polly. "Get away from me," he said.

Polly stumbled and fell. She looked up at Jason with hurt eyes. "I just wanted you to live long enough to see your child," she said.

Jason closed his eyes. "Child?"

"She's pregnant," I said.

Jason hung his head. "I'm sorry, Polly."

He moved too fast for me. His feet kicked my legs out from under me, and I dropped the gun. Jason had the gun in his hands, and I was on the ground before I could stop him. He aimed the gun at me. "I've realized something," he said. "I used to think that you should kill me, because I brought nothing but death to this world. But now I realize that if I should die, you should too."

Kieran put a gun to Jason's temple. "Stop," he said.

"He's not afraid of that," I said to Kieran.

Kieran pulled the trigger anyway.

There was an explosion of blood and bits of bone. I shut my eyes, and I felt it spatter against my face. When I opened my eyes, Jason was shaking his head like a wet dog and laughing.

Kieran stepped back. "What is he?"

Jason bowed low in front of Kieran, still laughing. "Haven't you guessed? I'm the messiah."

I got to my feet and plunged head first into Jason,

sending him sprawling on his back. "I don't think so," I said.

He reached up and stroked my cheek gently. "Last time we did this," he said, "I remember it being a lot more pleasant."

Suddenly, I was crying. "Kieran, give me your gun," I said. Kieran did. I put the gun in Jason's face. "You're crazy. You tried to kill Kieran. You mutilated people and sent us their fingers. You hurt Chance. You deserve to die."

"Do any of us deserve to live?" Jason asked.

I was still crying, because for some stupid reason, I was thinking of things that Jason had done that had made me love him. Like the way he always snored, or how he loved Guns N' Roses and would sing along at the top of his lungs to "Welcome to the Jungle."

"You gonna do it, babe?" Jason said, grinning at me.

"Yes," I whispered, fingering the trigger. "Jason, some part of me still cares about you. I'm so sorry." My tears were blinding me. I took one hand off of the gun to wipe them away.

It was only a second, but Jason took that second to drive his fist into my stomach.

I oomphed, doing my best to absorb the blow.

But before I could pull myself together, his other fist collided with my chin. My teeth crunched against each other. My head snapped back.

Jason was on his feet, his foot on my chest. He kicked the gun out of my hand. He stared down at me. His eyes were full of tears too. "As long as there's a part of you that cares about me, there's a chance for us," he said.

And then Jason was running. Kieran scooped up the gun and fired after him, but what did that matter? Only I could hurt him, and by the time I'd made it to my feet, he'd disappeared into the trees.

Maybe I should have gone after Jason, but I didn't. Instead, I stumbled over the dead bodies to the corpse of my little brother, Chance. I collapsed next to him, pulling his head into my lap. We could go west now. We could get electricity. But I didn't care, because my baby brother was dead. I looked into his lifeless eyes, stroking his cheek. "I'm sorry," I said. "I'm sorry."

EPILOGUE

I paced back and forth in the alley, gripping the cell phone tight against my cheek. "Yes, Phillips," I said, "it's very impressive that you always find a way to contact me."

I rolled my eyes at Kieran, who was leaning against the side of a building, a tiny blanket-wrapped bundle in his arms. Skyscrapers surrounded us, and the sounds of explosions underscored our conversation. Kieran made hushing noises as loud wails emanated from the blankets in his arms.

"Can you hear that?" I asked Phillips. "The baby's screaming."

Phillips' voice crackled a little. Cell reception wasn't great these days, especially since Jason's people kept knocking down all the towers. "The baby is Wodden's child, isn't it?" he asked. "Can't you see how risky it is to have him with you?"

"Little Chance is safer with me than he'd be anywhere else," I said. Why was I arguing with this dick anyway? I had better things to do. Like annihilate Jason's army. "Jason's already sending messages that he wants his son. There's no way I'm letting that happen." Polly hadn't made it through delivering him. There were too many problems

336

with the birth, and the doctor had tried to do an emergency C-section. There had been so much blood. She hadn't even been able to name her baby before she died. But she'd grasped my arm, stared into my eyes, and made me promise to take care of him. I was determined to keep that promise.

"Please, Azazel," said Phillips. "Please relinquish your command to the OF forces. You aren't trained to—"

"Phillips," I said, "stop trying to convince me to give up command. No one can fight Jason better than I can. I know what I'm doing."

Phillips' voice shook. "The destruction the two of you are wreaking on the country is—"

Phillips voice cut off as I lost the call on my phone. Good. I didn't want to talk to him anyway.

I went to Kieran and little Chance.

"The explosions are scaring him," Kieran said.

I touched Chance's grimy cheek. "What's going to happen to you, little man? Growing up in the middle of battles all the time? Watching everyone die?"

"Azazel," Kieran said.

I looked up at him sadly.

"Maybe you should turn over command to the OF," said Kieran. "The three of us could go into hiding."

I shook my head. "Jason would take over the world if I didn't try to stop him."

There was a loud crack as a bomb struck a building close to us. The ground shuddered.

"If there's a world left after this," Kieran muttered.

I sighed, refocusing myself on the battle. My army was gaining ground on Jason's, but that hardly meant anything. We fought so constantly, huge masses of people against each other, all over the United States, that one victory or loss made no difference. "I'll kill him," I said. "If I can ever get close."

I could see Jason's armies coming for mine, and I received messages from him—demands, insane ones. He wanted his child. He wanted me. He wanted our complete surrender, and he wanted us to join his fight for freedom. That's what he called it.

"If only we'd been able to find the grimoire," said Kieran.

I hated that he brought this up so often.

"Jason must have had it on him when he left Columbus," I said. "Let's get moving. This area is unstable. We need to find cover." With my mind, I pulled a few dozen men to cover us as we made our escape. I didn't tell Kieran I was doing this. It upset him that I forced people to protect us and didn't give them a choice. But it was the only chance we had to survive.

Kieran didn't move. "If we had that grimoire, we could get rid of both of your powers."

"I know," I said. Someday, I wanted that. I did. Someday, I'd tell Kieran that I'd found the grimoire in Jason's RV, and that I carried it with me, tucked in a pocket inside one of my packs. Someday.

I yanked on Kieran's arm. "Let's go," I said.

He followed me, then, handing me little Chance. I walked

338

with the baby snug in my arms, staring into his tiny eyes, so similar to Jason's.

Someday, I would get rid of both of our powers. But...not yet. Not now. I just needed to feel the power flood through me again. A few more times. And there wasn't any point in using my power without a worthy adversary, was there? I needed Jason to wreak this havoc. If he didn't, I didn't have any excuse. Did I?

Want more?

<u>Between the Heaves of Storm,</u>

<u>Jason and Azazel: Apocalypse</u>

<u>Book Five</u>

Keep reading for a sneak peak.

Want freebies, information on new releases, discounts, and more? Visit my website to join my email list.

vjchambers.com

BETWEEN THE HEAVES OF STORM, CHAPTER ONE

~joan~

"Can you see him?" asked Tessa, straining on tiptoe to peer over the shoulders of the crowd at the stage in front of us. It wasn't a large or elaborate stage, and it had clearly been made from timber gathered from various dismantled materials. The wood didn't match, but it looked sturdy enough. We'd just arrived, and I'd been so tired, I wanted to collapse on the grass. But being in the presence of Jason had energized me somehow.

"I can see him on the huge screen there." I pointed. Jason was standing on the stage, but closed circuit television projected his image onto several large screens. His voice was amplified through a sound system, and it boomed out over the rolling hills around the gigantic crowd of people. We were all squished up together under the blazing July sun, jostling together to get closer to him.

Jason.

"That's like seeing a video," said Tessa. "We're close to him for the first time. He's right there!" She craned her neck to look at the crowd in front of us. "I want to get closer."

Garth, Tessa's brother, laughed and shushed her. "I'm trying to listen to what he's saying."

I didn't know if it mattered what he was saying. He always said the same stuff anyway. He talked about peace and togetherness. He talked about freedom. He talked about how the Order of the Fly was a sham government that needed to be destroyed. It wasn't so much what he said as it was the way he said it. Something about his voice always made me feel weak and shivery. It called to me, awakened some deep part of myself. I adored him.

He did look different. I'd only seen him on videos — various clips of his talking that were passed from person to person, uploaded to cell phones or saved on digital cameras. The power was spotty most of the time, always interrupted by various skirmishes between factions of the OF and their enemies. The internet was slowly coming back, but it wasn't often anyone could really access it. Since the solar flare of 2012, which had fried transformers all up and down the east coast of the United States, the country had never really bounced back. Not really. Things were better than the first six months, when there was next to no power, but they weren't perfect. Of course, I didn't really remember that far back.

On the videos, Jason usually looked young and severe, with his short-cropped dark hair and bottomless dark eyes. He was beautiful in a haunting way, a way that let you know he meant business. Now, his hair was long — past his shoulders. It curled at the ends. He sported a full beard. Its dark shagginess framed his perfectly shaped lips. I couldn't see him clearly on the stage, but I could see that he wore a white flowing shirt and jeans. He looked like a guru or a yoga instructor. He had an air about him, something peaceful and powerful. Even his voice sounded that way, booming with authority but also soothing. He was still beautiful, I thought. He looked older now than he had in the videos. Wiser.

Jason was the first thing I remembered. Really the only thing. The sound of his voice. The feel of his pull. It was the only familiar thing I knew.

I had some kind of amnesia. I didn't know why. The first thing I remembered was two weeks ago—waking up in a strange apartment building in Washington, D.C., right in the heart of the Order of the Fly. Around me, there had been nothing but bland walls and closed-in hallways. I'd only been wearing pajamas. I'd torn through the halls, cement block walls streaming by me, until I'd gotten outside onto the street. All the time, I'd been thinking about Jason. I could feel him in my head, beckoning me. Telling me to come to him. I had to go.

It was odd, although I guessed it was pretty normal for amnesia. I could remember all kinds of things. I knew what year it was. I remembered everything that had happened with the solar flare. I even remembered the war which was raging between Jason and the OF Witch. No one said her name out loud. She was too awful. She used her powers to counter Jason, and to stop every move he made. Her attacks had slowed recently, but she was still out there. I remembered her. But I didn't remember anything about myself. Not my name, not where I was from, not if I had brothers and sisters. Amnesia sucked like that.

Tess and Garth thought that I must have suffered some kind of traumatic experience in D.C., and that was why I'd lost my memory. According to Garth, that was the reason most cases of amnesia happened. Trauma.

I didn't like to think about something traumatic happening. I wasn't sure, of course, but I had a sense of myself. I didn't think I was a particularly tough person. Something inside me felt very fragile, like I'd break into thousands of pieces if one thing went wrong. Of course, maybe that was why I'd gotten amnesia.

I was lucky that I'd run into Garth and Tessa. They were both on their way to see Jason, just like I wanted to do. They called themselves pilgrims. They said that lots of people felt the same call I did, the magnetic pull towards Jason. They were really nice people. They didn't know me (hell, I didn't know me), but they let me tag along with them. When I'd first met them, I'd realized that I didn't even remember my own name. It was a terrifying feeling. Being no one.

But Tessa had told me that I should name myself, and I had. I named myself Joan. I felt like a Joan. The three of us took off together, heading west. And after all our travelling (mostly by foot), we were finally here. Jasontown.

Nestled in the foothills of the Appalachians, this was

Jason's settlement. It was completely off the OF power grid, meaning that it relied on solar power and generators for its scant electrical needs. However, most of the people here lived in close connection with the earth, as Jason encouraged his followers to do. Tessa and Garth had told me all about it. Jason welcomed anyone and everyone who wanted to come here. He'd built a community where people lived together in harmony. They took care of each other, grew food together, built shelters for each other. It was a blissful place, from what they told me. With Jason, everyone was happy. Unfortunately, the OF was trying to stop what Jason was doing and tear down his utopia. Apparently, until recently, it had been difficult to get here, because the OF had blocked most people's entry. No one knew why, but it wasn't hard to get in anymore, and people were pouring into Jasontown. The OF was the only reason there was every any conflict. If the OF would go away and stop trying to get in the way of what Jason was doing, the entire country, even the whole world, could hear his message and feel his influence. We could all be at peace.

I sighed just thinking about it. The perfection of the thought was beautiful, and I wanted to be part of making it a reality.

Tessa grabbed my hand. "Let's get closer." She tugged at me.

Closer did sound good. I wanted to see Jason better too, not only his image on the screen. I followed her.

Garth touched my shoulder, stopping both of us. "Where

are you guys going?"

"Getting closer," said Tessa.

"We have to stick together," Garth said.

"Then come with us," said Tessa.

I reached out my hand to Garth, who looked at it for a second, then grasped my hand with his own. A train of three people, we followed Tessa's lead as she wound in between people, snaking through the crowd to get closer to the stage. It reminded me of being at a rock concert before the lights went out and everything changed. At least, it would have reminded me of that, if I had any memories. I guess what I meant was that it seemed like the atmosphere of a rock concert — the excitement in the air, the crush of bodies.

Surprisingly, people didn't jostle us or give us dirty looks as we pushed past them. There really was a lack of animosity here. It was as if Jason's presence wiped all that away. Instead, they let us by, some of them with amused faces. Maybe they'd already seen Jason a thousand times. We never had.

Tessa was nothing if not determined. I would have been happy to get just a little closer. But Tessa kept pulling Garth and me along until we were right smack dab in front of the stage, and we were mere feet from Jason.

I looked up at him as he spoke into the microphone, his arms wide as he gestured. "Welcome to all the new faces I see here today. It seems like we have more and more people every day, and this is a wonderful thing. We have the answer here," he said. "The answer is freedom. The answer is peace. The answer is everything the OF is against."

Yes! He was right. Here, close to him, the call I'd felt before was so strong. I was engulfed in Jason's essence. It flooded me with tranquility, like a cool spring breeze. I wanted to drink it up. Not even the intense heat or the smell of the sweaty crowd seemed to penetrate my mood. I breathed deeply, closing my eyes and savoring the sensation. I'd never felt anything this good before. I was at peace, and I could sense that everyone around me was too. We were all connected.

"But lately," said Jason, and his voice changed somehow. It got more menacing. "Lately, I've gotten reports from those closest to me that there are spies in our midst. The OF has sent people to infiltrate our happy home."

A collective gasp rippled over the crowd. I felt it, like a punch in the gut. How could someone betray Jason like that? Could these spies from the OF see what it was like here? I'd only been here for an hour, and I already thought it was the most wonderful place on earth. What was wrong with them?

Jason was nodding on stage, his expression grieved. "You won't know who they are. They will seem like anyone else. And they may have been here for a very long time, hiding out, gaining our trust." His voice began to thunder out over the crowd. "Anyone could be one of them. Your wife. Your brother. Your friend. The Witch of the OF is powerful. Her influence can be felt even here. She could have corrupted anyone. No one is above suspicion."

The crowd began to murmur softly. I looked at Tessa,

feeling concerned. Would they suspect us? They'd have to see that we were sincere. Wouldn't they?

"If you suspect anyone as a spy," said Jason, "anyone at all, you must turn them in for questioning. If they are innocent, they have nothing to fear. But we must remain safe. Safe from the OF, and safe from its Witch, that hag! She is a traitorous bitch, with the name of a demon. She controls the power of pure destruction. Nothing good comes from her. Beware, my people. Beware the influence of Azazel!"

Jason's eyes swept the crowd. His eyes smoldered. I felt fear clutch my insides. Dread ripped its way through my guts. He'd said her name. Jason's gaze started at the back of the crowd and zigzagged forward. It was almost as if he were looking into the eyes of each and every person gathered in front of him. The crowd was completely silent as he looked at us.

He finally worked his way up to the front, where we were standing. I saw him look at Tessa, and then Garth. Then his eyes met mine.

Suddenly, all the fear I'd felt burst. I didn't feel any fear at all. In fact, the undercurrent of peace and tranquility that I'd felt beneath the fear was gone. I felt...

Normal. Just a girl standing in the blazing sun with a bunch of people.

Jason knocked over the microphone and clambered off the stage, coming straight for me. He didn't look happy.

I took a step backwards.

He tackled me, his hand at my throat. We toppled to the

ground, Jason on top of me. His breath was hot against my skin as he whispered in my ear, "What the fuck are you doing here?"

***

~kieran~

I couldn't stop staring at the place where Lily's ring finger used to be. There was nothing there now, only a twisted mass of scar tissue. She was sitting across from me, behind her desk in her office. She absently tapped the eraser of a pencil against a stack of papers. I knew it was rude to stare at her missing finger, but I couldn't stop.

"You seem to be feeling better," Lily said. Her hair was pulled back into a severe bun at the nape of her neck. She was a middle-aged woman with tanned skin. She'd done her time fighting in the field. When I looked at her finger, I did my best not to let the flood of memories jolt my brain.

"The headaches are better," I said. The memories were like liquid, sloshing around in my head. I tried to dam them up and keep them out, but I wasn't very successful. It was disconcerting too, because when I saw Lily's finger, I got so many images. My own memory of the bloodied bundle in the grass in Columbus Kentucky. And then the other memories, the ones that were foreign to me, but made me feel like I'd lived them. Memories of another bloody bundle, of a wild-eyed woman screaming things like, *Which of you must die?* And always *his* face and the jumble of emotions that went with it. Adoration, disgust, fear, devotion. I waited for my head to begin throbbing, but it didn't. The headaches

349

really were better.

"Good." Lily toyed with the pencil, but kept her gaze fixed on me. "I suppose having all of that extra information in your brain must be uncomfortable."

"Are you going to lecture me?" I slumped in my chair. "Because I know what I did was a bad idea. I know that now. I want to fix it."

She put the pencil down. "No lectures. I only wanted to let you know that I've been working on a solution."

I sat up straight. "Did you find her?"

Lily shook her head. "Nothing like that. I simply meant a solution for you. A way to get all of that jumble and confusion out of your head."

I furrowed my brow. I didn't think there was a way if we hadn't found her. "I don't understand."

"It's simple, really," said Lily. "I can use the same spell on you. You'll go back to normal."

I thought about it. I could surrender all these foreign feelings and thoughts. Feel like I was just one person again. I hadn't realized, before this happened, how much I cherished my own identity. It did sound nice. But... "The spell wasn't supposed to strip memories, though," I said. "I thought you said that I must have made some kind of mistake. How are you going to duplicate that?"

Lily picked up the pencil again. "I've looked over the spell numerous times. It's difficult to translate something that ancient. It's possible that it is actually a transference spell, not a purging spell. The important thing, Kieran, is that those powers are a burden you don't have to bear. The President would feel more comfortable with them resting with someone like me."

I nodded slowly, understanding coming to me. "So you don't even know if you could take away her memories, do you? You just want her powers."

"I'm fairly certain that the spell would work to take away both the memories and the powers, Kieran."

I shook my head. She was lying. I could tell. I didn't know if it was because I was tapping into her jadedness or if it was because I was pretty jaded myself these days. "You'll split her up," I said. "When we find her, how will we make her whole again?"

"I don't think it's in the best interests of anyone for Azazel to regain her powers, Kieran. Not even if we did find her. We'd give her back her memories, of course—"

"You don't even know how to do that," I said.

"You can't tell me that you think she should be given back the powers," said Lily. "After all, you're the one who stripped her of them. You thought she was dangerous as well."

Lily was right, and I could feel the shocked betrayal of the strange memories seeping into my mind. "I never meant to steal everything from her. I never meant to hurt her."

"I know that. And even if there have been unexpected consequences, the OF sees your actions as a positive move. Azazel's powers have been integral to the OF's strategies. Without her, we would never have been able to make the strides forward that we've made. We're rebuilding society, and we can't do it without her powers. But she had become erratic and difficult. Now, her powers are disconnected from her, and the OF can use them. So I'll take them from you—"

"No," I said. "I don't want to give them up." They weren't going to pull what little was left of Azazel apart. I was going to hold her together, even if it meant my brain exploded.

"Kieran—"

"I'll do what the OF wants," I said. "I'll use her powers. But I don't want to run the risk of separating her. And if anyone should have her memories, it should be me. I love her." At least, I thought that was still true.

"The OF would simply be more comfortable with me having the powers," said Lily.

I shook my head. "I don't care. I'm not giving them up."

She sighed, laying the pencil down carefully. "You'll follow the orders of the OF without question? Use the powers for whatever operation they deem necessary?"

"Of course," I said.

"And there's nothing I can say to convince you otherwise?"

I shook my head again. "Listen, is this all? Because Chance is probably waking up from his nap, and he's going to be hungry. I've got to go make him a bottle."

Lily shrugged, standing up. "I'll talk to my superiors and see if your offer is acceptable." She held out her hand.

I shook it, but all I could think about was that there was

no finger. There were several painful flashes inside my head. *"Evil spawn," said a woman's voice. And then the sensation of Jason's lips —*

Ugh. Why did she have to have so many memories of him that were like that?

I got to my feet, one hand on my head.

"Are you okay?" Lily was concerned.

"Fine," I said. The painful sensation was already fading.

***

~kieran~

Chance had woken up alone in his crib and was already yelling. He was getting to a point where he got very upset if he was left alone or left with unfamiliar people. I had thought this was because he missed Azazel, but I did some research, and apparently, it was only a normal baby development thing. He didn't quiet down for a long time, even though I walked him around the room rocking him and trying to give him a bottle. Instead, he just howled, his tiny mouth wide open.

He wasn't the least bit interested in his bottle, so eventually I gave up on it and gave him a sippy cup of juice instead. He clutched the handles with his chubby hands and quieted.

Every day, he looked more like his dad, and as much as I hated myself for it, I didn't like it. I set Chance on the floor of the apartment I'd shared with Azazel until about three weeks ago. We'd been there for about four months or so. Originally, Azazel hadn't wanted anything to do with the

OF. We'd spent our time running from city to city, sleeping where we could. I'd convinced her that it wasn't good for Chance, and that going to the OF would provide a safer environment for him. So we'd come here. Chance's baby toys were strewn across the carpet, and he quickly abandoned the sippy cup for a large bright block, which he began to pound against the floor, laughing. The worst thing about losing Azazel was Chance.

We hadn't exactly been a conventional family, considering we were raising her ex-boyfriend's kid. But having Chance had been the only thing that had made the last few months of my life bearable. With Chance, Azazel was completely different. She was sweet and motherly. She held him and tickled him and sang to him.

And then, from inside her brain, she controlled the minds of thousands of soldiers and sent them on suicide missions to destroy people. And she liked it.

I couldn't handle it. It didn't make any sense for her to be so kind and wonderful in one situation and so ruthless and cruel in another. If it hadn't been for Chance, we would have ripped apart. And I'd done what I'd done only because I wanted to save her — the part of her that was Chance's surrogate mother. Not the part of her that was some kind of all-powerful being who didn't give a rip about human life. It was the magic that did that to her. I know it was.

When I met Azazel, she actively resisted using it, and once she gave into it, she changed. She grew more and more... well, evil. I know it seems weird to think of anyone besides cartoons as evil, but that's what she was becoming. She loved the power. Even though she was supposed to be working for the OF, she never listened to them. Azazel had to have her own agenda. She had to use the power however she wanted. It was like she was addicted to it. And that was disturbing, because, before, all she'd wanted was to get rid of it. In fact, we'd spent a lot of time searching for a grimoire, a book of spells, which had a purging ritual in it. Azazel wanted to use it to get rid of her powers.

Three weeks ago, I found the grimoire in one of Azazel's bags. She'd had it all this time. She'd had it for over a year. And she hadn't used it. She hadn't purged her powers, because now that she was this cruel all-powerful being, she liked it.

I was sickened. I was betrayed. And if it hadn't been for Chance, I would have left. I would have taken him with me and hidden. But I couldn't do that, because Chance loved Azazel, and I didn't want to take her away from him. I decided instead that I'd do the purging ritual myself. I thought that if I could purge Azazel's powers, I could bring her back. She'd be like she was, and all of the darkness in her would be gone. I wanted that so badly.

I remember the day I did it. It was late, and we'd put Chance to sleep. She was getting ready for bed, brushing her teeth in the bathroom. I was sitting on our bed, watching her through the crack in the door. I had the grimoire open on the bed in front of me. Maybe I shouldn't have said anything to her. Maybe I should have done it. Maybe that would have made it work the right way. But I had to know why she'd kept this from me for all these months.

So when she came back into the bedroom in her pajamas, I said, "Why did you hide it from me?"

She looked from the grimoire to me and then back again. "You found it."

I nodded. "Please tell me you have a good explanation for not telling me you had it."

She folded her arms over her chest. "I was waiting until we could get close to Jason. I can't purge my powers and leave his. He'll destroy the world."

I thought she'd say something like that. "We know where he is now. He's set up that weird commune type thing in the country. It's an hour's drive from D.C. We could go tomorrow. We could purge both of your powers then."

She didn't say anything.

I knew she wouldn't go for it, but I had to try. "You never had any intention of getting rid of your powers. You like them too much."

"I will get rid of them someday, Kieran," she said. "I will. Just not yet."

"You're lying," I said. "I don't know if you're only lying to me, or if you're lying to yourself too, but I can't let you continue this way. You're destroying yourself. You're destroying the world. And Chance and I need you." That was when I started reading the words of the purging spell aloud.

Azazel realized what I was doing immediately. She

356

started forward, trying to snatch the book from me, but the spell caught her. I could see it. It was like shimmering little strands of light, filtering out of my mouth and winding themselves around her body. It trapped her there and held her while I read.

Azazel lashed out with her power. I felt it like a tugging in my brain, a small voice that whispered to me to stop reading the spell. I faltered, struggling against the whispering voice. I knew it wasn't mine.

Azazel strained against the bonds of the spell, trying to break free.

But she couldn't, and I kept reading.

The light of the strands surrounding her body grew brighter and they began to make a sizzling sound. Tiny plumes of smoke emanated from them.

Azazel started screaming.

I wanted to stop. But I didn't know if I wanted to stop because *I* wanted to stop or because *she* wanted me to stop. We were connected suddenly, her thoughts were booming inside my head. She was thinking, *No, Kieran, don't. Kieran, you're hurting me. Kieran, please!*

And I kept reading.

Then there was an explosion of light and sound. It knocked both of us onto our backs. I sat up, looking for her. She was dazed, staring around the room as if she'd never seen it before. "Who are you?" she said in a small voice.

And before I could answer, my head began to throb. There was an influx of voices and sounds and pictures.

357

Sensations. Things I didn't know. Things I couldn't know. And underneath it all was a scaly whisper, slithering around inside my head, knocking against the inside of my skull. My temple pounded in pain. I clutched my head and screamed and screamed.

I woke up sometime later. Chance was crying. Azazel was gone. My head still hurt.

And I realized that I had purged Azazel's power. At least, I'd taken it away from her. But I'd transferred it to me, along with all of her memories. She had run away, no idea of who she was. And we still hadn't found her.

www.ingramcontent.com/pod-product-compliance
Lightning Source LLC
Chambersburg PA
CBHW061316170626
46817CB00001B/197